THE Dreyfus Collection

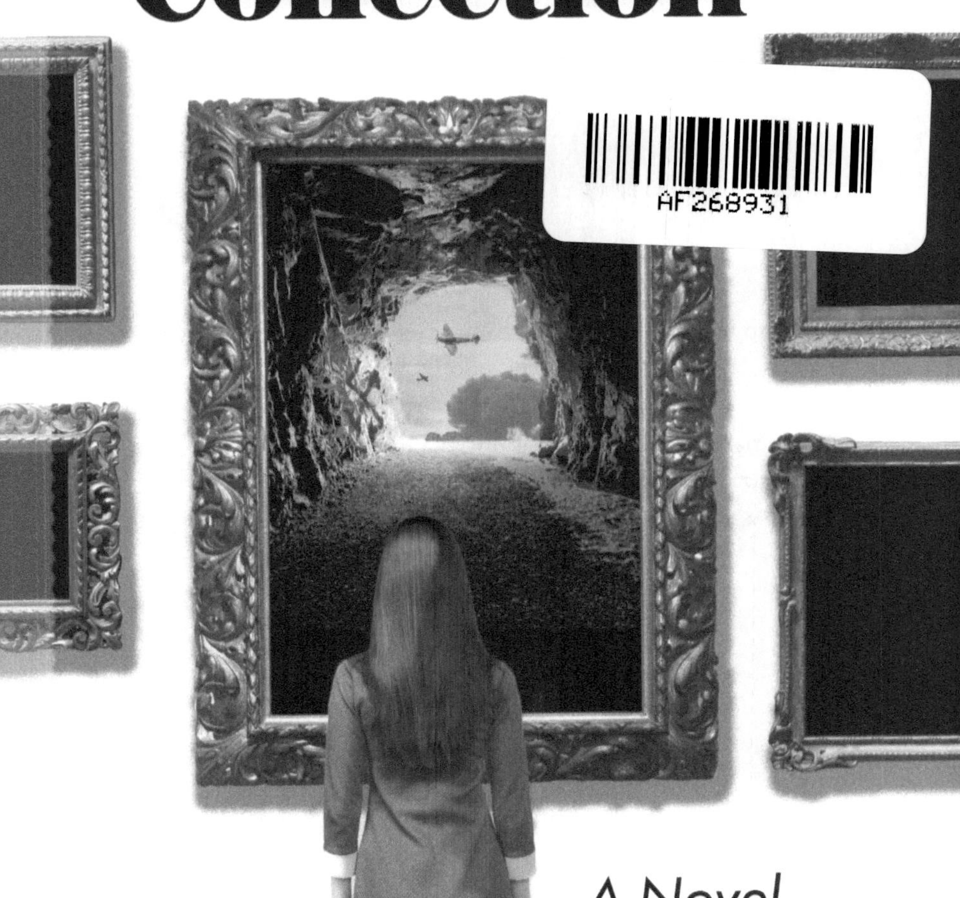

A Novel

By Estelle Rubin Brager

The Dreyfus Collection, a Novel: The Race to Find Priceless Art Stolen by the Nazis

Cover and Interior Designed by Siori Kitajima,
SF AppWorks LLC

Cataloging-in-Publication data for this book is available from the Library of Congress
ISBN-13:
eBook: 978-1-950154-58-6
Paperback: 978-1-950154-59-3

Published by The Sager Group LLC
TheSagerGroup.net

THE Dreyfus Collection

A Novel: The Race to Find Priceless Art Stolen by the Nazis

By Estelle Rubin Brager

To our beloved mother, sorely missed.
May her memory be a blessing.

Contents

Acknowledgments

After our mother died in 2014, my siblings and I self-published a novel she had written that was based on the memoirs of her own grandmother, who escaped the widespread persecution of Jews in Czarist Russia, emigrating to the United States with her family at the early turn of the century. After that book, *Gittle, a Girl of the Steppes*, went on to garner rave reviews from readers, we decided to self-publish another of Mom's novels, *The Dreyfus Collection*, a suspense thriller about the race to find priceless paintings stolen by the Nazis before the Russians found them. Mom had started writing this novel in the 1980s when very little had been published about the Monument Men (the Americans who searched for artwork seized during World War II, much of which had been secreted in the mountains of East Germany). If her novel had been published then, it would have been one of the first to chronicle this fascinating story of espionage and subterfuge. But Mom, always a proud woman, sent one copy of the manuscript to Simon & Schuster, and when she didn't hear back, pretty much gave up. A few months ago, my siblings and I were inspired to self-publish her book. I found an old USB drive with scattered chapters of the book, pieced them together, and did some editing. My siblings (Linda Bresler, Paul Brager, and Stuart Brager) and I are publishing this novel in honor of our mother, Estelle Rubin Brager.

—Alison Bass

Prologue

Lisa Warden stood quietly in one corner of her family's gallery, nursing a soda as she searched the crowd for her father's friend. Her father would have been pleased to see so many visitors to what he and her grandfather had built into one of the most prestigious art galleries in Manhattan, the Warden Art Gallery, on Fifty-Seventh Street. However, six months ago, Peter had disappeared on a trip to Europe to purchase art. Her stepmother, Claire, who had taken over the gallery's management, had given up hope that he was alive. But Lisa refused to believe her father wasn't coming home.

It was now mid-December and Claire was allowing fifteen-year-old Lisa to attend the opening exhibit of new paintings by artists whose names Lisa didn't recognize. The art on display was abstract and modernist, and she was not at all surprised at the brief time many of the spectators took browsing the gallery. But even as visitors left, many more were arriving.

With her dark hair softly cupped about her head emphasizing her sloe eyes, Lisa had no idea she was becoming a beauty, like her mother. Lisa barely remembered her mother, Ann, who had been struck and killed by a car when her daughter was only four years old.

A few days before the opening, a longtime friend of her father had called Lisa at home and said he was planning to come and hoped to see her there. As she surveyed the crowd now, she tried to remember what she knew about Tony Russo; he had always seemed such a mysterious person. Hadn't her father once intimated that Tony worked for the US government and was an operative of some kind? Peter had been in awe of him, and Lisa was convinced Tony could find her father.

Finally, she saw him approach, an imposing man, tall and dark-haired, dressed as if he were on his way to the opera.

"You must be Lisa," he said, smiling.

"Uncle Tony!"

"You've grown so, I hardly recognized you," he added. "But then, you resemble Ann."

He looked down at her upturned face to ask, "Have you heard from your father?"

Lisa winced. Where was he? She said softly, "Not since Daddy called me at camp and asked me to give you that message."

"The one about a rock and a tree?"

"Yes."

"You haven't told anyone?"

"You asked me not to say anything about that call."

"Good girl! That's just between you and me."

Tony was looking at her in a strange way, which unnerved her.

"You're going to find Daddy?" Lisa asked, her voice trembling.

"Of course. That's one of the things I do, find people." He hesitated, then asked, "How are you getting along with your stepmother?"

Lisa tried smiling, then admitted, "Barely."

Tony gave her a sympathetic look. "I hear that with Peter missing, the gallery's reputation has declined."

What was there to say? Her stepmother had terrible taste in art. Lisa looked up at him.

"Are you sure you don't know where Daddy is?"

He chucked her under her chin. "We'll find him. Don't worry."

Lisa could sense that Tony was holding something back from her. She suddenly felt hemmed in by all the people surrounding them, viewing paintings her father would never have featured. Without him, the Warden gallery and its openings no longer meant anything to her.

She felt Tony's hand on her shoulder. "Contact me the moment you hear anything, anything at all," he said.

And then he disappeared into the crowd.

PART
ONE

Chapter 1

Paris, June 1940

A glimmer of dawn penetrated the tall windows of their Paris bedroom, dispelling the darkness. They lay entwined, strands of Sarah Dreyfus's long blond hair laced against David's dark head. He faced her, their limbs resting on one another.

Even now, in the afterglow of their lovemaking, she remained attuned to the adjoining room, where their two daughters, three-year-old Rachael, and Ruth, who would be one in a few months, slept. It was the safety of these children that occupied their thoughts.

"You must go," he whispered. He put a finger on her cheek; it was wet.

"I can't leave you."

"For the sake of the children," he repeated, "you have to go."

"I love you," she answered.

"I'll be fine," David said. "Only a month or two before I join you in New York."

"Suppose—"

"No supposing."

He drew her close again, feeling the slender shape of her body, wanting more, but there was no time now that Adolph Hitler had invaded France.

Sarah drew away from him, filled with premonition. She had always been intuitive, and everything she was feeling told her they were all in danger.

Sarah stared at the wall opposite their bed, at a painting the now penetrating rays of sunlight brought to life, a glowing face, its intense expression staring back at her, the artist, Van Dyck. She heard her husband speak.

"I have your tickets. The ship leaves this evening from Le Havre. There's no alternative." She gasped. So soon! She hadn't known.

He rolled away from her and sat up in bed.

"Sarah," he said, frustration edging his words, "you have no idea how difficult it was to gain passage for you and the girls. Fortunately, I had connections."

She drew close to him, her voice pleading, "Why, David, why insist we have to leave now without you?"

He turned away from her.

Sarah sensed his frustration. She knew he was right, but stubbornness was part of who she was; she had always had a sense of surety. She hadn't changed since the first time he'd laid eyes on her when she was eighteen. But then, perhaps motherhood had tempered her a bit. She sat up in bed, feeling a pit in her stomach, and asked softly, "Why I must go and you must stay?"

Tears in check, she leaned against the headboard and continued to watch the early light illuminate their bedroom. Would she miss seeing the Art Deco–styled furniture by Guimard and Galle and the impressionistic paintings they had lovingly acquired that adorned the walls? Did any of this matter now? Through the open windows the morning was bringing forth the usual Parisian sounds, the voices of passersby, cars traversing the rue Saint-Honoré, even the clip-clop of horse hooves as vendors began their morning rounds, carrying fresh produce from the countryside to the markets.

"Damn it!" David said.

Sarah's eyes widened in surprise. David never swore in her presence.

"You know they breached the Maginot Line. They'll be in Paris soon. You may not be able to get away."

"And you?" she persisted. "What makes you think you will be able to leave France once they occupy Paris?"

He hesitated, then repeated what he had said to himself and to her many times, as if by rote.

"I'm an American citizen. The United States is not at war with Germany. I have my passport."

In response to the skepticism in Sarah's eyes, he added, "No one doubts I am in Paris on business. Germans respect business. Besides, I can't be encumbered with family when I finally leave."

She felt his touch. "I promise you I will arrange to pack up our best works of art and ship them to the States," he said.

"But this house, the paintings you don't bring home, what will happen to them?" Did she really care when her world was crumbling?

"Nothing. They'll be fine until we return. Besides, Pierre has worked for us these many years. He will keep an eye on our property, and Marie can continue to live here. You need not be concerned. I promise I will pack up those paintings we especially like and bring them back to New York." A crooked smile. "Didn't you tell me there's space in the Cape Cod house?"

Sarah wanted to believe him, needed to, but her mind kept picturing the dangers he faced in an occupied country. She wondered what more she could say. True, David's success in business, the wealth he had acquired, had enabled her to indulge her tastes. She was a frequent visitor to the studios of Majorelle and Galle and often purchased furniture designed by them. More important, together she and David, with the advice of the most prestigious gallery in Manhattan, had collected some of the finest works by French Impressionists and the precise Dutch and Flemish painters that curators termed Naturalists.

She listened as David, his dark eyes glowing, reminisced.

"Remember, Sarah, the first time I saw you in the Metropolitan Museum in New York. For some reason, instead of looking at the Monets I came to see, I couldn't stop staring at you, so petite, your blond hair reaching your shoulders, so self-assured. When you finally acknowledged me, you told me that you were an art history student on assignment to study paintings by Claude Monet. You showed the same interest I did in the series the artist did of the Rouen Cathedral and the haystacks."

David's smile broadened. "I haunted the museum then, looking for you. To my good fortune, we met again and I remember telling you why I visited the Metropolitan, that I had begun collecting the French Impressionists and wanted to learn more."

"Yes," she replied softly. "How could I forget that first time, how surprised I was when you approached me. I had seen how taken you were with the Monets. When you spoke to me, you said that paintings calmed your soul."

He reached for her then, pleased she remembered, gently turned her face and kissed her lips and would have enveloped her completely but Sarah eluded him and got out of bed, thinking she heard little Ruth cry out. Her youngest daughter was a delight, into everything. Her Rachael, older by two years, favored David. She had his dark hair and brown eyes and his quiet manner. But there was no sound in the adjoining nursery.

Sarah turned toward her husband. "How much time do we have?"

David reached over and pinched her bottom where she still leaned against the mattress.

"Glad you asked," he said, rolling over to the other side. "We leave Paris right after lunch. I had Marie pack your things and the girls' when you were out with friends yesterday."

Sarah bristled. Why had he waited so long to tell her!

He came around to where his wife remained standing stiffly at the side of the bed.

"Don't make this more difficult for me," he said. "You know I can't bear to see you go, but for the sake of our girls, you must get them out of Paris now before all doors close."

Sarah opened her mouth to protest once more, but said nothing. It was clear David had made up his mind. When he took her in his arms, he said, "I swear to you, I'll leave as soon as the ink is dry on the French contract. So go, Sarah, and don't give me any more tsuris, I can't bear it."

It was going to be a beautiful June day. The light, elbowing its way through the tall windows, held such promise. But her heart was breaking. Never had she feared for him as she did now, the possibility she might never again see this husband she loved.

Chapter 2

His men were tired, weary of driving all night, their green Wehrmacht uniforms stained with mud. Nonetheless SS Major Han Kunz was determined to carry out his mission. Riding in the cab of the Skoda truck, he paid no attention to the overcast sky, the possibility of rain.

All of them had heard rumors, filtered through from those still fighting, that the führer was sick, that Field Marshal Goering, who commanded the Luftwaffe, had sought safety from the advancing Russians by abandoning Berlin and fleeing to the allies.

None of that mattered to Kunz. He knew what he had to do. Despite the lack of equipment on the battle front, a line that was continually shifting, he had managed to commandeer a truck and with precious gasoline siphoned from vehicles abandoned by the Wehrmacht, his team made their way to the mine at Eisleben in the Harz Mountains, where so many secret depositories lay hidden.

It worried Kunz that he was unable to determine at that moment exactly where the Russians were or even how far the Allies had advanced. If it rained, the truck would find the route a muddy impediment to his plan. He stretched his cramped legs. He was squeezed between the driver and his Oberleutnant and all three men were tense, for they were driving over roads pockmarked by exploded shells.

The SS major didn't want to think about what he had to do. Instead, he focused on the comfortable life he and his sister would have once they sold a few of the paintings.

He had had such high hopes for himself. From the beginning of the German expansion, he'd been considered a trusted officer of the Rosenberg ERR when it was first organized to confiscate Europe's treasures. Alfred Rosenberg had assigned him to the early Gestapo teams that had begun removing valuable objects from the private collections of Jews and others who were enemies of the führer. Kunz had relished his role, enriching Germany by stripping decadent nations of valuables.

It was fortunate he spoke French fluently, a skill his superiors relied upon when Paris was occupied. His position suited him well. He had no scruples about what he did. More important, the ERR assignments kept him out of the regular army, which now was being decimated by the dual fronts on which the Wehrmacht fought. He'd just recently heard that General Wenck's Twelfth Army, which had been formed in the Harz Mountains, was being butchered.

What a mistake, Kunz thought, for Germany to have invaded Russia, to have had to endure the brutal winters there. That strategy had only weakened the army and imperiled the Reich.

His thin lips compressed. He was no military strategist, merely an art expert who had made himself invaluable. But even he knew Germany was doomed. It was time to feather his own nest. Others were doing the same. He alone knew the resting place of the paintings he had appropriated for his fürer from the Jew David Dreyfus in Paris.

Kunz thought back to that night, when he had surprised Dreyfus, he and his men. He smiled, remembering the shock on the Jew's face and his own suppressed excitement when, after forcing his way into the house, he saw the magnificent paintings. He couldn't wait to spend time admiring them. But first their owner needed to be dealt with. After all, his orders to appropriate the collection led him to believe neither Hitler nor Goering wanted witnesses. The river would do.

Now, five years later, Kunz knew exactly what it would take to provide a comfortable life for himself and his twin, Hildegarde. He felt it was his reward for following orders that had enriched his superiors.

Eisleben was not far from his birth village near Hasselfelde and the farm where his sister lived alone. He had stopped there a few weeks before, a short visit, but important to his future plans. Seeing Hildegarde again warmed his heart, but being with her permanently—that would have to wait.

She was the only person he loved. Certainly, he had never cared for his overbearing father nor his weak, insipid mother, both of them stupid enough to have visited relatives in Berlin just when a devastating Allied air raid commenced. He wondered at the time why his parents imagined they would be safe from the bombing there. He was grateful his sister had refused to accompany them to Berlin, showing a stubbornness so like his own. Thinking of Hildegarde strengthened his resolve for what he had to do.

As the truck bounced on the war-torn roads, his mind reverted to the one special mine that held the paintings he had brought from Paris, their careful packing personally supervised by him. Somehow, Hans Posse, Hitler's prime procurer, had lost track of the Dreyfus Vermeers, which would have been destined for Linz and the special museum the führer planned to build there for his magnificent collection. Once Kunz realized the oversight, he had moved the paintings from one German castle to another on the pretext of protecting them, and finally into the mines of the Harz Mountains.

The major smiled inwardly. He had obeyed orders, of course, but the artist in him gave rise to a nonconforming trait, a small deviation from the norm. He kept that part of his personality well concealed from his superiors.

Trying to ignore the sound of war as Russian explosives sounded in the distance, he and his weary men finally arrived at the mine in mid-afternoon. Seeing little activity, Kunz stepped down from the truck and ordered everyone to wait. He then entered the mine, greeted the custodian tersely, and descended to the depository's lower depths. Stepping from the lift, he strode to the far interior. The crates he sought, the ones he had carefully stacked against the far wall deep inside this mine, stood untouched.

Oh, yes, he had taken every precaution for his führer, always making certain, despite his many trips into occupied territory, that on his return to these mountains, none of these special crates had been moved or opened. Fortunately, no soldiers guarded the valuables that lay inside this mine, only a curator. That was no surprise; every able-bodied German was needed at the front. At the end, the Wehrmacht had refused to heed Field Marshal Goering's outlandish orders to relocate such treasures. They were safer in the mountains. All of Germany had been stung by the Allies' devastating bombing of Dresden in February, which almost obliterated the historic city.

Kunz was well aware that no one would dare question his removal of any art, especially as orders were arriving constantly along with the remnants of the ERR to move precious works to the west. Even the curators realized the situation was out of control, and there was always the fear of retribution if they interfered. The one caretaker who had looked up from his paperwork when Kunz entered the mine recognized the major and asked no questions.

When Kunz returned to the upper level, he found that his Oberleutnant had followed him into the mine, a worried look on his face.

"Herr Major, the men are asking, what do you want them to do. They are nervous, the Russians being so close. You can hear the guns."

It was true. They had little time.

The two men went together into the recesses of the mine, where the major pointed to the six crates, clearly separate from the others. He gave an order, "Get the men in here, schnell. You will have to help. Schnell, mach schnell!"

His men, long accustomed to handling crates of paintings with care, descended into the mine and, lifting the crates, returned to the surface with them and placed them in the truck. When one of his men asked about other crates that still remained in the mine, Kunz brushed off the question. He was only interested in the six that bore his special markings.

As they prepared to leave, his men awaiting further orders, he had a small change of heart. They didn't all need to accompany him, his Oberleutnant especially.

"Fritz!" Kunz took him aside, out of hearing of the others. "I only need to take three men."

Seeing his longtime aide about to protest, he stopped him with a fierce look and gave an order. "Achtung, you are to head west, on foot. We are close to the American lines. If you have any sense, you will give yourself up." He put out his hand and pushed him away. "No argument. Now, go!"

Turning his back on the stunned man, Kunz strode to the truck and, climbing aboard, told the driver to start driving west on a route that he knew would take them further into the Harz Mountains. Though his men said nothing, he sensed they were pleased to be heading away from the sound of the big guns. It was about an hour before they passed a town that only Kunz knew was the place where he was born, where his twin sister now lived alone on nearby family land. Too bad, he told himself yet again, their reunion would have to wait.

Eyes intent on his search, Kunz at last directed the driver to turn off from the local road they'd been traveling onto an unmarked road that was barely passable. To the driver's consternation, Kunz had him make yet another turn. This time the truck entered an almost imperceptible earth track that rose into the forest. It was a trail he knew well, for he had never forgotten what he and Hildegarde had once discovered, a place that formed part of his childhood memories.

As they neared a bluff, he instructed the driver to pull up in front of a huge pine tree and park. He saw the puzzlement in the driver's eyes as the man shut the ignition and looked at the major.

Kunz's voice was curt: "This is the place."

The driver got out of the truck. He had always trusted the major. In all the years he served under him, the man never made mistakes. Kunz stepped out and waited as the other two men jumped off the back of the truck, somewhat pale from the shaking up they had received. On his orders, the driver found the picks and shovels he had wrapped and hidden under the front seat while the other two men reached for the buckets that hung there. They were surprised when Kunz told them that he himself would lend a hand when necessary. A hand for what, the three men must have been wondering. Yet they followed him as he stepped behind a large pine tree and halted. All they saw were three large boulders strangely lined up beside the tree. Then, crowding behind the major, their eyes wide, they saw the narrow slit in the monstrous stone that stood upright against the hill.

Kunz allowed himself a smile seeing his men pause, their mouths open in surprise. The narrow opening was hardly big enough for a man to squeeze through, but on his order, squeeze they did. Once inside, in the light of his large flashlight, Kunz saw puzzlement on their faces just as he expected. The cramped space they occupied was almost too small for the four of them. It certainly could not accommodate the six crates.

Kunz lifted his flashlight toward his men so they were momentarily blinded and fingered his revolver. He would brook no rebellion, not now when his project was nearing completion. Wisely he had made certain these three were weaponless, having disarmed them of their MG-34 light machine guns as well as the Schmeisser 9mm pistols early on this mission, banking that they would not run into Russian troops.

"Herr Major, was iss?" The question came hesitantly, and for Kunz, the time had come to explain what he had in mind. In a matter-of-fact tone, he answered, "The shovels are for digging and buckets for dumping the earth in the ravine just outside." Then he pointed his flashlight to a hole, not easily seen and only big enough for a small person to crawl into.

"We need to dig a tunnel about six feet high and maybe two foot wide, just enough to move the crates through. There was a tunnel here once, I believe, but it collapsed over the years. You will find a new hiding place on the other side. Trust me."

He smiled reassuringly. "While you work, you are safe. The Russians can never find us and neither can those shells they're sending our way."

His men shrugged. Orders were orders. They trusted Kunz to keep them out of trouble. Hadn't he always looked after them? But so had their Oberleutnant. And where was he now?

Chapter 3

Harz Mountains, April 13, 1945

It was not until the early morning hours of the next day that a rough tunnel-like opening emerged. Kunz stood by as his men labored, keeping the flashlight steady, replacing batteries as needed during the night's work. In the confines of the narrow space just inside the entrance, the men shoveled out the residue, realizing as they dug that there had once been a tunnel, just as the major said. Finally, after the last shovelful of earth had been discarded in the ravine outside, he turned and motioned to the men to follow him, then stepped through the opening. Stooping slightly, for he was the tallest of them, Kunz drew them into a large space and watched them collectively draw a breath as they realized their major must have known beforehand that an inner cave existed. They stood dumbfounded by the unexpected size of the space.

As dawn approached, he had them transfer one crate at a time from the truck through the newly created tunnel into the interior cave. As they worked, Kunz played his flashlight about the walls so the men could see and feel air holes feeding this cave, a benefit he had discovered in his childhood explorations. Though lacking the salt residue from salt mines that sucked up moisture and made such repositories ideal for storing paintings, Kunz believed nevertheless that the temperature and air circulation in this particular cave would mitigate damage to the precious art he possessed. His work for the ERR team had given him important information on how to avoid mold and prevent buckling in the wooden backings of the paintings.

Even though Kunz and his men had not slept for more than twenty-four hours, he badly wanted to open one of the crates, lose himself in the color and line and depth of the paintings, but he knew couldn't afford the time. He drew a deep breath and subdued the urge. The six crates having been secured to his satisfaction, they all retreated from the cave.

Kunz gave new orders. He directed his driver to turn the truck around on the narrow plateau, then had the man move it two hundred feet further down the track, where he and the others who followed him on foot began covering the vehicle with a camouflage net.

Sunlight filtered through the forest. The men could hear the birds in full voice and see them flit through the trees. How fortunate, Kunz thought, the overcast skies the day before had produced no rain and therefore no mud to impede this mission. It was time to complete it, he decided, as he and his weary team walked back to the cave opening.

He himself carried their rations from the truck and suggested that after sharing the food, they reenter the small cave and bed down on the dirt floor. There, he told them, they could sleep for a few hours, safe from the enemy's bombs.

"We'll eat now and then we'll sleep. I'll keep watch. When it grows dark, we'll drive west. Better the Americans than the Russians, nein?"

Kunz could see agreement on their faces. He joined them in the meal, and watched them fall asleep after eating. If he was any judge, theirs would be a deep sleep, for all three had been constantly on the move for many hours without rest. As he sat stiffly against the tunnel wall, slowly marking time, he willed himself to keep awake. After a time, he stood up, stepped carefully about the sleeping figures, and exited the cave. Turning left, he found the tree stump he had marked among the trees, and reaching in, pulled out the canvas bag he'd placed there two weeks ago when he had visited his sister. Inside the bag were two small boxes marked "Danger, Ammonium Nitrate/Aluminum." He would have used an electric lead but didn't have one. Instead, he would have to use an ordinary fuse.

He took out the gun cotton he had hidden in the bag and located the fuses. Upon returning to the cave, he stepped carefully around the sleeping men and retrieved the flashlight he had left. He used it to position the box near the original crawl space he and his twin, Hildegarde, had discovered and his men had subsequently shoveled clear.

Kunz propped the light away from the men and opened this box. Stooping, he filled the canvas bag with gunpowder and, after straightening up, walked quietly among the three sleeping figures, distributing the powder in two-inch-wide swaths in a line leading to the front end of the just-unveiled tunnel and partially through it. Satisfied, he left the cave and walked back to the tree stump, where he picked up the second box and carried it to the cave opening.

Kunz was perspiring now in the humid atmosphere, but it wasn't only the air that caused his discomfort. It was what he was about to do. He was prepared to take chances, even with dynamite. He told himself he was no fool, nor could he afford a mistake. He thought he knew exactly the right amount of dynamite and the placing of it that would do the job he meant to do. His hand shook slightly as he lit the match and tossed it on the fuse.

The light went out. Scowling, swearing softly to himself, he bent closer this time to light the fuse. He saw it flare. Then Kunz ran wildly for the ravine. The shock of the explosion sent him over its side. He grabbed the shrubbery, slipping only a few feet below the plateau.

When at last he caught his breath and regained his courage, he lifted his head to the top of the ravine and peered at the cave. Dust was drifting out of the narrow crevice. Still, he remained quietly huddled against the earth at the ravine's side, listening, wondering, expecting to hear...what? Anguished cries?

Time seemed immeasurable as he hung there at the side of the ravine. Finally, he pulled himself up out of the ravine. He needed to know his plan had succeeded, that the men were dead and the newly dug tunnel had collapsed, sealing the opening to the inner cave. Even now, the Russian guns could be heard. Fortunately, his explosion, though somewhat muffled, had been one of many in the region.

Kunz hesitated for a moment, afraid of what he might find. A bloody figure? Perhaps more than one might emerge, staggering. Despite his intimidating reputation as a member of the Gestapo, he had managed not to do any of the killing, leaving the dirty work to his Oberleutnant or one of his men.

Kunz gathered his courage and entered the cave to find silence. His hand went to his side and he fingered his revolver. He hoped he wouldn't have to use it. He remembered an expression he had once read in a pirate book as a boy, "Dead men tell no tales."

As he passed through the narrow rock entrance, still a crevice, Kunz observed that everything remained unchanged. Holding a cloth over his nose to filter the dust that now filled the small space, he saw to his relief that the tunnel had vanished. It had been replaced by a wall of newly collapsed earth and rock. The narrow outer cave had remained much as it had been when he was a child, giving no indication that anything existed beyond the newly blasted wall. Except he knew there were now bodies lying there before him, hidden by a foot or more of earth.

Then he saw the hand. It lay on the floor palm up, sticking out from the fresh cover of earth and broken stone. He stared at it, at the skin newly callused from the digging. Kunz shuddered. He stood there, staring. The hand didn't move. Therefore, its owner was dead or near death as were the other two. But what was he to do about the hand? He couldn't leave it there, a dead giveaway. Dead! Certainly dead!

Kunz took a deep breath. Rather than hack it away, as had been his first thought, he would cover it. This he proceeded to do, returning to the ravine with a bucket to retrieve earth the men had dumped earlier. The hand slowly disappeared under the dirt.

The major gave one last look at the scene and turned away. Considering the risks, his plan had gone well. It was time to put the second phase into operation. Walking down the track away from the cave, he pulled the camouflage net from the truck and stuffed it behind the rear doors. Daylight was important to his plan if he wished to drive the truck through the mountains on unmarked roads. Fortunately, they were familiar to him, from the hiking he'd done as a boy. He suspected he had little gas, but the vehicle needed to be moved far from this new repository he had established, giving no hint of its location. He would use the truck in his westward flight until it ran out of gas, then continue his escape on foot. At all costs, he had to avoid running into General Field Marshal Schörner, the "Hangman," who hung any soldier found to be a deserter.

As expected, after only a few miles, the gas indicator showed empty but he continued driving until the truck came to a final jerky halt.

No matter. The major congratulated himself on his familiarity with the Harz Mountains and its back roads. He felt temporarily safe knowing armies traveled principal highways.

Besides, in these hidden mountain places, it might be some time before the truck was discovered.

He opened the door and reached into a small overhead compartment. Pants, shirt, and jacket, all dark colors, that he had earlier stashed in the truck cab, fell onto the seat. Kunz changed clothes, then took the time, using a shovel, to dig a hole at a distance from the truck. Regretfully he placed his uniform and anything that would identify him as a major, or a member of the Gestapo, in it. He then took a handy knapsack and stuffed whatever rations were left from his mens' final meal inside. Without a backward glance, he started walking west toward the imaginary line that would separate the shifting American Zone from the Russian Zone.

There had been rumors among his superiors that Bad Lauterberg or Göttingen on the Leine River lay across this line, and though he remembered to carry a compass he could only guess he was near the town of Andreasberg. Any of these destinations would require hours of walking, but he was prepared to do whatever it took to reach the Americans.

He had only gone a mile or two when he found a paved road and, though wary, would have stepped back among the trees, but suddenly several American jeeps with soldiers swept by and he was spotted. The jeeps screeched to a halt and several men jumped out.

Facing their rifles, he slowly raised his arms, but the smile on his face vanished when he realized the men were shouting at him in Russian.

For a second, he thought of making a run for it, but he didn't want to die in these mountains, not when he was now worth a fortune and might, someday, if he was clever, enjoy it with Hildegarde.

Chapter 4

Paris, September 20, 1945

Peter Warden left his hotel near the Place de Concorde in Paris at eight that morning. He walked briskly and carried a small package. A beautiful morning for a walk, he thought, even if he didn't have far to go. As he approached the Musee du Jeu de Paume, a building adjacent to the Tuileries, he couldn't help but remember the happy years before World War II. This little building before the war had displayed wonderful Impressionist paintings that the Louvre declined to exhibit when they first appeared in the 1860s.

On his arrival in Paris, he had questioned the concierge at his hotel about these buildings and been informed that as Allied forces neared the city, German POWs shattered windows in the museum and Frenchmen were placed on the roofs of the Louvre to fight possible fires from approaching Allied guns. Fortunately, Von Choltitz, the German general, surrendered Paris to the Allies with too much damage to its museums.

At the Musée du Jeu de Paume, Peter approached the reception desk and gave his name to the receptionist. While she dialed the person he had come to see, he looked about him. He had been told in Washington that the French had the foresight to remove their valuable paintings, thousands of them, at the first threat of war, and hide them. He wondered if two Claude Monet paintings, each portraying an exquisite lady with a parasol, had been returned. Were they hanging in their usual place? He remembered their title, *En plein air*. They took his breath away each time he viewed them. And that reminded him of the beautiful Monet in the private collection of his good friend, David Dreyfus. Peter grimaced. His friend had been murdered by the Nazis and his collection stolen. No one knew where it had been taken.

Hopefully, the woman he had come to see, Mme Rose Valland, might have some information about the stolen artwork. Rumors reached him and others in the States that she had quietly tried to keep track of artwork brought to the Jeu de Paume by the Nazis and dispersed by the ERR. They had used the museum as a temporary repository. His sources in Washington had been in contact with the normally tight-lipped French art directors and curators who nevertheless elected to provide the Americans with highly confidential information during the occupation. They told him that Valland was dismissed by the Nazis from time to time but was allowed to slip back to her job on the pretext that only she knew how to fix maintenance problems that kept afflicting the building.

He prayed Valland would talk to him. If anyone could tell him what happened to the Dreyfus Collection, it would be her. At that moment, he watched a woman walk toward him and decided she must be Valland. She resembled the photograph he'd seen of her and fit the description others had given him: almost manly, dark hair cropped short, eyes obscured by glasses, not a woman who would arouse the prurient interest of a conqueror.

"Monsieur." She shook his hand.

"Peter Warden, Mme. Valland. How kind of you see me."

"Non, not kind . . . pleased," she said as they spoke in French. I have heard of the Warden gallery in New York, its fine reputation. Now, how can I help you?"

"Perhaps we might speak privately," he suggested.

"Of course. Follow me."

Valland led him to her small office and pointed to a chair in front of her desk. She then took her seat. For moment, Peter looked about at bookcases jammed with volumes. Her window overlooked the vast gardens.

"The Dreyfus Collection." There was no need to beat around the bush with this lady.

She took a deep breath, remembering.

"Ah, oui, that poor man, murdered by the Nazis."

Peter tried to put the image of David's face out of his mind.

"Mme Valland, please excuse me if I get right to the point. As you know, the Dreyfus family willed their collection to the National Gallery of Art in Washington before the war. It has always been our government's contention that they did not belong to David and Sarah Dreyfus at the time they were confiscated. We were not at war with Germany then. It was understood by both parties the paintings would remain with the Dreyfus family until a new wing was added to the museum."

Valland interrupted. "Ownership did not matter to those barbarians." She paused to regain her composure and said, "Fortunately, our Louvre paintings and those in this building were moved in the summer of 1939 before the occupation. Would you believe we saved four hundred thousand works of art? But I am digressing, monsieur. Let me tell you what I remember."

Valland paused again, then said, "I was not here when they brought in Dreyfus's collection during the night, but I saw the paintings from a distance the next day when I came to work. There was a major in charge, a former Gestapo officer who commanded an ERR unit, an intimidating man."

She permitted herself a smile. "One listens, you understand, especially as I understand German and men gossip, as men will, when they are bored.

"This major would not permit any of our staff near the room where those particular paintings were lodged. That room is known, strangely, as *Room of the Martyrs*. Paintings Hitler considered degenerate were deposited there.

"However, shortly after their arrival, this major oversaw their shipment out of here. As far I have determined, the Dreyfus Collection was placed on a train to Germany and I have no knowledge of where it may have ended up or even if it remained intact."

She added, "I believe the Vermeers were intended for Hitler, for the new museum at Linz he planned. Goering would not have dared to keep any of those for himself."

Her next words resuscitated Peter's mission.

"I have to tell you, monsieur, it surprised me that this major spoke such fluent French." She hesitated. "That leads me to believe he lived here in Paris at one time and learned our language. This made him invaluable to the Nazis and the ERR."

"Describe him, please."

"A tall man, thin with sharp features, thin lips, and cold brown eyes that would frighten anyone. And a small mole on his lower cheek."

It came to him, the memory. Could this Nazi be the same person he'd seen years earlier, a student like himself, in the galleries, both at the Louvre and the Jeu de Paume, closely studying paintings that hung there, ignoring all else? Apart from noticing the mole, Warden remembered being struck by the intensity of concentration that student had shown, the thin narrow face. A coincidence? Strangely, this German student had made an impression.

"Monsieur?"

He blinked and came back to the present.

"I think I've seen that man before," he said. "He and I may have been students in Paris at the same time."

"Then I can be of help. We still have the old student records somewhere. I will find them," she offered. "Perhaps Jaujard, the director, knew him."

She paused. "Where are you staying?"

"The Crillon."

"Ah, oui," Valland said. "They have finally removed the machine guns from its roof." She added: "The notes I kept during the war, I don't keep them here." Her lips tightened. "Non, notes would be too revealing while the Germans occupied Paris. Afterwards, would you believe Jaujard and I along with others from the museum were taken prisoners by the Free French for a short time on charges of collaboration? Sanity finally prevailed. Of course." She allowed herself a smile. "We did try to give that impression for our own safety during the war."

A moment's hesitation and then she said, "Monsieur, I will contact you. Just give me a little time to investigate the matter."

Peter hid his impatience. He had to have faith in her.

He stood. "Mlle Valland, I hope France recognizes your bravery and rewards you in some way. My father and I have known Jacques Jaujard for many years. We in America who deal in the fine arts are aware of how both of you struggled to save France's treasures."

She thanked him and then confessed, "I have spoken freely to your Lieutenant James Rorimer. I trust him and have told him much. He says he is a former curator at the Cloisters in New York. You might want to talk with him also."

Peter smiled. "I already have. You, if anyone, understand how these American Monument Men get around especially as they were sent by my government to locate and restore art to their rightful owners."

He refrained from including himself as one of them, for his mission had been congressionally arranged.

"They are doing their job, monsieur, and I, for one, will help them as I plan to help you," she said.

"You will call me, n'est pas?" he asked as Valland rose from her chair. "My room number at the Crillon is 301."

"Certainement."

He'd almost forgotten. The package on his lap. He placed it in her hand. "This is for you."

"But, why?"

"Silk stockings. My wife insisted I bring them for you from New York since we understand they are impossible to obtain in Paris."

Valland said nothing at first, overcome by gratitude. Then she smiled. "Monsieur, I cannot refuse the gift. Please convey my appreciation to your wife. Merci beaucoup et adieu."

Chapter 5

Paris, September 20, 1945

The leaves on the trees outside Luxemburg Gardens on this September morning remained green, not yet ready to embrace autumn. More importantly, Peter saw before him a city freed from German occupation, its people smiling.

Suddenly he missed Ann, his wife, and their daughter, Lisa, only four years old, wanting to share Paris with them. But he had work to do.

The morning had been fruitful. He and Rose Valland now had a lead, possibly giving them the identity of the man responsible for David Dreyfus's murder and the theft of his paintings. The student he recalled seeing in Paris years ago could be a German who became a Nazi ERR agent.

Peter headed in the direction of the art galleries that tended to congregate on the Left Bank. Arriving at broad rue Saint-Germain, a street once famed for its galleries, he was not entirely surprised to find one of his father's old associates doing business in the same location. The dealer's sign still hung there.

He mounted the stoop and rang the bell.

"Peter!"

He heard his name called out from the rear, disbelief in the man's voice.

Peter replied, "Michael, my old friend!" He had known Michael Dupont since he was a teenager accompanying his father on trips to France.

"Ca va?" He reached the dealer and shook the man's hand.

"And you, how are you?" the man replied in English, genuine pleasure in his voice.

Despite the dim interior, Peter could see that the Frenchman had aged. His physique, however, was the same, short squat, broad-shouldered, with a round face. Hair that had once been bushy and dark was now sparse and streaked with gray. Michael's lips curved in a broad welcoming grin.

"So, Paris is a siren song, pulling you back now that the dogs have gone!"

"You might say that."

An awkward silence, then Peter spoke. "And you, Michael, you suffered while I was safe, n'est pas?"

His remark caught the Frenchman off-guard. Michael's shoulders sagged and he said, "You couldn't possibly know, Peter, what we went through. I kept my head down, went along, but it didn't matter for my Jewish friends. Their lives were forfeit."

Michael added sadly, "There are no Jewish art dealers in Paris any more. Pity!"

He paused, then said, remorse in his voice, "We were useful to them, the Nazi spoilers. How else could they dispose of stolen art, sell what they didn't want to keep for themselves, make lots of money."

"I've heard this, dear friend." Peter tried to stem his old friend's confession.

"No! You haven't heard it all."

The ensuing silence hung heavy.

Then the Frenchman smiled. "I forgot to say, Peter, I'm glad to see you. And, of course, we can always do business." He grew serious. "I heard about your father passing. My belated condolences. A special friend he was. Knew ten times more than I'll ever know about paintings. I'm sure he taught you well."

The dealer couldn't stop talking. It seemed to Peter there was so much Michael wanted to tell him now that he could speak openly, now that Paris was liberated. He saw tears in the man's eyes. Was it regret for the unbearable years of occupation, he wondered, or tears of joy?

The Parisian took a deep breath and rubbed his eyes with the back of his thick hands. "Come! I'll make us a cup of coffee," he said. "Paris is just beginning to import the real thing, if you can afford to deal in the black market."

Peter hadn't taken his eyes from the art dealer. "And Sophie, is your wife safe? Your daughter, Yvonne?"

"Yes, yes, we have all survived. We were hungry, perhaps, but the Nazis needed me. It was better for us than for others. They used us to enrich themselves." He cast a glance. "And you, Peter . . . a wife? A handsome young man like you."

Peter blushed. "I'm lucky," he said, "I married a wonderful person. I have a daughter, Lisa. She's four years old."

"Congratulations! And who is looking after the store?" Michael asked.

Peter smiled broadly. "My wife, Ann, is there. So is Sarah Dreyfus, David's wife. She helps me. She knows as much as I what is genuine, what's not."

"Interesting!"

While Michael busied himself with the coffeepot and the mugs, Peter looked around the shop.

"I see you have quite a few paintings," he said. "Any my gallery would be interested in?" He knew that what Michael needed was a return to normalcy, French francs in his bank account. His remark brought an instant response.

"Peter, I always knew you to be a life saver. Naturally I have paintings you will like. Authenticated, of course."

Peter grinned. "Of course. In Europe, every canvas seems to be up for grabs regardless of provenance. New York is full of frauds. I've spent the war years turning down stuff refugees staked their lives on."

The Parisian was not offended. "Peter, you know I won't sell you a fake." Handing him a mug of coffee, Michael added, "Others maybe, not you. We go back too far."

Peter laughed, "Yes, I know that. Besides, as you hinted, my father taught me well."

"But when you seek elsewhere, be careful," Michael warned. "Other dealers may not have the same scruples I have. As a matter of fact, a score of German and French dealers who serviced the Nazis, selling stolen art, are still operating openly." He smiled furtively. "Although, Peter, I must admit to you, I do have a few fakes. But I'd never stick you with them."

"Naturally."

Michael paused, then admitted, "I might have unloaded some on German visitors." He asked, "Did you know your father was acquainted with Henri Vollard, the most important dealer in Impressionist paintings at the turn of the century? There was some competition between the two of them at first."

"I remember my father telling me how in Vollard's memoirs, the French dealer confesses to not understanding the real value of a Van Gogh," Peter said. "Later, he writes how wrong he was."

Michael changed the subject. "So, what are you doing in Paris so soon after Germany's defeat? You can't be lacking for paintings for your rich clients. People did manage to get out of Europe with some of their wealth."

"David Dreyfus didn't!" Peter's remark was unintentional. It surprised them both.

"Oui," Michael said. "All of us, the art dealers, heard about Monsieur Dreyfus, his misfortune, and that's when we knew we were in trouble, Jews especially. At least he had the good sense to send his wife, Sarah, and his daughters away in time."

Peter changed the subject, saying, "I shouldn't be misleading you, Michael. I'm not in the market just yet. I wanted to see if old friends like you were still around, and ask a few questions."

"Tu es une merde!" The Frenchman let the expletive hang. After a moment, in control of himself, he asked, a shrewd look on his face, "Tell me. Any word on the Dreyfus Collection?"

When at first Peter didn't answer him, Michael added, "All the dealers in Paris are wondering about those Vermeers and the rest of the collection. None of them have turned up on the market. That's strange, now that the war is over."

Peter understood the intent behind the dealer's question; they both knew that finding the Dreyfus Collection would be a dangerous game because of its immense value. He remained silent and Michael said finally, "Well, perhaps too soon, n'est pas?"

"I would like to find those paintings."

Michael grinned. "So! Truth will out. Peter, my friend, let's be candid," he said. "Why would you hear it from me? After all, I can find a market for them too. Finding them, selling them, would make my fortune." He added, putting his cup down: "If the Russian trophy brigades get to them before the American Monument Men, they will disappear into the Pushkin or the Hermitage. You won't see them again, not in our lifetime."

What Michael said was true, but Peter refused to accept the possibility of the Dreyfus Collection being in Russian hands. "The United States government will pay more, much more, if the collection surfaces," he said. "Europe is impoverished just now, will be for some time. The U.S. wants those paintings. Depend on it, you will make your fortune."

"Can't ask for more than that, can I." Michael's eyes were shining at these words. The search was on, and his American friend was a major player.

He dared to ask one more question. "The Botticelli, did Dreyfus keep it here in Paris or New York?"

"It was also stolen."

"Pity. I liked it. Your father outbid me on that one and then sold it to Dreyfus."

They chatted a few moments longer, promising to keep in touch. Peter put down his coffee cup and the dealer walked him to the door, where they shook hands. No further words were needed.

Later that same afternoon, strolling through the east bank of Paris pungent with memory, Peter attempted to see another former friend of his father's. He found the art gallery was no longer at that location and wondered what had happened to that dealer, for he remembered the man well.

Then, deciding to make still another visit, he discovered a new owner at the third location. To Peter's dismay, the dealer was anxious to pump him for information regarding the Dreyfus Collection.

"Has it been found?" this dealer asked slyly. He seemed to know who Warden was, that he and David Dreyfus had done business together.

Peter didn't respond at first. The truth about David's murder gave him painful pause. He finally found his voice and changed the subject. Once the dealer realized the information that he sought was not forthcoming, he began to press paintings on the American, early sixteenth-century Dutch works he insisted were genuine and valuable. Looking them over, Peter didn't think his clientele would be interested in any of the canvases, and when this became apparent, the dealer's attitude turned hostile.

"Why so particular?" he said. "Your American clients wouldn't know the difference."

Even now, Peter realized, the peace was too fresh, the memories of the occupation too raw. America, safe across a wide ocean, had been isolated from the nightmare that had enveloped Europe. He bid adieu, promising to stop back on his next visit to Paris, and walked slowly back to his hotel, satisfied that at least he had made some attempt to reestablish ties with Parisian art dealers, if only to discover that the vanished Dreyfus Collection was a prime topic of conversation. That told him that not a single item of the collection, its paintings all well known to these astute gallery owners, had reached the market. Monets, Cézannes, Vermeers, all of them rare and invaluable. It meant that he would have to continue the search.

He would call Sarah shortly. She was his partner in this, the only one besides himself who knew exactly what the collection contained and could identify the paintings once found. Wasn't she one of the reasons he had taken on this task apart from his obligation to the powers in Washington? And David. For his sake, he needed redeem his friend's legacy.

Entering the Hôtel de Crillon on the Place de la Concorde, he first checked the reception desk for messages. Finding none, he went up to his room. Not that he expected to hear from Rose Valland this soon, but he was anxious to learn the identity of the German student, his only lead. The wait made him reluctant to leave the hotel for dinner. Besides, he had no appetite. He would use this interlude to catch up on sleep, the time lag between New York and Paris beginning to affect him now that he was no longer laced with adrenaline. He called down to the desk and had the reception clerk send a telegram to his wife, saying he was fine. He had had an uneventful trip, he said. He missed her and Lisa and loved them. He closed his message advising Ann that he expected to be home shortly. If there were problems with the gallery, wire him immediately. Peter loosened his tie, took off his shoes, and lay down on the bed. He tried to sleep but his mind gave him no peace. He had a recurrent nightmare from the episode he had witnessed five years before. Peter saw once again the Gestapo pushing David into the black car as he hid a short distance away, afraid to intervene. It tormented him, as always, that he had done nothing to help his friend, making him no better than all the others who turned their backs on evil.

Only in Ann's arms when he awoke in a sweat was his distress mitigated. She alone knew the truth of this nightmare. She had extracted a confession from him one sleepless night, that he had slipped into occupied France on orders from the U.S. government to warn his friend. He had just left David's house, annoyed the American was so blind to his vulnerability, and started to walk back to his safe house when he saw the large van without lights drive up and park. It was followed by a car.

Slipping into a recessed doorway, he'd worried that he may have been spotted by men he was certain were Nazis. But he remained undetected and watched in dismay as his friend, protesting, was shoved into a car and driven away. As he remained scrunched against some door, he saw David's paintings, covered in quilts, being removed from the house and stowed in the van.

A tall, thin uniformed officer directed the operation. Though the night was dark, a lamp on the pavement outside David's house enabled Peter to observe and commit the man to memory, this tall narrow-faced Nazi, so determined to perform his service to the Third Reich. Even then, there was something naggingly familiar about this man, a feeling he had seen him before, sometime in the past.

He had stood frozen, unable to move in the time it took to empty the house of its paintings. At last, he saw the officer seat himself beside the driver as men mounted the rear of the van, closing the doors behind them. Only then, after they had driven off, did he abandon his post in a state of shock. He remembered that same night running to the American embassy, telling them what he had seen, entreating them to do something to save David. The official on duty said there was nothing he could do until David was brought into Gestapo headquarters. But he never was.

Two days later, a French informer told Peter his friend's body had been recovered from the Seine, his death declared a suicide by the German authorities. Peter was engulfed in remorse and guilt; he had played the coward.

Chapter 6

Paris, September 21, 1945

A deep sleep finally carried Peter Warden into a new day. When he awoke, he discovered he was wearing the clothes he'd worn when he first lay down. Chagrined, he took them off, showered, and dressed in fresh clothes. He went down to the Crillon's café to have breakfast, but first he stopped at the reception desk to determine if there were any messages. Finding none, he sighed. Patience was not one of his virtues, as his father had frequently pointed out to him when the pair were negotiating for a stunning piece of artwork.

He enjoyed a breakfast of croissants and coffee, and then walked about Paris to pass the time. Crossing the bridge, Warden revisited Sainte-Chapelle on the Île de la Cité, wanting to gaze at the magnificent stained-glass windows in the ancient church. He then decided to have lunch at Les Halles. These familiar forays pleased him and he returned in a better frame of mind to his hotel room.

He was napping when the phone rang and, picking up, he heard the reception desk announce a visitor. He made his way to the bathroom, quickly splashed cold water on his face, ran a comb through his hair, and was fully awake by the time he heard the tapping on his door.

A young man in student garb handed him a letter, waiting only long enough for Peter to tip him generously. As soon as the messenger left and he shut the door, he sat down at the desk, certain the letter came from Rose Valland.

It did. In neat French script, she had written the name of the German ERR representative who delivered the Dreyfus Collection to the Jeu de Paume that July night in 1940. She wrote that the same man had been a student at the Louvre in the mid-'30s. His name was Hans Kunz.

Valland's letter continued: "I was working late that July night, a problem with mold that the Paris humidity spawned. At least, that's the excuse I gave them because so much artwork came into the Jeu de Paume after nightfall. I remember how strangely this officer acted that night, and afterwards I learned David Dreyfus had been murdered. This Kunz never once left the museum while the paintings were there.

"I saw him studying the art, obviously taken by their beauty. There was a cot in the room where they'd been stacked, and his men brought him food. I overheard him tell them his orders were to pack the paintings carefully in crates and saw him use those crates, their corners bound with flat strips of metal. They stood about five feet tall by six feet wide, possibly ten inches thick, with packing between the rows. When all these paintings were secured, I noticed he identified the contents of the six crates, with some code evidently.

"As I remember, they were to be immediately shipped to Carinhall, the immense estate Goering was building in Prussia. I overheard the SS men say there were railroad cars attached to Goering's special train bound for Berlin, even then, waiting.

"The men spoke freely, unaware that I understood German," she wrote. "They talked mostly about how Goering planned to present Hitler with the Dreyfus Vermeers when the Führer visited Carinhall."

Valland closed her letter saying it was likely Goering had moved the paintings from Carinhall when the German offensive against the Russians collapsed to protect them from the advancing enemy troops.

"There were so many possible depositories, and as the paintings may have been moved more than once, it would be difficult to locate them, if indeed they survived the war."

Valland wished him luck, thanked him for the silk stockings, and signed the letter "Rose." She added a postscript, writing that she hoped someday to be invited to Carinhall to see and identify what works of art might still hang on its walls if the Russians hadn't removed them.

Peter put her letter down and took a deep breath. So! The man responsible for David's murder was named Hans Kunz. All he had to do now was find him if he was still alive, and if he was, Peter had a gut feeling Kunz knew what had happened to the Dreyfus Collection.

Elated, he prepared to go out to dinner, a small celebration perhaps. As he opened his door to leave, he heard his phone ring and turned back to answer it.

It was a call that changed his life.

His face devoid of color, Peter sat watching from his seat beside the window as his plane approached the Idlewild airport on Long Island. He recognized Cape Cod and the islands, Nantucket and Martha's Vineyard, as they appeared briefly below him. The plane flew over Long Island, losing altitude quickly. But Peter wasn't thinking about the landing, his mind was elsewhere. Even taking a breath was an effort, he was in so much pain.

How did it happen, the accident? Why Ann? He couldn't believe his lovely wife had been hit and killed instantly by a car on New York's Fifty-Seventh Street, the driver running a red light just as she started to cross.

The plane touched down smoothly, moved off the runway, and was guided close to the terminal. At the captain's signal, Peter stood and began disembarking following the other passengers down the gangway to the tarmac. As the press of exiting passengers held him up, he paused on the elevated steps, feeling the cool afternoon air, very different from the Manhattan heat he had left behind when he'd flown to Paris only days earlier. But he didn't register the raucous calling of gulls, annoyed their space had been usurped by aircraft landing.

When Peter entered the terminal, the sense of loss overwhelmed him. How could it be that Ann was gone? Then he saw Sarah Dreyfus watching for him, holding the hand of a little girl. He ran toward Sarah and Lisa, desperate to hold his daughter in his arms.

Chapter 7

Soviet Union, June 1956

Hans Kunz slowly regained consciousness. The former SS major lay crippled and consumed by pain. He wanted to get up off the straw-covered cot, but then he realized he was no longer in his barracks. His jailors had separated him from his fellow prisoners. His uneasiness continued to grow. When he tried to lift himself once more, he couldn't move. There were broken bones in his body.

Lying there helpless, Kunz acknowledged he had brought the beating on himself, so obsessed had he been with the need to escape the Russians and find his way back to Germany. He had almost succeeded. His plan had been well thought out, but when he fled the camp at Tambov, the dogs tracked and found him in the woods that surrounded the Soviet internment facility.

Pain gripped him. His mind refused to acknowledge it. Was it only six years ago that he and other prisoners had been transferred in crowded boxcars to Tambov, a camp located halfway between Moscow and Volgograd? This distance from his East German home where his sister waited hadn't deterred him from flight, for Kunz was a determined man. Sooner or later he intended to be free, and although there were recent rumors that all Soviet internment camps were to be abolished, he refused to put stock in them. Hadn't he heard the same drivel for years? Nothing had happened that would give him hope.

However, for the first time since his capture by the Russians eleven years ago, he was fearful. He knew he had been delirious due to the intense beating they dealt him. He had babbled, he felt certain, and was frightened he may have said something in his delirium that would somehow compromise his release. Could he have mentioned Dreyfus and his stolen art collection? He recalled the Jew's despairing look as he was forced out the door of his own home. Now, his own life hung in the balance.

He remembered the beginning of his misfortune, the day he planned to surrender to the Americans as the Third Reich imploded. Instead, the Russian Army plucked him from the side of a road in the Harz Mountains not far from where he was born. He been sent to a vast improvised prison camp in a suburb of Berlin that had once been a cement factory, grateful he had stashed his crew's rations in his knapsack before he was apprehended because no food was given prisoners the first few days. He had studied his surroundings and the habits of the guards and was poised to break out on a dark night when, unexpectedly, he was put aboard a cargo plane and flown with other German officers and some looted valuables to Moscow.

He soon learned that the Russians knew his rank and suspected his SS connection. Kunz didn't know how they had obtained that information, but he quickly realized that officers were being treated differently than ordinary soldiers because of information they could impart to their conquerors. He was told several times by his captors that he was a lucky man to find himself sent to Moscow rather than Siberia, where prisoners were worked to death in the mines. Due to his status, they said, he and other German officers would wind up in a camp just outside Moscow. On arrival, he saw the sign over the gate. Krasnogorsk 27/II. It was a camp located, he later learned, twenty-two kilometers from the Kremlin. How convenient a location for the NKVD and, later, for KGB interrogators.

In time, it became even clearer to Kunz that his captors were looking for Germans they could recruit and train to be their spies once they were returned to Germany. He had wrestled with his conscience. It was a way out for him, a chance to return to Germany and Hildegarde, but he had been told he would be hunted down and killed if he didn't perform his new duties, and he never doubted his captors.

Kunz finally decided he would not be forced into a role he abhorred, and as the years passed, he stopped counting on rumors that the camps would be shut down. When it became clear he was not being released when others were, he planned his escape.

His body again seized up in pain. He tried to ignore it. He had taken good care of himself while imprisoned, exercising regularly, walking everywhere he could within the camp, doing calisthenics, an hour at a time. It was equally important to keep his mind sharp, especially since he was interrogated regularly by the NKVD. He had been careful always to keep his story the same, allowing no deviation that would give them cause to doubt what he told them. Fortunately, he managed not to trip himself up. He explained he was not wearing his uniform when they caught him, saying he had hoped to melt into the countryside as a noncombatant, though it pained him to admit to the Russians that he was a defector. When they asked him what he was doing away from his regiment, he acknowledged being a member of the Schutzstaffel, the SS, an elite group, and told his captors that with Hitler's suicide, he had no further reason to pursue the war.

Kunz lay there on the cot, eyes closed, panicked for the first time in his life. Again, he wondered, had he in any way blurted out his secret during the beating, unwittingly disclosed knowledge of the Dreyfus Collection? Certainly, he had known of the competition between the Soviet Trophy Brigades and the American MFAA, the Monument Men as they were called. Both had rushed to locate and save stolen artwork—that is, until the Americans and Brits pulled out of what became the Soviet zone, allowing the Russians to hunt through East Germany to their hearts' content.

News was scarce at Krasnogorsk. Only rumors prevailed, and he wondered if, years later, the Soviets were still searching for hidden treasure in the East German zone they now controlled.

He convulsed suddenly, then wondered where the doctors were, why his broken bones hadn't been set. And then, he felt the presence of someone in the room. He opened his eyes and realized that, like a cat, this man had entered quietly and was now looking down at him. Kunz shrank inside himself. This was the man who had him beaten, who, when he began to babble, sent the brute out of the room and continued the punishment himself, smiling all the while.

In German, his tormentor said, "So, Major. You are feeling better?"

Silence.

"Don't shrink away. I'm your friend. I was under orders to punish you. It was hard for me to do it."

Kunz could only stare at this man, not tall like himself but powerfully built with sandy hair and cold blue eyes that stared down at him, eyes that belied friendship.

"Your sister, Hildegarde. You spoke her name. I can help arrange your release. You've heard, haven't you, the rumors. The camps are finally going to be shut down. Party Chief Khrushchev wants this."

Kunz knew then. He would never have mentioned his sister's name except in delirium. He had compromised the one person he loved. Again, he wondered what else he had disclosed. He had written Hildegarde one last time before his attempted escape. He remained silent.

"Hans, I can help you. Tell me what I need to know and I'll reunite you with your sister in a week."

It was all too clear to Kunz. If he had revealed the hiding place of the paintings, this man would not be standing beside him now, wanting answers. No! He would leave Kunz to rot once he had the information, or worse. In his delirium, he must have said something that indicated he had secreted treasure.

Kunz finally spoke, his voice barely audible, "You can't believe what a tortured man says."

"Indeed I can, Hans. You made much sense, about the art. I checked. Those paintings you spoke of have never been found."

"How can you know that?" Kunz was pleading.

"We NKVD people know everything."

Kunz accepted the inevitable. Hildegarde didn't know where the Dreyfus Collection was. She was not at risk. The card he sent probably made no sense to her. He knew now he would never enjoy his stolen treasure, so let the Jew's paintings decay in that hole. Broken as he was, he would not survive his attempt to flee.

So be it.

He closed his eyes, then and remained silent until fingers wrapped around his throat and his eyes popped.

Chapter 8

East Germany, July 10, 1956

The sun rose slowly above the ridge of the Harz Mountains. Peter Warden pulled off the narrow East German road and parked behind a bank of fir trees, the ground softened by a heavy cover of needles. For some reason, he felt it important to conceal his rented car. Traveling anywhere in East Germany had become a nuisance, the authorities making it as difficult as possible for foreigners to get around. Washington had warned him about this, the expectation that all foreigners were spies.

Fortunately, he had so far managed to escape notice.

When he stepped out among the trees, he could smell the fragrance of pine and fir that permeated the woods. He was reminded of Christmas and his fourteen-year-old daughter, Lisa. Sadly, theirs was a reunion that would have to wait.

Peter stood for a moment getting his bearings. At the age of forty-two, he was once more on a mission for the U.S. government. He'd been told by his American sources that an unclouded sunrise was rare in summer, that moisture-laden clouds coming from the northern plains produced constant rain, and in winter, heavy snowfall. Standing there evoked the memory of the summer when, as a young boy, his father took him to visit the Dresden Art Museum. They had stopped to see the old fortified Hanseatic town of Quedlinburg with its engaging timber houses dating to the fifteenth and seventeenth centuries. It had rained then.

In briefings, he'd been told that many of the scattered towns in the valleys and plateaus of the Harz range had long been resorts catering to hikers or skiers in season. But the region's real economic value lay concealed. These mountains, rising abruptly from a plain on every side, had for centuries yielded copper, lead, gold, silver, and zinc. The extracted metals produced wealth to those who owned the land and mined it.

These mines were the reason he had returned to Europe at Washington's behest. More than a decade ago, the Third Reich had used them for a different purpose. With caves deep beneath their surface, they had become the perfect repositories for German valuables as well as European and Russian art systematically plundered by the Nazi regime. From the mine at Grasleben alone, forty-five crates of the best paintings from the Kaiser Friedrich Museum were recovered.

Peter removed a topographic map from his coat pocket and checked for a mountain trail that lay just beyond his hidden car. It would lead him to a high elevation less than a mile ahead and from there he could unobtrusively survey the scene below. He would then descend on another trail to the farm he knew lay isolated in a corner of the valley.

He'd made the decision to not drive directly to the farmhouse, reluctant to risk an immediate confrontation with the woman who lived there, Hans Kunz's twin sister. Instead, he would present himself as one of the many hikers who frequented the region.

As the summer day began heating up, producing the humidity for which the Harz range was known, Peter climbed steadily through the mountain forest, past the fir and spruce and beech that filled its woods. It pleased him to discover that although he had celebrated his birthday in the States weeks earlier, age hadn't appreciably slowed his pace. His mind harked back to the years following World War II, remembering the phone call he'd gotten in Paris about his wife. His daughter had been his only consolation after Ann's tragic death. He had always made time for Lisa and took pleasure in watching her grow. He also had thrown himself into his work at the Warden Art Gallery and was pleased to see the Manhattan gallery become well known. When the directors of the National Gallery of Art in Washington pressed him to resume his search for the missing Dreyfus Collection, he had been reluctant at first to leave his daughter and his business.

But then, Claire, his new wife, assured him the Warden gallery could survive without him for a brief period. With Lisa in school and busy with academics and sports, Claire insisted his daughter would not miss him too much. He thought about Claire, the way she seemed to fit into the business, the ease with which she charmed his customers when they visited the gallery. Is that why he married her? Peter wondered. Certainly, Claire was beautiful and he believed he loved her, but not with the same intensity and passion that he had loved Ann. Her loss haunted him still, especially as Lisa reminded him so much of her mother.

Now, working his way up the steepening path, Peter considered the information he had gleaned the past week. He had gone to East Germany, to the town of Magdeburg on the say-so of Lamont Moore, a former employee of the National Gallery of Art and a Monument Man during the war. Moore knew of Peter's search for the Dreyfus Collection and guessed that Tony Russo, Peter's Washington contact and longtime friend, would have told him about the Harz Mountain repositories. Moore and Russo knew each other. Both men had begun hunting for confiscated European art even before the war ended.

At one point, when Lisa was still a baby, Peter had been asked to be a Monument Man but he declined, citing the pressing needs of family and his gallery. Even so, he remembered Moore telling him that as late as 1944, the Nazis had used the nearby Schönebeck salt mine with its great caverns as an important repository. When the Russians began their advance into East Germany, Lamont had said, the region became a combat zone, valuable art works feverishly moved by the Germans from place to place.

Then a decade later, Lamont had visited him in New York and suggested that Peter resume his search for the missing Dreyfus Collection at the behest of the National Gallery, which had been promised the collection when David and Sarah Dreyfus died. As Peter and Lamont lingered over coffee, the former curator had said he believed the Soviet Trophy Brigades had gotten their hands on the paintings, adding they were probably languishing either in the basements of the Hermitage or the Pushkin Museum. But Peter had his doubts about that. Surely they would have heard something about the collection if that were the case. And David's widow, Sarah Dreyfus, was convinced they were still somewhere in the Harz Mountains.

Sarah Dreyfus continued to live in New York with her two daughters. Peter saw her often and had even visited her at her summer home on Cape Cod. With Washington's sanction, he had enlisted her help shortly after the war ended. Who else besides himself and Sarah would recognize those paintings that he and his father had sold the Dreyfus family?

Besides, he owed David for having failed him.

Anticipating that a painting or two would have fallen into the sticky hands of soldiers, German and American alike, as both combatants managed to purloin souvenirs during the war, both he and Sarah kept careful watch of the markets. They began attending New York art auctions, knowing that dealers lucky enough to acquire such rare paintings would not want to keep them off the market long.

When Peter couldn't leave the city for business or family reasons, Sarah would fly to London, Paris, or Switzerland in his place, being certain not to miss what had become the most valuable auction of all, *Important Old Masters* at Christie's in London. And on buying trips to Europe for his gallery business, Peter made it a point to visit the owners of those galleries with whom he kept in touch. He stressed to those gallery operators that it was in their interest to alert him should any paintings that the Dreyfus family owned appear on the market. At the same time, he knew full well the temptations these dealers faced, considering that valuable works were bringing such escalating prices now that Americans were buying Impressionists. A quiet sale of a masterpiece to a wealthy collector where it might not resurface for generations would make any dealer's fortune.

Peter reached the ridge overlooking a valley not far from the town of Hasselfelde. He leaned against a fallen tree trunk and rested, turning to watch two hawks swoop gracefully among the trees and soar down through the valley below. For a time, he allowed himself the pleasure of watching the peaceful summer scene. It was during this pause he recalled the first important break in his hunt. It occurred in Eisleben, a sixteenth-century city where he found a curator retired from the Dresden Museum who, after a few beers and a fine dinner, talked freely of the time he worked in the mines around Eisleben, cataloging and protecting the artwork that kept inundating the repositories. The man boasted of the Schönebeck salt mine near Magdeburg, a great cavern with vaulted roofs and electric lights two thousand feet underground where he had been temporarily assigned.

This curator spoke of other repositories where paintings were preserved. The coolness at those depths and the salt there captured the moisture in the air and prevented mold. He made a point of lamenting the removal of Dresden Museum objects found in a castle at Meissen by a Soviet team. He had been grateful, the man admitted, as the Allies mounted their offensives and Germany fell apart, to be in a place, underground, protected from the bombs.

In sympathetic agreement, Peter mentioned he had once met an SS major familiar with the mines, a man named Hans Kunz.

Yes, the curator replied, hardly pausing to look up as he cut himself a piece of schnitzel. I remember him. What an intimidating person. Those steely eyes! Scared me half to death each time he appeared. Always had the feeling he'd as soon shoot me dead as speak to me.

The German drank his beer, then gave Peter a sly glance before remarking that Kunz turned up surprisingly often at the mines when he worked there, especially after he and his men had deposited six wooden crates there.

"When these crates first arrived, and only, mind you, after I was certain he and his ERR team had left, I inspected them," the German said. "They had special markings that seemed to catalog whatever was inside. Naturally, I never questioned. Why ask for trouble?

"Kunz came one last time, just after we received word from Hamburg radio that Hitler had committed suicide at the end of April. He had a truck and four men.

"I recognized his Oberleutnant. That man was always with him. The others I did not know," the curator recalled. "He had the crates loaded onto the truck and drove off, and of course, I assumed he was taking them to still another hiding place, especially as the Russian Army was so close."

The curator pursed his lips and looked around to make sure no one was listening. Then he leaned forward and whispered to Peter, "I followed them from the repository for some fresh air and thought it strange he did not take his Oberleutnant with him that time. He left him behind, and I saw the man start walking, to the west."

Now standing atop the Harz Mountain ridge, Peter's thoughts shifted to the problem confronting him, how best to approach Hans Kunz's sister. She was the reason he had returned to Europe. He surveyed the village and farms nestled below in the long narrow valley. He saw a timeless scene, a world that hadn't changed for a century.

Tony Russo, his friend and the man to whom he reported, had shared with him information from the partisans who aided the Russian advance. These fighters claimed that countless German soldiers, especially officers, had been rounded up in that final push through East Germany and had been detained in a holding place nearby before being flown to Russia. Russo believed Kunz was one of these unfortunates.

Kunz' disappearance troubled Peter. He had discussed all the possibilities of finding him, not only with Russo but with Sarah Dreyfus, before he left. She believed the sister, Hildegarde, might know her brother's whereabouts, especially as sources in Germany informed Washington the two were twins. Sarah felt Kunz would have made some attempt to contact his sister as his only living relative. Their parents were dead, killed in the war. Hildegarde now lived alone on the family property on the outskirts of Hasselfelde.

Peter glanced at his watch. The encounter with Fraulein Kunz could not be put off any longer. He began walking downhill through the trees, finally emerging onto the open field. As he stepped carefully around some kind of crop, he saw a woman working in a garden patch close to the building that probably served as a barn. It was probably Hildegarde.

He walked toward her slowly, not wanting to frighten the woman by coming upon her unexpectedly. He needn't have worried, for as he stood there, she straightened suddenly and whipped around, pointing a rifle at him. Startled, he lifted his arms, then stared. The resemblance to her brother was uncanny. She had the same tall, skinny figure, the hard eyes, the narrow features. Twins certainly, but not identical.

"Was wollen sie von mir?" No mistaking the threat in her voice, nor the trace of fear.

Peter replied in German, though he'd been told she spoke English. "I came to talk to you about Hans."

"Hans! You know him?" Her voice caught.

He slowly lowered his arms. "I didn't mean to frighten you, fraulein, but I am searching for things that have been lost and I believe your brother may know where they are." She continued to stare at him, her rifle pointed at his chest.

"You're not German," she said finally.

"No. I'm American," he admitted, surprised she could tell the difference. They stood for a moment looking at one another, her inspection more intense than his. Then, lowering the rifle, she pointed to the house. They should go inside.

He followed her, hesitating at the open door, trying to wipe the dark soil from his shoes on the mat lying there.

Once inside, she turned to face him, her eyes narrowed and her mouth grim.

Peter, glancing about, saw the room was immaculate. What surprised him most were the walls. They were completely covered with paintings, landscapes mostly. Some he recognized as scenes from Paris, others, perhaps, the local countryside. She watched him, saw the surprised expression on his face, then spoke proudly, "Hans's work. All my brother's."

She shoved a wooden chair toward him. "Since you came so far, sit!" For the first time, she put aside the rifle.

Encouraged that the woman was showing less hostility, he pointed to Hans's artwork. "I recognize Paris," he said. "I believe your brother spent time there."

She sank into a chair that faced his. "You know that?"

Then she looked away and said morosely, head down, "But what does it matter. Hans is dead. I feel it in my bones. For a while, I didn't think so, but I do now. He and I, we understood one another. Knew what the other was thinking. No words were needed."

Peter sat quietly, wondering if Hildegarde's instincts were true. He'd heard twins were clairvoyant. If so, was it possible she knew where David's paintings might be? Keeping his voice sympathetic, he asked, "When did you last hear from your brother?"

She looked up then and he saw tears.

"You want to know. Well, I will tell you. It was just before the Russians came. He said he had a plan to make us rich, but he wouldn't tell me what it was. He said he trusted Americans more than Russians. He would head west where the American and British armies were and surrender to them.

"It didn't happen that way," she said bitterly. "I received a card from him finally. It came from somewhere inside Russia. He was their prisoner."

Was? Had he escaped?

Peter leaned forward. "What did the card say?"

She answered him defiantly, "Why should I tell you?"

No reason, he wanted to say to her. His head ached. No reason except that he needed to avenge David's murder, make amends for his cowardice.

He sensed that his silence was discomfiting.

Hildegarde finally asked him, "Who are you, anyway? Why did you come all the way from America to find me?"

He decided he had no recourse except to tell her the truth. He spoke of the missing Dreyfus Collection and its rare paintings. He even told her about David's murder without implicating Kunz. Instead, he stressed the interest the United States and the National Gallery of Art had in finding the collection promised to them.

"Your brother was the last one to move several crates we think contained the collection," he said, "That's why I'm anxious to know what the card said."

"You didn't tell me who you are!"

"Fair enough. My name is Peter Warden and I have an art gallery in New York," he said. "I'm often in touch with the National Gallery of Art and they value my expertise. I came to Paris at their request in 1945 after the war ended and learned your brother was involved with finding artwork for his country. I also discovered he and I both studied in Paris at the same time."

Hildegarde's eyes widened at this.

"I would have come after the war to see you, to try to find your brother, but . . ." It was hard to speak about Ann's death, even now.

"But what?" Hildegarde regarded him with curiosity.

"I received a phone call from America. My wife, Ann, had been struck and killed by a car in New York. We had a daughter. So I returned to the States immediately. That is why I have not pursued this search until now."

"Your daughter is now how old?"

"Fourteen. It was hard to leave her. She and I are very close."

"Like Hans and me, yah!" Hildegarde was actually smiling. "What is her name, your daughter?"

"Lisa."

Peter saw the thaw in her demeanor. She was less tense. He waited for her to speak.

Hildegarde, her voice flat as if nothing mattered anymore, said at last, "You want to know what Hans's card says. Stay here. I will get it for you."

He watched her enter a side room he guessed must be a bedroom and wondered if the card would be of any help and why she assumed her brother was dead.

When she returned, she stood over him and declared, "You speak German. Can you read German script?"

He looked up at her and thought it politic if she read it to him. When he made no move to take the card, she admitted,

"I question if Hans really wrote it. It sounds so strange, but, of course, it is his handwriting."

"Strange? Why do you say that, Fraulein Kunz?"

"It wasn't the usual. He speaks of our childhood and asks if I remember what fun we had exploring the mountains. He says here," and she began to read directly, "'We'd slip inside and only as children could we continue on and emerge in a place we treasured. Remember?'"

"What else does he say?"

"'Be warned. There are spirits left behind since you were there last. Ignore them, cast them out, and rejoice in what you find.'"

She looked at Warden questioning, "What is he saying, my brother? What does he want from me?"

When the American didn't reply at first, she added, "Perhaps it is because the Harz Mountains are supposed to be haunted by witches. There is a legend they convene on the highest point, Broken Mountain, on Walpurgisnacht, the witches' sabbath."

Peter didn't know about witches, only murderers.

"I would guess, fraulein, because the Russians censor prisoners' mail, he was sending a message whose meaning only you would know."

Her composure failed her. She sat down heavily and put her hands to her face.

"Herr Warden, I am so afraid Hans is dead. They tell me only that he is in a hospital and has been very sick."

"They?" Peter stiffened. "Who's they?"

"Two days ago, a man visited me, a stranger. I am certain he was Russian, though he spoke my language well. He came in a car with a driver. I don't like him. I don't trust what he tells me. That's why I carry the rifle when I go outside my house. If he comes back and threatens me, I will shoot."

Her words alarmed Peter. "Tell me what he said."

"He said he had been in the Soviet navy stationed at Leningrad but that he had spoken against the government and was sent away to the prison, where he found Hans. He said Hans was desperate to escape and finally did, but was caught and brought back."

Tears filled her eyes again. "He told me Hans was badly beaten and became delirious. He spoke my name and mentioned treasure. This man explained that as he had expected to be released soon from the prison, he promised Hans he would look me up and help me find the treasure. We would use it to bribe the guards to set Hans free."

Hildegarde dabbed at her eyes with a handkerchief. "I know what he said about Hans escaping is true. My Hans would have the courage." There was sudden anger in her voice. "But this man lied about himself. I know he did. The look in his eyes told me."

Peter nodded. He would have to trust this woman's instincts; after all, she was Kunz's twin sister. He turned his attention to the coded message in the card her brother had sent her, repeating the words.

"A place we treasured. What do you think he meant? Did the Russian say what the treasure was?"

"No."

"The card, Fraulein Hildegard, will you let me see it?"

A moment's pause and then Hildegarde handed it to him and studied his face as he read it. When he looked up, there was a question in his eyes, one she anticipated.

He asked, "In your childhood, was there a special place just you two shared?"

"Yes. We played hide and seek all the time, Hans and I. We didn't need anyone else. As we grew older, we would walk beyond our property, up into the forest. Once when we were exploring along a mountainside, Hans noticed a slit in the rock face. It turned out to be an entrance to a small cave. That day we had fun pretending all sorts of things."

She sighed. "We went there again to play inside. Hans noticed a small opening. Always daring, he got down on hands and knees and crawled inside. I expected to see him back out and waited, frightened for him, but no, he came out head first. I remember wondering how he could turn around inside such a place.

"He wanted me to do what he did, but I was too afraid and refused. But the next time we went into the forest to the cave, he brought a flashlight. This time, he insisted I follow him through the opening. If you knew Hans, he could be unrelenting. To please him, I got up my courage and slowly crawled behind him on hands and knees, certain we would get stuck and die, but after what seemed forever, it ended and I could stand up.

"Hans flashed on the light. I gasped at the size of the cave I now saw. It was immense, at least to a little girl. We walked around, holding hands, and finally crawled back through. Hans made me promise never to tell anyone about the place, especially our parents. We never went back there together, though I think he did, until he grew too big to fit the hole."

Peter tried to keep the excitement out of his voice. "Would you be willing to tell me where it is?"

Hildegarde did not respond.

He tried again, asking, "Will you come with me and show me the place?" There was no doubt in his mind about the card's message. The missing Dreyfus Collection had to be stored there.

"No! I will not go. Didn't you read what Hans says? There are spirits there. He wants me to be brave, but without him, I have no courage."

She lowered her voice. "All these years I have been so lonely and I will go on being lonely because Hans was the only one who made me feel whole and everything that speaks to me of him tells me he is dead."

Her face contorted in pain while Peter sat helplessly by, wondering what he could do to mitigate her grief. Finally, he stood up and went to her, and gently lifting her from her chair, held her in his arms. He knew what lonely was. But at least he'd had Lisa. Hildegarde had no one.

The two stood together until Hildegarde pushed him away. "Whatever is there," she said, "Hans wants me to have it, but I don't want it. I don't need riches now." She sighed heavily. "I have no one to share them with. I'm too old to have children, even if I were to marry. Supposing the treasure turns out to be the paintings you seek, you tell me they belong, not to us, but to America."

She took a deep breath, having reached a decision. "I wash my hands of this, Herr Warden. You deal with the spirits."

Hildegarde went to a desk that stood by the window. Finding a pen and paper, she began to slowly draw a map. He stood by, holding his breath.

After a few minutes, Hildegarde handed him the paper. Then she explained what landmarks to look for. "Remember to turn the corner on the plateau beside a ravine or you won't see the narrow entrance, she said. She began moving toward the door. "Come outside with me," she commanded.

He followed her into the shed, where she handed him a flashlight. When they emerged, with the summer sun full on them at midday, she pointed a forested hill behind the barn. Peter thanked her and began walking in the direction she had pointed him. Behind him, he heard her say, "Good luck. Come back soon and tell me you found what you were looking for."

Chapter 9

East Germany, July 10, 1956

Peter held Hildegarde's map in his hand, glancing at it from time to time. When he reached the tree line at the end of the field, he followed the trail Hans Kunz's sister had clearly marked. She had said it would take less than an hour to reach the cave, reminding him, a faint smile on her thin lips, that as young children familiar with the mountains, she and Hans had made it in half the time, running most of the way.

He began a steady climb through an increasingly dense spruce forest interspersed with pine. Though he took a wrong turn or two and had to retrace his steps, the map Hildegarde had drawn and her spoken directions kept him from getting completely lost. As he climbed, he passed several dark wooded ravines and wondered how the children had found the cave in the first place. Checking the map one more time, he turned a corner, skirted yet another ravine, and saw the large pine tree and several huge boulders.

Holding his breath, he peered behind a shield of bushes and saw a narrow cranny. The slit in the rock wall was more than six feet high and perhaps twenty inches wide, certainly enough to slip a crate through, he reasoned. Gathering courage, he inched in sideways and once inside found he could stand in the small interior space.

He had brought a flashlight with him, jammed in his pants pocket. Pulling it out, he flashed the light around along the earth floor looking for the little opening Hildegarde had described, the one she said she and her brother had crawled through on hands and knees when they were children.

It wasn't there. Peter cursed soundly. Why would anyone believe six crates could fit the space he was in, especially if it took two men to carry them inside. There was no opening through which the two children could have crawled. The woman was confused. Perhaps Kunz had found a different cave.

Peter felt sick, defeated. He might as well give up his search, admit to Washington and finally, to Sarah, that the collection was indeed lost. Weighed by disappointment, he stepped back against one wall, almost stumbling as his heel connected with a pile of earth. In his frustration, he kicked back at it, but the earth wouldn't move. Turning the flashlight on the obstruction, he gasped. A human hand lay exposed.

Breaking out in a cold sweat, he understood now what Hans had meant by "spirits" and why Hildegarde, guessing Hans's meaning, wanted no part of the search.

Peter shivered, his mind racing. If he quit now, what would he tell Tony Russo, that he had found a hand? He took off his jacket, looked around again, and noticed a shovel lying half-buried in the dirt. Extracting the shovel, he began to dig.

He found a body attached to the hand. It was dressed in a now faded and torn green Nazi uniform. Trying not to look at the face, Peter turned the corpse over, seeking some identification. It was then that he discovered a package lying partially concealed under the body. Only after he had removed the dusty wrapping that covered it and unrolled a small painting hastily cut from its frame that he realized he had found the hiding place of the Dreyfus collection.

The poor bastard. He had stolen the painting and Hans Kunz never guessed.

The puzzle suddenly came together for him. He was certain that beyond the collapsed wall, the collection stood untouched in the larger cave that Hildegarde had described. Kunz must have obliterated any opening using explosives to resemble a natural cave-in.

The little painting he now held in his hand, by Antony van Dyck, gave promise to what he might at last find. He recognized the painting, having himself sold it to David Dreyfus, one of the first deals his father encouraged him to make when he returned from his studies in Europe and entered the business.

Sobered by the find, Peter re-rolled the Van Dyck carefully, picked up his jacket, and slipped the painting into one sleeve. Laying the jacket aside, he took up the shovel once more and with the same earth he had earlier dug away, covered the body over. He had the same difficulty Kunz had concealing the outstretched hand. With a sigh, he parted the arm at the elbow and placed it alongside the man, then buried it once more.

Recovering his jacket, Peter exited through the narrow opening, relieved to breathe fresh air again. His initial exhilaration that he had succeeded in his long search gave way to deep sadness. He wondered if this powerful melancholy was inherent in the beauty of these strange and wildly formed mountains. Had they affected him? He took a deep breath and resolved that witches were not his thing, not unless they appeared in a painting. Hildegarde had called Witches' Night Walpurgisnacht. What a spectacle such a painting would make.

As Peter began walking back to the farmhouse, the shovel still in his hand, he decided that what assailed him was not euphoria or melancholy, but hunger. He hadn't eaten anything in hours. Perhaps Hildegarde would feed him.

As he approached the farmhouse, however, Peter suddenly halted. A car had just pulled up. He saw a heavyset man get out of the car and walk to the front door. The stranger stopped abruptly when Hildegarde appeared at the door, her rifle pointed directly at him.

Something snapped in Peter. He threw his jacket to the ground, forgetting the precious painting enclosed in the sleeve. Using the shovel as a weapon, he charged the stranger like a crazy man, remembering how he had once failed his friend, David Dreyfus. The man turned and, seeing Warden's wild approach, dove for the car.

But the car did not drive off.

Peter slowed, having realized how foolishly he was acting, how out of character. Sheepish now, he came up still panting beside the car. The dark-haired driver who sat at the wheel stonily refused to look at him, but the man Peter had been prepared to assault opened the car door and stepped out. There was a smile on his face now as if what he had just witnessed was an everyday occurrence.

He stopped Peter cold when he said in perfect English, "You must be the American who keeps asking questions about Hans Kunz."

Glancing at Warden's weapon, he added, "What were you doing with a shovel?"

Peter realized then what a mistake he'd made. He had to have raised questions in the man's mind especially if these men were who thought they were.

The stranger smiled more broadly. He, too, wanted to play the episode down. "Hey," he said, "Better a shovel than a gun."

The man's words did nothing to mollify Peter, his smile so patently false.

"Why are you here?" Peter demanded in German.

"Calm down."

"You didn't answer my question."

"Do you speak for this lady?" The heavyset stranger pointed at Hildegarde, who still held her rifle aimed at him.

Peter surprised himself when he answered, "Yes, I do."

Just then, Hildegarde approached the two men standing beside the car but kept her rifle raised. Her face contorted in anger as she shouted to Warden in German.

"He's the man I spoke of, the one who kept saying he was Hans's friend in prison. He lies. Hans is dead. I know it. Make him get off my property and never come back."

As she continued talking, the man turned toward his car. Suddenly he whipped around, and this time, he held a gun in his hand, surprising both Peter and Hildegarde. She stiffened and shot him in the shoulder.

The stranger screamed and dropped his gun. The driver suddenly opened his door and, leaping out, a revolver in his hand, shot Hildegarde in the chest.

Stunned, Peter ran to her, oblivious to the stranger's screams of pain and rage. But then he heard the wounded man, speaking Russian, berate his driver for shooting the woman. She was a source of information, he heard him scream. Now, she would be unable to tell them what they'd come here to learn.

Shutting their voices out, Peter bent down and cradled Hildegarde in his arms. Blood seeped from her mouth. He watched, horrified, as her eyes, fixed on his face, slowly lost their focus. Only when he heard the car motor start did he force himself to look away from her in time to see the car disappear down the road.

Hildegarde died in his arms a few minutes later. Holding her limp body, it took Peter several anguished minutes before he realized that if he was found in this compromising position, he could easily be accused of her murder. No one would believe his story about some Soviet agents. Struggling under her weight, Peter carried Hildegarde into the house and laid her on her bed. When he straightened up, still distraught, he discovered that his clothes were bloodied. His instincts kicked in then. He knew what he needed to do. Using a handkerchief to cover his fingers, he first searched the house until he found the card Kunz had written to Hildegarde from prison.

He began opening closets, looking for clothes that could fit him. In one closet, he found pants and shirts, and though he wasn't as tall as Kunz had been, still, they fit, more or less. He exchanged them for his own bloody garments and hitched up the pants. He then started a fire in the fireplace to burn Kunz's card and his own bloody clothes but thought better of this and, stepping outside, he retrieved the shovel where he had dropped it after he rushed to Hildegarde's aid. Returning to the farmhouse, Peter placed the remains of his bloody garments from the fireplace into a bucket, then buried them behind the shed, spreading straw over the newly dug earth. He wiped his fingerprints from the shovel and stood it in the shed, not forgetting to obliterate his prints from the shed door. Reentering the house, he continued to carefully remove prints from anything he might have touched.

Finally, he left the farmhouse and, walking through the field, located the jacket he had flung aside when reason failed him and he mounted his attack on the stranger. He checked; the Van Dyck portrait still lay concealed in the sleeve.

Once back on the trail that led through the mountain forest to where he had hidden the rented car, he decided to place an anonymous call to the authorities at Hasselfelde as soon as he found a public phone, telling them where to find Hildegarde's body. After that, when he returned to Washington with the location of the collection finally established, he would let the two governments, East Germany and the United States, arrange details, duke it out if need be, whatever it took to retrieve David's paintings.

Peter would be done with it at last. The search was costing too many lives.

Chapter 10

Naples, July 17, 1956

Peter sat at in the shadows of a café in Naples, waiting impatiently for the man he had arranged to meet. The café was on the Rettifilo, a broad thoroughfare not far from the harbor. The day was hot and muggy and Peter felt uncomfortably sticky. While he had passed through Naples before on the occasional trip to look for Italian paintings, this was the first time he had been in Naples in July and he promised himself he would never come to the city again in the depths of the summer.

He had chosen this shabby café for the rendezvous deliberately. It was well off the tourist grid, and he was certain he was being hunted. Since fleeing East Germany, he had become convinced that the men who murdered Kunz's twin sister were now looking for him through a vast network of spies. He wasn't just being paranoid. When he had checked in for his flight at the Frankfurt airport a few days earlier, he had seen several beefy thugs closing in as he approached his boarding gate. One had even drawn a weapon and Peter was astonished to think that they might attempt an assault in such a public place. He didn't wait to find out. He sprinted through the nearest exit door and managed to elude them by hanging unobserved on the far side of an empty baggage cart that was moving off the tarmac. Later, from a concealed place outside the airport, he saw the same men leave the terminal and heard them speaking not German, but Russian, to each other.

It had to be the Dreyfus Collection they sought. The men he encountered at the farmhouse represented some organization or government that desperately wanted David's paintings and the wealth their sale would bring.

Peter concluded that if Frankfurt, an international hub, was under surveillance, no doubt the Paris airport would be closely watched. He decided to take a train to Vienna, hopping aboard the last car at the last minute. On arrival he took a cab from the station to its airport, but after asking for the driver's indulgence, continued to sit inside the cab for a few minutes. To his dismay, he became aware of men in pairs, scanning new arrivals. He realized that if he sought help from security personnel, he might be turned over to the East German police and questioned in connection with Hildegarde's murder.

He decided to ask the driver take him to the American embassy in Vienna. But once there, he again saw several loiterers resembling the men who had pursued him in Frankfurt. At that point, Peter had begun to wonder whether he would ever get out of Europe with the crucial information he possessed. He had to phone Washington and tell them about the cave, but getting home with the exact information that Hildegarde provided him seemed an increasingly remote possibility. Yet he had to try. If he fell into the hands of the Russians, they would torture him for the information they sought and then kill him. Yet another disturbing thought struck Peter. Was he actually dealing with the Soviet government, or with international thieves?

He finally had the Viennese cab driver deposit him at a busy corner of the city. When he was certain the cab had gone on its way, he walked for a mile or two and found a seedy hotel in a neighborhood he knew Americans did not frequent. He had hardly slept since Hasselfelde. Even though it was still daylight, exhausted as he was, as soon as his head hit the pillow, he fell soundly asleep in his clothes and didn't wake up until the following afternoon. He washed and shaved; fortunately, he had with him the small carry-on bag he had planned to take aboard the flight in Frankfurt; it contained his toiletries and the rolled-up Van Dyck painting he had found in the cave in Hasselfelde.

After leaving the hotel, Peter had gone to the cavernous Vienna train station. There he had slipped into an enclosed phone booth and tried to phone his contact in Washington, his old friend Tony Russo. But Russo was not at his desk and Peter declined to leave word with a secretary he didn't know. He tried Tony at his home, but no one answered.

He thought of calling Sarah Dreyfus. She would be at her summer home on Cape Cod. He wanted to confide in her but couldn't remember her Massachusetts phone number. In addition, Tony had warned him not to entrust information to anyone except a select few who worked in U.S. intelligence. But he couldn't reach them, either.

Weighing his options, Peter decided to try to leave Europe from Italy, a country he knew well. He took a series of buses, one after the other, heading south from Vienna through the Alps, then along the National Road from Rome to Naples. In the small towns where the bus briefly stopped, unshaven with clothes wrinkled, Peter knew he no longer resembled an American tourist. Two days later he had arrived in Naples. He'd had plenty of time to think about his predicament on the tiring journey and had concluded that he had to somehow record the information he carried in his head in case he didn't make it home. At a small way station near Naples, he again tried to contact Tony and failed. It was then that Peter decided to arrange a rendezvous with an Italian he'd known and trusted for years.

Now, as Peter sat in the Naples café waiting for his old friend, Rodolfo Siviero, he tried to stifle his growing impatience by reminiscing about how they had met. The Italian had been head of the Italian secret service attached to the

Allied Command, and he and Siviero had surreptitiously met several times in Rome during the war. When peace was declared, Siviero, a descendent of an old Venetian family, became the first Italian ambassador to Germany.

Peter knew his friend had made it a practice, all these years, to learn where the retreating Germans had taken their stolen Italian masterpieces. Like a bulldog hanging on to a pant leg, Siviero tenaciously kept track of those paintings, much to the dismay of art dealers throughout Europe and the United States who had hoped to turn a dishonest dollar. There had been times when Peter had attended auctions in the Europe and noticed Italian works he knew to have been stolen by the Germans. He had passed this precious information along to Siviero, enabling the former undercover agent to retrieve important Italian paintings for his country.

Finally, Siviero showed. As usual, the Italian was dressed impeccably.

"Rodolfo, over here."

Siviero's mouth dropped open at the sight of his friend's unkempt appearance, but he quickly masked his surprise. The two men shook hands and the Italian took a seat across the table from Peter.

"Ciao, Peter. Shame on you insisting I come to Naples when you could have met me in Rome."

Peter noticed Siviero's hair had grayed and, as always, he favored English tweeds. He thought of teasing his friend about his sartorial tastes, but instead got right to the point.

"I need your help, Rodolfo," he said. "I can't tell you why, but I must get back to the United States." No point in endangering his friend with too much information.

"So get on the next plane out of Rome!"

"I tried that in Frankfurt. They were waiting for me. I barely eluded them."

Siviero frowned. "They?"

Peter ignored his query.

"Tell me, Rodolfo, where I can go to put information on one of those plastic magnetic tapes that we perfected during the war. And can you steer me to someone you trust who won't talk about it to anyone?"

Peter paused. "I also need a different passport."

Siviero sighed. He chewed at his lip, thinking.

After a moment, he said quietly, "Mario will do it for you. He has the microphone and the equipment and I know he keeps up with the latest technology. He lives here in Naples. During the war, his father owned a fishing boat that proved useful to us when we had to go undercover. He's a good boy. He won't betray you."

Siviero studied his American friend. "Okay, I won't probe," he finally said. "I will take you to Mario and let him know it's for me you are making the tape. But I won't stay for the taping. Obviously, the information is private and I have too many irons in the fire just now to get scorched by yours." He smiled. "I won't even ask if it has anything to do with the missing Dreyfus Collection," he said. "We both know none of it has turned up so far." He shrugged. "But that's your thing."

Peter said nothing; it was best if he didn't place his friend in jeopardy by telling him what had happened. Siviero waited just a minute and then stood up.

"Okay, mi amici," he said. "Let's leave this hole in the wall and do our business."

"You better go first, Rodolfo. Find a cab. I'll hop in at the last moment."

"Right."

As they sat beside one another in the rear of the cab, Siviero said in a low voice, "You know I can smuggle you out of Italy. Not all the way to America, but Turkey, if you like, or Greece, or across the Straits, to Morocco."

"Thanks, Rodolfo, but I have a plan that I think will work and I don't want to involve you deeper," Peter replied, warmed by his friend's offer. "Italy has too many communists."

"At least, my friend, it's not the Italian Mafioso who give you trouble." Silviero chuckled and reached for his wallet.

"You'll need money."

"Yes, thanks! I was afraid I might run short."

As the cab entered an alleyway in a different section of old Naples and drew up to a small house, Peter said, "I'll need a change of clothes, simple stuff."

"Mario will have what you need."

"I also want to make a phone call to the United States."

"No problem. He has a phone."

As they pulled up to a nondescript house, Siviero asked the cab driver to wait for him. A handsome young man opened the door to them. He had curly black hair, worn long, and dark eyes that momentarily expressed amazement at seeing them. But he greeted Siviero warmly and invited them in. The pair entered the house and found the interior darkened and cool, a welcome relief from the sultry heat. A brief conversation ensued between the two Italians.

Siviero then turned to Peter, assuring him, "You are in good hands. Mario understands what you need and I have asked that he refrain from listening to your message while you record. Now, my friend, I need to get back to Rome."

Siviero gave Peter a warm hug. "Va bene."

Mario shut his front door and went to get the equipment Siviero told him was needed. When he returned, he carefully explained to his guest how it operated and then, glancing once more around the room to make sure all was in order, he left Peter alone.

Following Mario's instructions, speaking clearly to the tape, Peter addressed himself to Tony Russo. He kept the message precise, trying as best he could to replicate the spoken directions Hildegarde had given him. When he had finished, he called for Mario, who returned to the room and showed him a small stainless-steel box and some plastic covering.

Peter carefully wrapped the miniature tape in the plastic, sealing it twice. He then inserted the wrapped package into the small box that would fit into his pockets and further sealed it in heavy plastic. He placed Tony's name and address in it. Only then did he let Mario lead him to another room, where the young Italian had laid out the clothes he would need, everyday Neapolitan work clothes he had requested as well as a package of hair dye.

"Mario, what do I owe you, for all this?"

"Rodolfo took care of everything," the young man answered. "You owe me nothing." He paused. "He said you wanted to make an international phone call. When you have changed your clothes, I will show you the telephone. Do you know how to place the call?"

"Yes."

At this, Mario left the room, closing the door behind him. Peter showered in Mario's bathroom and dyed his blonde hair brown, using the dye he had asked Mario to find for him. When he joined Mario in the kitchen, the young man, making no comment on Peter's altered appearance, showed him where the phone was and left him again.

Peter tried one more time to reach Tony. He let the agent's phone ring for minutes – to no avail. He swore softly to himself and hung up. He then placed a call to the New York Adirondacks, praying the counselors at her summer camp could find Lisa quickly. It seemed like an eternity before he heard her voice through the wires.

"Daddy?"

"Lisa, sweetheart. How are you?"

"Fine." Her young voice was thin. "I miss you. When are you coming home?"

"Honey," he said, fighting to keep his own voice even. "I can't know for sure when that will be, but if I am delayed in

Europe, tell Uncle Tony that I called and when. He may come from Washington to see you."

"Okay." Her voice trailed in disappointment.

"Honey, I'm bringing a little painting you will like. You can keep it for a while. It's by a painter called Van Dyck and it's a portrait. The colors are beautiful." He didn't want to stop talking, to break the connection between them.

"The edges are a little jagged, but we'll find a frame for it. Tell Tony I found it in the Harz Mountains near Hasselfelde, but tell him you don't know exactly where. I didn't say. Just tell him there's a cave opening beside an old pine tree and a cluster of three large rocks like sentinels alongside the pine."

He heard her sob and wondered if she heard him. Then she said, in a small tight voice, "Daddy, I can't wait until you come home. I'm sure the painting is beautiful. I love you."

"I love you too, Lisa. I need to go. Goodbye, sweetheart." Reluctantly he hung up.

The next morning, Peter walked slowly toward the Stazione Marittima, the steamship wharf built after World War II. He looked up at the sleek ocean liner lying at its pier, its hull black in stark contrast to the white upper decks. At that moment, the decks were lit by the late morning Neapolitan sun highlighting a single funnel that rose emphatically near the ship's bow.

It was reassuring to see passengers in the process of boarding. There were several different gangplanks separating the first-class and cabin passengers from the large groups of Italian families emigrating to the United States. Peter understood the element of safety these immigrants provided him. As he took his place in line with the noisy, excited Italian families moving toward the ship's lower gangplank, he knew the clothes he wore stamped him as one of them. Even so, he kept his head down and affected a slouch while carrying a scruffy suitcase, one Mario had given him. At the last moment he realized he would need some kind of luggage to carry off his disguise as well as a place to hide the Van Dyck painting. Mario had also supplied him with a new passport, one with an Italian name.

Mario had left Peter at his house that evening and returned a few hours later, the document in his hand.

"Hey, Giuseppe!" he said. "Giuseppe DiSanto. You like it?" He laughed, the first sign of humor Peter had seen in the young man since they had met.

Peter had grinned back. "You couldn't give me a better name than that, Mario?" he teased.

Before meeting with Siviero the day before, Peter had passed the Stazione Marittima and spotted the proud ocean liner lying at her berth, preparations being made for departure. The idea had struck him like lightning; why not pass himself off as Italian and board her? He spoke the language well enough. If anyone was stationed at the gangplank looking for him, they would hardly be paying attention to the immigrant Italian families who would be occupying C-deck, the cheapest and smallest of the cabins aboard the huge ship.

The next morning, Mario, in a scratched and dented old car, had driven him to the pier. Peter made his way to the ticket office, where he managed to insert himself into a group of emigrants as if he were one of them. When it came his turn, the ticket agent looked up at Peter's blue eyes but noting his shabby appearance expressed no surprise when Peter asked politely for a cheap cabin. Looking through his sheets, the man explained that if he wished to share a cabin, it would cost less, but Peter wanted the luxury of being alone. He had the money to pay for it, in part thanks to Siviero's generosity. As the agent took his money, he informed him, "That's one of the last single cabins in C-class."

As Peter waited to walk up the gangplank, he noticed a man, dressed like a stevedore but with binoculars, studying the ascending passengers. However, this man seemed to be concentrating on the affluent travelers. But then he saw two more men, burly individuals, on the dock, continually glancing at the stevedore as if awaiting a signal from him.

Peter moved closer to two families who were boarding C-class. He smiled at a young woman, hoping there was no husband to make a nasty scene. He stepped beside her and, speaking in Italian, introduced himself, explaining that he too was emigrating to the States. He said he expected the voyage would be a pleasant one and continued the one-sided conversation as they slowly moved up the lower gangplank onto the ship.

Once on board, they parted ways and Peter approached a steward for directions to his cabin. He finally found it, amidships, on the starboard side of the huge vessel. There was still one important matter he needed to attend to, the disposition of the tape now fastened securely around his waist. If anything happened to him, the tape had to be in a separate place with the address inside the waterproof packing directing the finder to send it to his friend, Tony Russo, at a Washington, D.C., address. He paused in the tiny cabin, wondering where the package would be safest.

Peter was familiar with ocean liners, having sailed frequently with his father to Europe on pleasure as well as business trips. He knew that pursers sometimes stored passengers' valuables in the ship's vaults and the captains often had their own safes. That's where he would have the package stored. The voyage would take nine days, plenty of time to secure the tape, catch up on his sleep, think about the future. He looked forward to seeing his daughter again.

Having resolved that dilemma, Peter put down his suitcase and looked at his ticket again.

It was the *Andrea Doria* that would carry him home.

PART
TWO

Chapter 11

Mattapoisett, May 1967

A heavy New England fog had invaded the Massachusetts coast. Lisa Warden felt its soft dampness on her long dark hair as she drove, windows open. Her eyes ached. It was the first week of May and Lisa had fully expected her trip would be made in daylight. But that wasn't to be. The fog slowed traffic and the light had begun to fade. She had been on the road for several hours when the fog crept in from Long Island Sound, making it increasingly difficult for drivers to see what lay ahead.

The change in weather surprised her. When she left Manhattan in the late afternoon, its tall buildings were wreathed in sunlight. Now she found herself in another world altogether, straining to see the white line that divided both lanes of Route 6. Lisa glanced at her watch. It was after seven. Straining to see the road, she felt the urge to get out of her car, stretch her limbs, and rest her eyes. She was on her way to Woods Hole, where a new job awaited her, as a graphics artist for the Woods Hole Oceanographic Institution. She was grateful that her degree from the Manhattan Art School had offered her this opportunity. But whatever awaited her in Woods Hole could wait.

Approaching an intersection, she looked for a place to pull over and, despite the thick fog, saw a sign close by the road advertising a real estate office. She had reached Mattapoisett. Lisa decided this was as good a place as any to take a break.

She made a right-hand turn and pulled over to the curb in front of a store. She parked and shut the engine down. There, surrounded by fog, she took a deep breath, relaxed back against the car seat, and closed her tired eyes.

In the quiet of an apparently deserted street, she couldn't help but reflect on the reasons that brought her to Massachusetts from Manhattan, a place she no longer considered home. She had no family now. Her mother had died when she was four years old. Her father had remarried when she was eight but after he disappeared when Lisa was fifteen, her stepmother had run his gallery into the ground, exhibiting art that his regular customers didn't much care for. When Lisa complained about what was going on, Claire had enrolled her in a Manhattan boarding school to get her out of the house. The gallery soon went bankrupt, and since her father had not left a will, Lisa didn't inherit anything. She was able to go to art school only because her mother's mother, who died shortly after her mother did, had left her a small trust fund.

Everyone who had known her mother, Ann, remarked on how much Lisa looked like her, the same slight figure, pale complexion, and brown sloe eyes. But she couldn't really remember her mother or mourn her. Her father's strange disappearance was a different story—it had devastated her. She was now twenty-six, but sorrow and emptiness hovered over her like a cloud that refused to go away.

She suddenly remembered the last time she had seen Mattapoisett. It was when she, her stepmother Claire, and her father had stopped there for lunch one summer afternoon on their way to the cape. She had been ten years old and they were taking a long-anticipated vacation. It came back to her, how bright the Massachusetts sky had been that day, how impressed she had been with the simple cottages that sat back behind small gardens blooming with summer flowers.

The memory of white picket fences supporting vibrant rose bushes and sheltering red, yellow, and purple flowers filled her with nostalgia. She wondered, Could that have been the beginning of her desire to paint nature?

On that brilliantly sunlit afternoon, she and her father had spied sailboat masts over the rooftops of several cottages and gone to track them down, leaving Claire to scout out a restaurant where they could lunch. They found the path to a small marina, one that seemed in her childish eyes to be holding the swaying sailboats in the water, captive. As they stood together in a freshening breeze at the end of a pier, her hand in his, she remembered her father had tried to explain how the waves in Buzzards Bay responded to wind and tide.

Tears sparked in her eyes. She missed her father so much. In sudden anguish, she called to him, her cry echoing within her. Where are you now? What did I do to make you abandon me?

His disappearance had been almost too great to bear. When he didn't come home, others came looking for him. The Tony she had always called "Uncle" appeared at the Warden Art Gallery the evening her stepmother allowed her to attend an important art exhibit. He took her aside and she told him then about her father's telephone call, the one he had made when she was at summer camp. She tried hard to remember her father's message, even the name of the painter who had painted the small picture he said he was bringing her. That night, it was agreed between them she would never tell anyone about the phone call, including Claire.

Sadly, she hadn't seen Uncle Tony since.

There had been a second man, heavyset with a round flushed face and small narrow eyes, who came to the gallery that fall when Lisa happened to be there. She was sure he was only pretending an interest in buying a painting. He had asked Claire a lot of questions, and then, turning to her, asked where her father was. Claire had been charmed by this stranger, Lisa could see, but no one, not even Claire, had any idea what had happened to Peter.

When this overbearing stranger attempted to question her, Lisa lied to him about hearing from her father. Her stepmother had soon intervened, thinking the man wanted to buy a painting. This gave Lisa her excuse to slip away into the storeroom and out the back door. Lisa wondered how this man had come to know her father as he claimed. From the questions he asked, he certainly didn't know where Peter was.

And there was the woman who came to the gallery, apparently wanting to know if, after her father's disappearance, his daughter was provided for. At least, that was the gist of her conversation with Claire that Lisa overheard. The woman's name was Sarah Dreyfus and Lisa recalled her father having mentioned her name in fond terms. He said this woman had met Lisa before as a young child but she didn't remember that. That day in the gallery she had listened to the two women talking, dismayed because their exchange became heated. And then they moved too far away for her to hear their conversation.

Suddenly restless, Lisa decided she needed to replicate the walk she'd had with her father to the pier where the boats were anchored. Perhaps then she could lay her lingering grief to rest, a final memory that might help her deal with his loss. She pulled the key from the ignition, opened the car door, and stepped out into the fog.

Walking past the store that was closed for the evening, she noticed the day's unsold newspapers bundled on the step, to be picked up at the next morning's delivery. The headline on the front page stared back at her, "Russian Trawlers Fishing Cape Waters."

As she walked, the fog allowed her to sense rather than see where the houses stood, barely discernible, dabs of yellow light signifying there were people inside. She followed the sidewalk a short distance and instinctively stepped off on a path to continue on between two widely separated cottages. It was an act of memory that defied logic and the fog. Fifty feet further, she trod on wooden planks. This must be it, she thought, that dock I remember that juts out into the bay. For several long moments, Lisa stood at the end of the pier engulfed in memory.

If she dallied, it was because she and her father had always liked the sea. Perhaps that was why she decided to take the job on Cape Cod. Not yet the season for boats, but still there were a few vessels tied to the pilings. The lapping of water against their hulls carried the message of their presence.

Slowly Lisa began to experience a feeling of detachment from her past, a feeling she had been desperately seeking. Alone on the pier, she imagined herself the only human being in the village. Breathing the moist air deeply, she was able for the moment to will away the tenseness and melancholy that so often plagued her since her father's disappearance. But as she stood there alone, she began to sense there was someone nearby. She turned and peered uneasily through the mist but saw no one. Lisa shivered suddenly. She began to carefully retrace her steps to the car. She reached it without encountering anyone, slipped quickly behind the wheel, and continued on her way to Woods Hole.

Chapter 12

Woods Hole, June 1967

The wharf extending behind the Bigelow Building was unusually noisy that morning. Matthew Chambers refused to allow the sound to bother him. He had already noticed the cause: heavy oceanographic equipment being loaded onto a ship's deck. He remained seated at his desk fixed in thought, unconsciously drumming his fingers against the desktop.

In his mid-thirties, Chambers knew he was considered young for the position he now held as acting director of WHOI, an institution dedicated to marine science. But he was confident he could handle the job through the next few months, at least until the director returned. According to the scuttlebutt, his boss was enduring a difficult recovery from appendicitis and not expected to resume control of the institute until fall.

Chambers normally headed up Ocean Engineering, one of WHOI's five major departments. Well liked and respected, he had a reputation for getting things done. He was six feet tall, had a square-shaped face and hair that was reddish blond, with hazel eyes. Everyone in his department called him Matt.

It had been a surprise when the Oceanographic's board decided to temporarily fill the director's position and chose Matt. The board told him they felt convinced the summer program was too important to allow the institute to drift without a director. Matt was only just beginning to realize the scope of the duties he had taken on. He had had no idea what was involved. He had to admit his least favorite part of the job was squiring around official visitors, usually politicians, who came to assure themselves that the nation's tax money was being well spent while they themselves spent the taxpayers' money on a semi-holiday. They arrived with hardly any advance warning, obligating him to make scarce time for them. But what choice did he have? Since the federal government had begun funding the Oceanographic Institution in the '40s, legislators and the military had come to expect special treatment.

Just two weeks ago, he had had to quickly arrange an overnight trip on the institute's vessel, *Atlantis II*, to New Hampshire. There, Matt had welcomed the vice president of the United States, Hubert Humphrey, on board for a short trip down the coast. Although Matt had been anxious about the trip, everything went well and Matt had been impressed by the vice president. At fifty-six, Humphrey was witty, articulate, and very attentive when Matt showed him around the vessel. Having deposited its distinguished guest back in Washington, the ship was back at Woods Hole and in the process of completing final preparations for a long scientific voyage.

A loud commotion disturbed his thoughts. He pushed back his chair and walked to the open window overlooking Woods Hole Harbor. A small submersible was being hoisted aboard the *Atlantis II*, the crew in vehement disagreement over how to lift it properly. Finally, the captain intervened and quelled all argument by supporting his chief mechanic's opinion.

Matt reluctantly turned away from the window just as the door to his office burst open and a young man rushed in.

"Hey, Matt! Heard the latest!"

He winced. His cousin, Ben, never stood on ceremony. Their mothers were sisters.

"What's up, Ben?" he asked.

"You mean you haven't heard about Adam Stillwell?"

Matt eyed his brash young relative who had been working at the institute the past two years.

"Yes, I've heard," Matt said, his tone dry. "You mean his brush with the Russian trawler."

Ben Williams was six years younger than Matt, about the same height, blue-eyed and blond, but more contentious than his cousin. He had a protruding jaw that Matt remembered aiming at when, as boys, the two of them tussled, Matt sometimes getting the worse of it. Still, he was forced to concede that his cousin not only was an outstanding athlete but possessed an intellectual curiosity he envied.

Even so, it had been a complete surprise to him when he learned that Ben had been hired as a biologist by Nils Hansen, head of Personnel. He hadn't known his cousin was applying at WHOI. Matt soon discovered to his chagrin that Ben habitually burst into his office without notice. Still, Matt couldn't bring himself to say anything about these intrusions. He wasn't given to ceremony, and besides, the two of them had too close a history growing up.

"I spoke to Adam myself," Ben said excitedly. "He's a good friend. We fish together. The way he tells it, he was curious about all those boats out there and he went in close. Could hardly believe it when one of those Ruskies tried to ram him. Says he turned away in time and hotfooted it back to Woods Hole to lodge a complaint with the Coast Guard. Told them he was pretty far out, about fifty miles south of Nantucket, when the incident occurred."

Matt nodded. He'd heard about the incident. Ben sat down hard on the director's leather couch, disappointed his news was stale.

"I guess you heard from the Coast Guard," he said.

Matt remarked wryly, "Doesn't seem to matter these days what President Truman said in '45 about the high seas contiguous to the United States being subject to its jurisdiction and control."

"Those Russians certainly aren't paying attention to that," Ben said.

Matt pointed to a thick folder lying open. "A report of their activities, Ben. I was just about to read it when you barged in. I grant you they are becoming a problem. Not just overfishing, but, as you said, they tend to harass boats that venture too close.

"Incidentally," he added, "I've been discussing the matter with navy public relations officials. For political reasons, they don't want publicity, no more than necessary, so keep it under your hat."

"Politics," his cousin retorted scornfully. He changed the subject. "Hey, Matt, did I tell you I'm taking tomorrow off? I'm doing a dive. Been wanting to try out a new regulator."

Matt flinched. Was it envy? In his new position, he himself didn't have the excuse of a day off, certainly not when the institute was being flooded with visiting oceanographers, biologists, chemists, meteorologists, all beginning to descend on the small village of Woods Hole for the summer hoping to mix scientific research with a little camaraderie and vacation fun. And the islands of Martha's Vineyard and Nantucket beckoned, a ferry ride away.

Matt had learned it was his responsibility to not only integrate all the visiting scholars and scientists with regular staff but to find time to escort visiting dignitaries and eminent scientists through the laboratories and aquarium.

"In case you've forgotten," he reminded his cousin, "some of those phytoplankton organisms you're working with need to be monitored daily. Are you accounting for that?"

"Naturally!" Ben grinned. "I've asked the new intern in my department, Sam Norris, to check on them for me. Admit it, Matt. I'm part of a revolution in marine biology brought about by scuba divers. Thank Jacques Cousteau for that. He made collecting underwater creatures that much easier."

Matt was curious. "Who are you diving with?"

Ben shrugged. "No one."

Matt blanched. "No sane person dives alone!" he said. "Don't be a fool, Ben." Another thought occurred to him. "The cruise departing in August deals with your biologic specialty, plankton. New species need to be observed in deep water. But you haven't signed on to that cruise yet. Why not?"

"I'm needed here," Ben retorted. "You can't tell me my work here isn't important!"

Matt frowned. "Nils is on my neck to assign you that ship. I kept you off the *Atlantis* this time but if you refuse to join the *Gosnold* when she sails in August, he wants to fire you and I won't be able to overrule him."

Ben jumped up from the couch and moved toward the door, his face flushed. He didn't need his cousin to remind him of his research obligations. But before Ben reached the door, he halted. Something else had crossed his mind.

"You know the new girl who was hired? Lisa Warden. She's nice looking. I see her in the Redfield Building on occasion and introduced myself yesterday. Is she one of those MIT research students they've begun sending as part of the new degree program?"

Matt sighed. Ben always knew when to change a subject. Matt had seen this young woman working in various departments sketching marine creatures and equipment. He had to admit she was attractive.

"If the girl is who I think she is, Nils hired her as an artist," Matt said. I understand she's from New York, graduated from an art school there. From what I hear and from what I've seen of her work, she has talent. Nils tells me he is pleased with her and will probably keep her on after the summer."

He couldn't help adding, "You planning to ask her out?"

"Maybe." Ben stood for a moment by the door. Then he said, "Hey, I'm out of here. Got to do a day's work. Isn't that what I'm getting paid for?"

Chapter 13

Woods Hole, June 30, 1967

With summer under way, vacationers flooded Woods Hole Village. They filled the streets adjacent to the ferry wharfs, parked their cars in long lines, and waited to be transported to the islands. It seemed as if all of New England descended on Cape Cod the weekend before the Fourth of July. The lucky ones had reservations for the ferries. All the others were on stand-by, having made a late decision to vacate the cities for island breezes even if it meant arriving in darkness.

In his office at the Oceanographic, Matt had just hung up the phone, mystified by the conversation he'd just had. A visiting professor from New York had just called saying he wanted to meet him and his cousin Ben. The professor had told him that he and Ben were working on some research; Ben had been a student of his at Columbia and they had similar research interests.

It irked Matt that Ben was choosing to work on scientific projects that did not involve interacting with the other scientists at Woods Hole or venturing on one of the institute's short exploratory trips. But he acquiesced to the caller's request, curious about what he and Ben were working on.

When Matt contacted Ben about the luncheon, they agreed to meet in the Bigelow Building lobby at noon. As usual, Ben was several minutes late, but Matt said nothing about it as they crossed the busy street to the White Chowder Café, a popular restaurant overlooking Eel Pond.

It was Ben who first spotted their guest sitting in a quiet corner. Approaching the table, Matt saw a bear of a man, in his fifties perhaps, his hair sandy despite some gray at the temples. He had a round, youngish-looking face, the blue in his tie matching the color of his eyes under bushy eyebrows. A big-boned man, he was dressed expensively in a suit Matt wished he could afford.

Ben took it on himself to make introductions. "Professor Alexander Kirov, Columbia University and the Sorbonne; Matthew Chambers, director of the institution, and my boss.

"Dr. Chambers! Kind of you to meet me this afternoon." Their guest spoke softly for such a big man.

He smiled at Ben. "Good to see you again." He spread a napkin on his lap with a flourish.

Kirov's name was suddenly familiar to Matt. The professor had published numerous important scientific papers on marine biology. How interesting, he thought, that Ben knew this esteemed scientist.

Matt took a seat followed by his cousin and the three men began scrutinizing the menu. A waitress appeared and took their orders. All three chose the local fish.

"I'm glad you took time to visit, Professor Kirov," Matt said. "I've read your work on ocean currents. Very interesting!"

Kirov smiled. "Thank you." He paused and then said, "Since I arrived on the cape, Ben has been telling me about the exciting things you scientists are working on here in Woods Hole. Has he mentioned I am particularly interested in the National Oceanographic Data Center? Such findings would no doubt fill in facts pertinent to my newer theories."

Ben jumped in. "You would be interested to know, Professor, that gamma rays were used off Cape Cod to determine sediment density in depths over eight hundred feet."

"Interesting. That's why I'm here, to educate myself about new discoveries," Kirov said. "I need to prove my theories correct."

Matt changed the subject. "You indicated that you and Ben know each other from Columbia University."

"Yes, we do."

Kirov failed to give any particulars. Instead, he began speaking knowledgeably about the cape, about visiting Woods Hole and the islands. Lunch arrived and the light talk continued.

Sometime later, over coffee, Ben said, "Alex, have you heard about the incident with the Russian trawler?"

Matt instinctively kicked his cousin under the table for having ignored his warning not to discuss the incident publicly.

"What's that about?" Kirov asked.

"Just some loose talk," Ben backtracked.

Kirov, his eyes narrowing, looked from one scientist to the other. He waited to hear more but when nothing was forthcoming, he continued in another vein, "I understand the *Gosnold* has just returned from exploring the ocean's Atlantic ridge. When might that data be made available to me? I hear you use that small submersible, *Alvin*. Was it helpful?"

Matt wasn't ready to talk about this voyage. The data was too new and probably classified. He was about to question Kirov about his latest work when Ben again referred to the Russian trawlers. "You know, they carry electronic equipment, those trawlers."

When Matt didn't shut him up this time, Ben continued, "They not only carry special gear, Alex, but we know they're charting our own coastline. With submarines, naturally."

He turned to his cousin. "Admit it, Matt," Ben said. "We've found devices on the ocean floor that look like position markers, unmistakably Russian-made. They even use ferrets to probe our experimental systems. And these so-called fishermen try to make hash out of our air defense exercises by monitoring radio communications. Don't you remember they even jammed ship-to-shore radios in New Jersey?"

Kirov turned to Matt and asked, "Does the navy plan to do anything about the trawlers?"

Matt didn't answer at first and Kirov's mouth turned down. "I guess I need to make it clear, Dr. Chambers, that although I'm of Russian descent, I am not a communist," he said. My parents fled Russia. They were White Russians. I am American now and prepared to do anything to protect this country."

Matt was surprised that Kirov was so defensive. He hadn't even been thinking about the professor's allegiance. He was wondering why Ben was talking so much about the Russian ships. He quickly reassured the visitor: "Of course, Professor Kirov," and then added, "I don't think the navy will do anything as long as they remain outside the three-mile limit."

Turning to his cousin, Matt said, "Look, let's put this in perspective. In a sense, we're doing the same thing, exploring oceans with our submarines, close in to foreign shores. As a matter of fact, General Dynamics in New London is building the first nuclear-powered research sub right now. Each time our Oceanographic boats go out, we add to our stock of marine information, much of which will be used eventually by the military. After all, they're paying some of our bills.

"It's not the same thing," his cousin insisted.

"Perhaps we're not doing it on as large a scale as the Russians, but then our fishing fleet isn't as extensive as theirs, nor as efficient, yet. I understand the Russians have equipment that may be recording motor and other mechanical sounds that our individual submarines and warships make."

Frowning, Kirov asked, "What do you mean?"

"The propulsion machinery of each boat gives off sound waves that are as individual as a, what should I say, a fingerprint, perhaps. We suspect there are underwater listening devices aboard those trawlers that are tape-recording these signatures. If so, they will ultimately be supplied to the Russian navy. That advantage will make it possible for the Soviets to identify any one of our ships anywhere in the world."

"Is the government developing new technology to prevent this?" Kirov asked.

"I have no idea," Matt said. He changed the subject. "Professor, I remember reading your paper on the waters of the Black Sea. I was impressed with your account of the weakness of the currents there and the effect on fish. Your paper implies there is very little oxygen in the Black Sea."

The professor's face lit up. "True! I'm pleased you are so familiar with my work. You too would have concluded that much of the same water remains in the depths of the Black Sea. The outlet is narrow and incoming water-bearing oxygen is limited. This creates anaerobic conditions."

Kirov stretched his legs, pushing back his chair. "But right now, I'm more interested in the work being done here. As a matter of fact, Ben, I've leased a boat during the next few weeks. Want to come along?" He added, "I know diving is your thing. Perhaps I can accommodate you."

"Sounds great!" Ben's eyes glowed. "But if you head south of Nantucket, remember, watch out for Russian trawlers. We've been plagued by them lately," he said.

"That's right," Matt added. "We've had reports of boats being harassed if they approach too close. No real damage, mind you, but a kind of warning to keep your distance."

"Thanks for the warning," Kirov said. He stood up and reached across the table to shake Matt's hand and then Ben's. "Thank you for lunch and such good conversation," he said.

"I will be seeing you both around this summer now that I have consent to use all of WHOI's facilities."

He headed out toward the street. Matt sat frozen. Kirov's parting words had surprised him. He didn't remember giving the professor blanket permission to the Oceanographic's resources, but then realized he couldn't very well deny a visiting scholar access to scientific information once it has been declassified. Matt had always operated on the assumption that knowledge spawned creativity.

Sighing, he initialed the luncheon bill, telling the waitress to put it on his tab. He wondered as he crossed the street how many more important personages he would have to feed before he could go back to being the director of engineering.

Chapter 14

Woods Hole, July 10, 1967

Pushing his papers aside, Matt sat at the large desk in his office and began drumming his fingers against its polished surface. He was finding it difficult to acknowledge he had a duty to perform, one he dreaded. If he could, he would have put off what promised to be a ugly confrontation with his cousin, who was still refusing to join the institute's scientific expedition scheduled for August. So obstinate! At least, he reasoned, Ben couldn't plead seasickness, not when he was an avid ocean fisherman and an expert scuba diver.

Matt stood up and walked over to the window. He fixed his attention on the research ship, *Gosnold*. Now that this ship was back in port, it would be fitted with new experimental equipment recently developed by his own engineering department. The ship had recently arrived back from an exploratory cruise in the North Atlantic, easing into the slot on the same Oceanographic pier the *Atlantis* vacated when that vessel sailed two days earlier.

Matt frowned. The problem was that Hansen was insisting that Ben be on board when the *Gosnold* sailed, pointing out it was part of the contract Ben agreed to when he was hired. Hadn't Nils complained several times that Ben was setting a bad example to the other scientists? While Matt was forced to agree Nils was right in wanting Ben's compliance, he wished his role as acting director hadn't made him a party to it. He understood Nils's position. But he didn't relish the idea of reading the riot act to his cousin. He had enough to deal with, arranging funding and approvals for the forthcoming expedition in addition to all his other temporary responsibilities.

Well, he consoled himself, he wouldn't be acting director much longer. From medical reports received that morning, his boss, the highly regarded director of the Oceanographic Institution, planned to resume his duties in September, if not sooner. But that wouldn't get him off the hook with Nils before the *Gosnold* sailed.

Nice day, nice view, Matt wished he could find time to enjoy it. He glanced at the swift-flowing , that linked Woods Hole Harbor with Buzzards Bay. The water sparkled in the morning sunlight and allowed the cluster of rocks off the Steamship piers to show teeth at low tide. His gaze then lifted past all this to the outline of Martha's Vineyard island in the distance, a view he never tired of.

He turned away from the window, put on a proper jacket, and left the office. Walking down Water Street, he paid little attention to the vacationing throngs that filled the pavements.

He found Ben in one of the laboratories hunched over a table, peering through a microscope at material sited on its stage. His cousin barely looked up and without turning his head, said, "Hold it, Matt. I'll be with you in a minute."

Still refusing to look up, he exclaimed, "Damn, I get excited whenever I study this strain of algae. I don't understand why it's not feasible to cultivate it underwater." He shifted the glass slide under the microscope. "You have to agree, what Professor Keogh wrote is true, every cubic meter of sea water contains nutritious value. We should be farming the seas."

Matt joined him at the lab table, encouraged by his cousin's enthusiasm. "We will one day, when either private enterprise or the government sets up a pilot project close to shore, or when food becomes scarce," he said. "Count on it happening."

"The Japanese are already doing it."

"Yes, but they depend much more on the sea than we do. And we're not starving yet."

Ben grinned, spun the stool he was perched on, and at last looked up at Matt, "Well, you're not here to talk about underwater farming."

"Dead right! I'm here to talk about your professor friend, Kirov, and something else."

"Yeah, well, yesterday I had a long talk with Alex. I've been wanting to tell you about it."

Matt was curious. "What did he say?"

"He filled me in on his work. Says he wants to look into sound. Not a new theory, of course, but important to American defense. I'm certain the navy will be interested." Ben paused, then said, "Alex is curious about those sound channels in the oceans."

"Oh!" Matt was surprised. "Is that why he's after ocean-ographic data? Someone—was it Iselin?—several years ago remarked, 'There isn't an ocean in the world big enough to lose the sound of a pistol shot fired at the right depth.'"

"Alex is looking for these channels, and that's not all he's interested in. He mentioned warm water pockets and phantom bottoms."

"Every navy in the world is investigating them," Matt said. "Submarines can't be detected under one of those pockets or bottoms. Our government is well aware how important it is that we find out about them because right now we have no foolproof underwater warning system." He paused and warned, "But Ben, it's not a good idea to discuss these investigations openly."

"Alex's work is important," Ben insisted. "We have to find those channels before our enemies do. Incidentally,

Alex asked me how soon you can grant him access to the information he needs."

Matt frowned. "It's not that easy. Much of what your professor wants is classified. I've no right to divulge any of it unless I get permission from the navy." He hesitated. "But I'll look into it. Any discovery he comes up with will help us as long as he promises not to publish right away. I'm sure he understands."

Ben stood up, straightening his back and shoulders. As he prepared to transfer the slide from the microscope to the walk-in incubator across the hall, he grinned and said, "I may get to first base with that good-looking artist we hired this spring."

"Lisa Warden?"

"Yes. Kirov offered his boat to me on a weekend. I may entice Lisa to Nantucket for a day. She says she's never been there." Ben grinned. "With women, Matt, you never know what makes them deliver."

Ben's trysts had never bothered him before. He wondered why he was feeling protective toward this new hire. Fortunately, from what he'd seen of Lisa Warden, she didn't strike him as easy prey. The assurance and skill she displayed working in the various departments and laboratories indicated that she was a person who knew her own mind.

An awkward pause followed; time was running out.

Matt said, "I didn't come to talk shop. I came to warn you that Nils is determined that you follow up on your experiments on the high seas. He wants you aboard the *Gosnold* when it leaves in August for the Sargasso Sea. I can't overrule him anymore."

"Can't or won't!"

"Have it your way!"

"Don't do me any favors!"

"Be reasonable. Your specialty is zooplankton. Marine biologists, yourself included, have been studying them in relatively shallow waters. Even you've admitted, we need to know more about deep-water species and the fish that depend on them. That's where the *Gosnold* will be going. And you're going with it."

When his cousin made no response, Matt grew angry. "Grow up, Ben," he said. "You're part of a team and you can't always have it your way."

Ben's reply surprised him.

"I have a month or more to decide if it's goodbye Oceanographic," he said, "so don't push me."

He stalked out of the lab, leaving Matt standing there, a worried look on his face.

Chapter 15

Quissett Harbor, July 15, 1967

If it hadn't been raining steadily all morning, Lisa would have been tempted to wiggle out of Sarah Dreyfus's invitation to lunch, only because she treasured her weekends for the time they gave her to paint. On Saturdays and Sundays, Lisa would lug her easel, some stretched canvas, and her box of oil paints and brushes to remote places where sand, woods, and water came together. Painting these views absorbed her completely as she tried to capture on canvas the remarkable color compositions nature provided. Painting had become her passion, as had flying. She was grateful she could continue the flying lessons she had started in New York at the Falmouth Airport, only a short drive away. Sometimes, if the temperature climbed into the high eighties, she went instead to the beach and swam. And then, she would call Rob Flanders and ask if he was willing to give her one more flying lesson.

A few weeks ago, however, an elegant older woman had accosted Lisa in the Woods Hole bookstore. She had introduced herself as Sarah Dreyfus and said she knew Lisa's father and her mother, Ann. Lisa, she said, bore a remarkable resemblance to Ann. Sarah said she had a summer house just up the road in Quissett Harbor and had insisted on giving Lisa her phone number and asking for hers in return. Since that unexpected encounter, Sarah Dreyfus had phoned Lisa several times to chat and learned of her proclivity for painting. Just the day before, knowing that Saturday's rainy forecast would dampen Lisa's artistic urge, she had called and asked if Lisa would join her for lunch at her summer home.

At first, Lisa was reluctant to accept Sarah's invitation, if only because she had no desire to reexamine the past or the reasons she fled New York. Even so, she found herself responding warmly to this woman who seemed truly concerned about her. It surprised her that Sarah Dreyfus had known her father so well. Any link, she decided, was important to finding out what had become of him. So she listened carefully as Sarah gave directions to her house at Quissett Harbor.

On Saturday Lisa followed Sarah's instructions, but before continuing on to the Dreyfus house up the hill from Quissett Harbor, she pulled over for a moment at the landing. Boats of all kinds moored in quiet repose, their cockpits abandoned and made indistinct by the steady rain. She resolved to someday come back and paint this idyllic scene, but stayed only a few moments, not wanting to be late. She found the mailbox that signaled Sarah's driveway. A low stone wall separated the property from the road. Driving up a hill, she parked in front of a Cape Cod–style house and shut off the engine. The house, she decided, must hold some history. Its wood exterior was shingled and weathered gray much like the day, rain dampening its color further and blurring its lines.

She stepped out of the car, put up her umbrella, and walked to the front door.

Sarah Dreyfus had been watching for her and opened the door wide despite the rain. She welcomed Lisa warmly, drawing her into what her guest saw was a cozy living room with windows that looked out over the harbor. Seeing where Lisa was looking, Sarah smiled.

"You'll notice not a single sailor is venturing out today. We have a small sailboat moored out there. My daughters sail. So do I on occasion when I have a friend with me."

Lisa noticed that a table and two slender wooden chairs were positioned so she and Sarah could look out at the harbor scene, dismal as it was, while they lunched. A smaller table close by held a platter with sandwiches. She took a moment to admire the lovely porcelain tureen that Sarah said held cream of asparagus soup.

As she was about to sit down at Sarah's invitation, a painting on the wall caught her attention. She found herself asking, "A recent copy?" It couldn't be otherwise.

Sarah looked up and followed Lisa's gaze. "You mean the Monet?" She paused. "It's an original."

Seeing Lisa's astonishment, Sarah said, "We bought that painting from your father. It's not part of the collection we planned to give away. We always intended to keep this one. The Seine near Giverny, early morning."

Lisa couldn't turn away from it. Her eyes feasted on the brushstrokes, the merging of greens and purples and grays that achieved the artist's vision of mist. Sarah interrupted her concentration when she said, "You couldn't know, could you, that Peter's favorite paintings were the two Monets that the Jeu de Paume museum in Paris exhibited in a small room there. Each painting features a woman under a parasol, and in each, the women face in a different direction. He told me about them, how he would stand mesmerized before the paintings on his trips to Paris."

Lisa caught her breath, picturing him. At the strained look on her face, Sarah changed the subject. "I don't know what you like to drink. I prepared both tea and coffee," she said. Then, as Lisa sat down, still feeling numb at Sarah's recollection of her father, her hostess picked up two bowls and ladled soup in them.

After a moment, searching for something to say, Lisa decided to speak about Peter. She asked, "Did my father ever tell you about the visit he and my grandfather made to Giverny when Claude Monet lived there?"

"No. Monet died in the twenties. Your father had to be quite young."

"He told me I was his age at the time, ten, going on eleven. He said he remembered a large rambling pink house with intricate gardens and ponds in the Japanese style. Inside on the walls were Japanese woodblock prints, lots of Utamaros and Hiroshiges, hung in places where the sun could not reach them because he said the colors faded under bright light. He learned later how popular these prints were with Impressionist painters. He said Van Gogh owned some."

"I've seen the Van Gogh prints," Sarah said. "They hang in a museum in Amsterdam." Lisa needed to shift ground. She asked, "Do you live here year-round?"

"No, I don't. Like you, I'm from New York. David and I have always had a house on the West Side of Manhattan. I have it still."

"Don't you find going back and forth a drag?" Lisa remembered her own prolonged trip a month earlier.

"Naturally. But I have friends who have small planes and sometimes I hop a ride with them."

Sometime later while they were having coffee, Lisa said, "Mrs. Dreyfus, if you wouldn't mind, I'd like to paint Quissett Harbor, this view, someday when the sun is shining."

"Of course! I'd be delighted. You can sit outside on my patio and paint to your heart's content. And please, call me Sarah."

She passed her guest a plate of oatmeal cookies, admitting, "My best recipe."

Munching at a cookie, Lisa listened as Sarah spoke proudly of her daughters.

"I'm about to become a grandmother. My daughter Ruth is expecting." She added pensively, "Unfortunately, my David will never see his grandchildren."

Sarah sat back in her chair, collected herself, and said after a moment's pause, "You don't really know who I am, nor what my connection with your father is other than being a customer of his gallery, do you?"

A strange statement. It caught Lisa's attention.

"It's about time you knew the truth. You were too young to know your father was on a mission for his government and for me, or even that my husband was murdered for the paintings we had collected through the years."

Lisa stared at Sarah, her eyes wide.

"Peter was in Paris that night in 1940 when the Nazis invaded our house and stole our paintings. He saw them push David into a black car and drive off with him. Days later, my husband's body was recovered from the Seine.

"At the behest of Washington, Peter went back to Europe twice afterwards to find the collection. As you well know, in 1956, he never came home." She added, "The relationship between Peter and my husband and me was special. We were more than friends."

Lisa mouth dropped open. She had not known any of this. Sarah reached for her hand, saying, "You and I have each suffered a terrible loss because the German Third Reich was bestial as well as greedy. She hesitated, then said, "David and I, the paintings we owned thrilled us with their magic. Your father understood this each time he and your grand-father sold us one. When the collection disappeared, Peter wanted to help recover it. You see, Lisa, it's because of our relationship with Peter that you mean so much to me."

The older woman's words stunned Lisa and she struggled to find something to say. They sat together in silence, as Lisa absorbed what Sarah had said. Finally, she asked, "What does the government have to do with my father's disappearance?"

"You probably didn't know that the collection actually belongs to the United States. David and I willed it to the National Gallery of Art. Congress was planning a new wing to house it. As young as you were, you couldn't have known your father was trying to find the collection and bring it home. He was operating undercover as a government agent while the larger world knew him as a prestigious American art dealer."

Sighing, Sarah reached out and squeezed Lisa's hand. "What I just told you, Lisa, is confidential. Washington hasn't given up the search. Surprisingly, none of the paintings have surfaced to date. That could mean they are intact somewhere."

Lisa couldn't believe what she was hearing. Her father a government operative? She felt a surge of anger and adrenaline; this might explain why he went missing. Could he still be alive somewhere?

Her throat dry, she gave voice to her thoughts. Sarah looked discomfited. She cleared her throat.

"I think you may have to accept the fact that Peter is never coming back," Sarah said. "I say this because knowing how much he loved you, I'm certain if he was alive, he would be here for you."

Sarah stood up abruptly then. "Let's have another cup of coffee, and please, more cookies?" She filled Lisa's cup and after a moment, asked, "Do you remember Tony Russo?"

Lisa stared at Sarah in surprise.

"Tony? Uncle Tony? I haven't seen him in years. The last time was at the gallery after Daddy didn't come home." Lisa pictured him in her mind's eye and remembered her father's last words to her, "Tell Tony I called," and then, "Tell him about the painting, the Harz Mountains." But hadn't Uncle Tony warned her not to tell anyone else?

Lisa saw that Sarah was watching her closely and heard her say, "My dear girl, you still don't realize how closely allied we are, you and I. I wish you would trust me. Tony does. Your father always did. There's very little I don't know except what happened to him."

Lisa put down her cup, afraid she might drop the delicate china. How should she respond? And what exactly did Sarah Dreyfus know?

It surprised her when Sarah added, "I know about the phone call, the one Peter made from Naples when your father told you about a painting. I know he cautioned you to tell only Tony, but you see, Tony tells me everything. We're in this together, Lisa."

On the verge of tears now, overwhelmed by Sarah's unexpected revelations, Lisa blurted out, "I don't want to be reminded that Daddy is gone. What's the good of rehashing, dredging up the past?"

Sarah sat back in her chair. She seemed troubled her words had brought this anguished response. She sighed. "I'm sorry, Lisa," she said softly, "I was wrong to do this to you, burden you with my own ghosts."

Shame that she'd been unable to control her emotions overcame Lisa. Still, all the links that defined her father led through this woman, connections she could now never shake. Did she want to share Sarah's futile search for some paintings? And if she did, could she ever hope to escape her past?

Sitting there in the Dreyfus summer house, rain pelting the windows, hearing that her father had engaged in clandestine activities, she was no longer the same person that had come to the cape, seeking solace. What had Sarah said? Burdened with ghosts?

Chapter 16

Nantucket, July 22, 1967

Ben Williams piloted the large motorboat slowly into Nantucket's Madaket Harbor past Eel Point. Running aground was not an option for him, especially since he had borrowed Professor Kirov's chartered boat. His sole passenger, Lisa Warden, sat in the cockpit, intently observing this little village at Nantucket's southern end.

"Nice, isn't it?" Ben asked.

"It's different."

"You've never been here before?"

"No, I haven't."

She continued to stare at the scene before her, at the few cottages entirely surrounded by grasslands, simple gray shingled residences close to water. She'd been told that between Nantucket Sound and the Atlantic Ocean, the island lay flat and narrow. Ben's cautious approach to its western shore allowed her time to survey the seemingly endless grasslands. She promised herself that someday she would return to paint this serene view.

It had been sunny all week, but that morning they had heard a prediction of rain and ignored it. Neither she nor Ben was willing to give up their planned excursion with the sun shining brightly. But now Lisa saw evidence of weather closing in. Dark clouds were gathering in the east and had begun to obscure the morning sun.

"Do you think the rain will hold off?" Lisa asked. "I don't want it to spoil things."

"Forget the weather. It won't rain for a long while. We've got the whole day."

Sitting quietly in the stern, she turned her attention to the boats moored throughout the harbor. It was obvious that while smaller boats held to the shallows, bigger craft similar to the one that was bringing them to this corner of Nantucket Island were moored or anchored close in to the same deeper channel their own boat was now hugging.

"We could have headed for Nantucket town, if you wanted excitement," Ben said. "You'd see all the old captains' houses, cobblestone streets, shops and art galleries, all of that. Some consider the town a tourist's paradise, especially as it has a history as a famous whaling port."

Lisa wondered why Ben hadn't given her the choice earlier. Then she remembered he had remarked when he invited her that he wanted to get away from crowds. As they approached a small dock, Ben put the engine in neutral and glided smoothly in to dockside, kicking fenders overboard just before the boat gently nudged it. Jumping off onto the pier, rope in hand, he quickly fastened the craft to piling, allowing for the tide change with a spring line.

The engine shut down, Lisa stood, took Ben's proffered hand and stepped up onto the pier's wooden planks. She was struck by the isolation of this island, thirty miles from the Massachusetts mainland. The pair picked up their bags, left the pier and began to walk through the sand along the shore. She and Ben strolled steadily for a time, until, looking back, they could barely see the village. Still, as they kept walking along the beach, they spied an occasional cottage showing behind a dune. It was another ten minutes before Ben found a spot on the beach that suited him and halted finally.

Looking east, Lisa again noticed a lowering of clouds that gave pause to the earlier sunshine. She felt a freshening breeze and was certain now the clouds presaged a change in the weather. Glancing back toward the village, she saw flags atop their tall poles lift slightly.

Ben dropped the picnic basket he'd been carrying. "You okay with this?"

"It's a lovely beach." She put down her own bag.

"Different, isn't it, Nantucket," he said as he looked about. "It attracts well-heeled property owners with its privacy, lack of access."

He added, grinning. "Only it can't help being overrun with tourists in summer. Keeps the locals happy."

Ben bent over, took a blanket from his bag, and began to spread it out on the sand.

"Normally, I bring scuba equipment wherever I go, you know, a tank and stuff. Sometimes I take a boat over to Great Point, search for specimens. But let me warn you, Lisa, the current around this island is scary. Swimmers have to be careful."

He straightened up then and said, "I'd like to teach you to dive. There's a wonderful world just waiting below the surface."

"Oh, but I know how to dive," Lisa said. At the surprised expression on his face, she explained, "I took a NAUI course with a friend when I was in college and became certified, but I haven't practiced much."

Ben grinned and asked, "What other surprises do you have for me?"

She seated herself, smoothing the sand under the blanket. "You didn't bring your diving gear, and I didn't bring my paints and easel when they normally go with me everywhere, so we're even."

Gazing up at him, she said: "I get so absorbed in what I paint, I'd ignore you completely."

"Understandable. Especially as this is a 'getting to know you better' trip."

"The meetings at WHOI, bumping into one another, not enough?"

"Hell, no!"

Still looking down at her, he said, "I figured you'd be different."

"Different, how?"

"After all, you're a New Yorker, like myself, an artist, even. Not some local gal."

Lisa thought about Ben's remark.

"I may be more cape-oriented than you imagine," she said. He didn't need to know and she didn't intend to let on that she hadn't dated much.

He plopped down, joining her on the blanket.

She guessed that he wanted to say more and decided it would wait. They had most of the day. He asked, "Want to rest awhile or go for a swim?"

"A swim."

Still, neither moved.

She said, consumed by curiosity, "I know so little about you. Did you grow up in New York?"

"Let's not talk about me."

"Why not?" She persisted, refusing to be put off, "I know you went to Columbia University where you met Professor Kirov. He's mentioned it, that he knows you. He seems to have free run of the Oceanographic and he always says 'hello' to me."

Ben hesitated before he answered her. "I guess you'll learn someday I had an alcoholic father. He couldn't keep a job, knocked me about a bit. But luckily. I had a mother who convinced me I needed to do something with my life, insisting I had the smarts to go to college like my cousin Matt did."

"Matt?"

"Matt Chambers."

Lisa's eyes widened. She'd had no idea they were related.

"Anyway, I do my own thing," he said. "People say I inherited my father's temper. His got out of hand when he drank, and sometimes when he didn't. But I'm working on that."

Ben smiled wickedly. "Fair is fair, Lisa, now that I've unloaded, what about you? What kind of temper do you have?"

"Oh," she answered archly. "I'm a poor orphan. I can't afford a temper."

"Why do I think there's more to your story than that?"

"Well," she said, getting off the blanket to stand up. "Any story I have to tell can wait. Let's swim."

She removed her big hat, sunglasses, and her coverup, noticing Ben seemed to like what he was seeing, a slim figure in a two-piece bathing suit.

Ben stood and divested himself of his shirt and long pants, again cautioning her.

"The currents around this island can be wicked. The only safe beach is near the entrance to Nantucket Harbor. They call it the Children's Beach. So don't try to swim out too far in these waters. I'll be swimming with you. You'll be fine—with your scuba training."

He added, "By the way, I'm always looking for a partner."

"In your dreams!"

She laughed and ran toward the water, Ben right behind her.

They dived into the surf and yelled at contact with water chillier than either one of them expected. Exhilarated, they struck out along the shore away from the village, Ben keeping alongside Lisa.

It wasn't long before she encountered a strong current. Unable to fight it, she turned around and allowed it to become a joy ride that carried her parallel to the shore toward Madaket Harbor. Ben, who had steadfastly maintained a position beside her, called out gleefully, "I told you."

Well before the two swimmers reached the harbor, they struck out diagonally toward shore. Lisa was happy to regain her footing as Ben emerged from the surf. Trudging beside him back to their beach blanket, she was chagrined to discover that while she was somewhat winded, Ben was not. They had no sooner reached their spot on the beach when Ben asked teasingly, "Want to do that again?" And laughed when she threw her towel at him in answer.

Retrieving it, Lisa rubbed herself dry while Ben did the same. Glancing about, she noticed the tide had crept closer while they were gone.

Ben broke their silence. "I could eat a horse. Where's the food?" Without waiting for her answer, he reached into the basket and fumbled around. She reached also and slapped his hand, then smiled and said, "Maybe not for a horse, but enough for the two of us."

She brought out paper plates and filled them with sandwiches she had earlier prepared, then reached in again and found cupcakes and peaches. Finally, she produced cans of beer she had placed in a special container to keep them cold. Without much conversation, she and Ben finished off all the food she had packed.

Contented now, neither one showed any inclination to stir from the blanket, stomachs full. Eventually, Ben got to his feet, tossing the last empty beer can into the basket while studying clouds increasingly darkening the sky. Seeing his glum look, Lisa realized she was grateful they had access to an enclosed cabin on the powerboat for their return trip. She shivered and reached into her bag for a sweater, feeling the drop in temperature.

"We'll be fine going back." Ben assured her.

She saw he had no intention of cutting short their outing until it became absolutely necessary.

"Nantucket Sound is seldom a problem this time of year unless there's a hurricane."

Ben seemed relaxed. He leaned back on his elbows. "At times they do have bad storms out here," he added. "Natives call them nor'easters. They can produce shipwrecks, currents washing most of the debris ashore."

Positioning himself so he could look directly at her, he said, "In case you didn't know, Nantucket natives as well as Vineyarders have made a living off shipwrecks for centuries."

Lisa grew restless. She kept glancing at the sky.

"Come on, Lisa, stop worrying! Any rain is hours away." Then, wanting to divert her attention from the approaching weather, he remarked, "There are stories about Cape Cod you haven't heard, being new, ones that go back to the founding of America."

"What stories?" Her interest was aroused.

"Way back when Henry Hudson sailed to the new world, the voyage took him to these parts. From what I've read, he was approaching Monomoy Island at the tip of Cape Cod about to enter Nantucket Sound when he spotted dangerous waters ahead. Today, mariners know the place as Pollock's Rip. The upshot is, he changed his mind and continued on south to New York, sailing up the river that bears his name."

He smiled. "And have you heard the one about the *Mayflower*?"

"Plymouth Rock?"

"From old reports uncovered in England," he said, "we understand the captain was heading for New Jersey but on seeing the turbulence at the entrance to Nantucket Sound, he bore off, turned north, and, sailing past Provincetown, landed at Plymouth Rock."

Lisa laughed. "Goodness, Ben. You're full of stories."

He yawned. "Mind if I catch a quick one?"

"Course not!"

Pushing sand about under the blanket to afford him the most comfort, Ben lay down. "Don't let me sleep too long. There are things to see even in this remote place and I promised I would show them to you." Hearing no reply, Ben quickly relaxed into sleep.

In the quiet that ensued, Lisa took time to bundle their trash and put it in the basket. Then, feeling drowsy herself, she lay down, placed her broad-brimmed hat over her face for darkness, a towel over her body to fend off the cooler air, and fell asleep.

How long she slept was uncertain, but she awoke to feel pressure on her chest, a hand on her thigh, massaging it. Her hat had fallen off her face and she was looking into Ben's eyes, realizing from the heavy pressure in his groin that he was lying on top of her in a needy way. She couldn't move.

"Get off!" Fully awake, Lisa struggled to free herself, frightened and angry that Ben would dare to take advantage.

"You want this as much as I do," was all he said. He had removed the towel and was lifting her hips, pulling at the bottom of her two-piece bathing suit.

"No, no!" She fought him and only when she began to scream loudly for help did he roll off her, bewildered by her reaction.

"What's the matter, Lisa," he asked, his erection subsiding. "What's wrong with you and me having a little fun?"

She rolled away from him and got to her feet, feeling unsteady for the moment. Without answering him, she adjusted her bathing suit bottom, put on her coverup, and picked up her bag. She looked down at him then, her heart pounding.

"Not that kind of fun, Ben." She drew a deep breath. "If I gave you the wrong impression, I'm sorry."

His face reddened and he apologized. "Wrong move, I guess! I thought . . . well . . . I don't know what I thought . . . . but usually, dates are willing."

"Not this date," she snapped.

He stood up then and reached for his pants and shirt. "I guess you want to go back or . . . you'll let me show you the island as I promised."

"Your promises aren't worth much."

Angered that she had misjudged him, Lisa reached a decision and flung the words at him. "I'm not going back with you," she told him. "You said the ferry leaves at four. It's still early and I mean to be on it." Holding back tears, she began to walk away.

"Hey! The weather's changing. It's going to rain soon."

He ran after her and attempted to take her hand. She pulled away and continued to walk off. She hadn't expected this behavior on a first date.

"Don't be a fool, Lisa," he called after her. We'll go back to Woods Hole. I won't touch you again, not unless you want me to."

"Not good enough," she called over her shoulder. "I don't trust you worth a damn. Then she remembered the island's isolation and the approaching storm and relented a bit. She called back, "Just stay away until I get over this, if I can. I don't ever want you to hit on me like that again."

Ben shouted after her. "Walk it off then. I'm not going anywhere without you. I'll be waiting at Madaket with the boat till you decide to come back. I don't care what time you turn up."

Lisa walked past the curve of the beach and only then looked back. Satisfied to see that Ben was no longer in sight, she began to run. Minutes later, halting, she turned one last time to see if he was following her and was greeted by the imprints of her bare feet in the sand. She continued her run then, but at last, out of breath, she stopped and walked.

Still, she encountered no one. Feeling the beginning of a drizzle, she crested a dune and found the road that paralleled the beach. Before her lay land lost in a cover of mist that had crept in from the sea. She began walking again until, seeing a sandy path diverge from the macadam, decided to follow it, wondering if she might be in the vicinity of the long narrow pond that stretched far to the center of the island, a pond she had seen on a map of Nantucket before she and Ben left Woods Hole. Perhaps she might find a house, people in it where she could phone for a cab to take her to the ferry in town. She hadn't yet decided if she wanted to return to Woods Hole with him.

Then, through the mist, at the path's end, she spotted a small cottage, gray and weather-beaten. She approached it, noticing the protruding chimney and small windows. The panes of glass, it seemed to her, lit by interior lights, glowed like eyes. As she drew near, a woman appeared at the door holding a cat in her arms, an elderly woman who looked up at the dark sky, and then at a clothesline close to the house. Sheets had begun to toss in the wind as if beckoning a visitor on. Lisa watched undecided until a strong gust whipped the coverup she wore, followed by another gust and still another, each with increasing force.

A sudden heavy downpour made the woman put down her cat and run to her clothesline in an attempt to pull sheets off. Lisa saw the woman, suddenly whipped and imprisoned by the cloth that wrapped around her body, begin to lose her balance. Her hair flying wildly about her face, Lisa went to help the woman, first dropping her bag on the ground.

Their eyes met. Together, the two women gained control of the binding cloth and, ignoring the downpour, unpinned each sheet from the line pushing them deep into a basket.

"Here," Lisa said. "I'll carry it for you."

She found her bag, placed it in the basket with the linen, then moved toward the door. The woman, her face etched with wrinkles, was already there, waiting for her. Both women spilled into the cottage.

"Where should I put the basket?" Lisa asked, as she and the cloth dripped water on the floor. She heard a thin reedy voice answer, "Drop it beside the stove."

Its owner, putting her weight against the door, forced it shut, then fetched a towel and handed it to Lisa. She then disappeared into what Lisa guessed was a bedroom and reemerged shortly in a dry wrap-around garment, having divested herself of her wet clothes. She carried a similar wrap-around cotton garment that she now insisted Lisa put on.

"Child," she ordered. "Get rid of those skimpy wet things. They'll need drying."

While Lisa retreated to a dark corner behind a sofa to take off what she was wearing, the woman said in a querulous voice, "Ain't never seen you before. A visitor?"

Dry at last and wearing nothing but the borrowed dress, Lisa felt grateful to have found shelter from the storm outside. She rejoined the woman at the kitchen table and asked, "You live here year-round?"

"Not exactly. Me and Catnip, my cat, we live in Nantucket town during the winter; have for generations. Summers, I rent my house in town and come out to this end of the island to live.

My husband built this fishing shack a long time ago. Me and Catnip like it here."

"Is your husband a fisherman?"

"Was. He died about five years ago."

She took Lisa's garments and laid them beside an old iron stove, then bustled about, lifting the kettle that had already been heated.

"Well," she said, "the least I can do is offer a cup of tea."

"Thank you. That's very kind of you." Lisa sat down at the table and added: "I'm Lisa Warden from Woods Hole. I was visiting Nantucket with a friend. We're supposed to go back later today."

The woman raised an eyebrow skeptically, as if to say where's your friend now. Lisa felt compelled to add, "I went for a walk alone and lost my way."

"Guess you ought to know my name," the woman said. "It's Mary Moore. Family's been fishing folk on this island longer than I care to remember. Our ancestors were whaling men bound from Nantucket."

She poured cups of tea for Lisa and herself.

"I don't see many people in summer, except when I go to town for supplies, but on this island, they know me well." Mrs. Moore offered a glass jar to Lisa.

"Here, try my homemade jam. Spread some on these crackers." She smiled for the first time. "Was right nice of you to trouble yourself about my laundry. Do appreciate it."

The woman had placed her gnarled hands on the table. She noticed Lisa staring at them.

"It's arthritis I got in my hands. Makes it hard to do work right." She sighed and pulled them back, laying them on her lap out of sight.

"Lisa didn't know what to say. She felt sorry for this elderly woman.

Mrs. Moore's next words were hesitant. "I have a letter I been meaning to write to my sister in Boston, only my fingers don't work well. I don't hold with having a telephone here. We don't talk often."

"It's not a problem," Lisa said. "I can write it for you."

Then, unaccountably, she shivered, feeling a chill despite the warmth in the room. She wondered why. After all, the cottage was sheltering them both from the storm that raged outside.

Chapter 17

Nantucket, July 22, 1967

Mrs. Moore excused herself and went into the bedroom to find a pen and stationery for the letter she wanted Lisa to write to her sister. While Lisa waited, she decided to look at the pictures that hung in no apparent order on the walls. She studied them with interest, old photographs and equally old watercolors of sailing ships and what was probably the town of Nantucket years ago, many in faded sepia colors. But what made her pause and catch her breath was a single oil painting that hung between two windows. The frame was homemade, roughly wrought of pine, but the oil painting itself glistened despite the soft light in the room. It was a portrait of a man from another century, an intense expression on his face. What engaged her interest was the technique, an early Flemish style of crust and glazes. Lisa had been well schooled in art all her life and she was puzzled to find such a fine painting in this simple cottage.

Mrs. Moore emerged from her bedroom and was watching her.

"What a beautiful painting," Lisa said. "Where did you get it?"

Mrs. Moore sat down abruptly, frowning. She motioned Lisa to come away from the painting.

"Sit here with me," she said, pointing to her sofa. She seemed to be struggling with what to tell Lisa. When she spoke, her voice was apprehensive.

"I like that painting," she said. "I wouldn't want anyone to take it from me."

"I don't understand."

"Cain't say as it's honestly mine."

The woman hesitated, then asked, "Do you remember the sinking of the *Andrea Doria*, the Italian ship that the *Stockholm* sliced into in a fog?"

"Hardly." Lisa was being honest.

"People round this way don't talk about the *Andrea Doria* anymore. There was a time, summer of nineteen fifty—oh!" Mary Moore paused. "Can't think just when. John was alive then and we were here in this same house when we heard on the radio, it was July, I think, that the big ship was in trouble.

"My John was a fisherman. He owned a boat. Though I called him a fool and tried to dissuade him, he went to the *Doria*. Told me later he wasn't needed by the time he got there. There were other ships. One was the *Ile de France*. He said that the little boats that went out only got in the way."

She snorted, "And would you believe, while he was gone, the people who turned up on the beach!"

"Sightseers?" Lisa ventured. "But what could they see from here?"

"They wasn't sightseers. Oh, no! When John finally got back, he was kept busy keeping them people off our property."

She paused and gave Lisa a significant glance. "Course you know they were here for another reason."

"Another reason?"

"Half of them people were scavengers, measly lot." Mrs. Moore's mouth puckered in distaste. Lisa asked, "You mean people were waiting for wreckage from the *Andrea Doria*?" An appalling thought! Then she remembered what Ben had told her.

"This beach's a great place for wreckage," Mrs. Moore said. "Half the wood that built this house come off some old sailing ship battered to pieces in a storm. Before John and I married, there was a shack here his family owned. John just made it more comfortable for us."

Lisa's widened. "Was there wreckage from the *Andrea Doria*?"

"Yes. A'course that ship was metal, but there was stuff did wash up on this island. Not right away, a'course. The sea was calm that night. I remember they said there was a fog out that way. That was the reason there was a collision."

"So the scavengers were looking for salvage?" Lisa asked, intrigued despite herself.

Mrs. Moore chuckled. "Salvaging has been going on since the Indians lived here, even before the white man came. People used to make a living that way, collecting what the sea cast up."

"Are you trying to tell me that the painting came from the *Andrea Doria*?"

The woman nodded sheepishly. "You won't tell anybody now, will you?"

Lisa nodded and the woman sat back.

"You're the first person I've ever told, that I got this pretty painting that way. She glanced at Lisa, then continued, "My John said he stood off a bit while the first-class passengers were being rescued. He told me later he was just trying to stay out of the way of those big boats when a suitcase bobbed up beside him, or it may have been floating in his direction.

"Anyways, he had a net and managed to haul it aboard. Wasn't terribly big. John said later it was a cheap piece, nothing like the expensive luggage from first class.

"The painting was in it, free of seawater as it turned out. John might have turned the whole suitcase in to the sheriff, but wasn't much good in it, only the painting. Easy to see it was well wrapped, but when John removed its covering, he said it looked like it had been cut out of its frame. He made a frame for it from driftwood after I told him, no way did I want to give it up. I liked it too much."

Lisa was intrigued by the woman's story but she realized it was growing late. Mrs. Moore noticed she was looking at the clock and suddenly stood up.

"The letter!" Mrs. Moore sat up. "I near forgot about the letter." She gave Lisa the pen and paper she had earlier retrieved from her bedroom. While Lisa waited for Mrs. Moore to collect her thoughts, she turned the pen idly about in her fingers and noticed an inscription.

She felt herself grow light-headed, the pen spinning in her line of vision. It rolled out of her hand and she fell to the ground.

Lisa had no idea how long she had been unconscious. Her eyes fluttered open and she could see Mrs. Moore's anxious head hovering above her, eyes fraught with concern. Lisa felt her hands being rubbed.

"Child, child," Mrs. Moore was murmuring. "I can't lift you. Oh, dear, please don't die on me."

Lisa struggled to sit up. Her head was aching. She felt Mrs. Moore pull on her and manage to plop her onto the sofa.

"Mercy!" The woman sat down beside her and regarded the girl. "Whatever happened? Your face got white and you toppled over." Her fingers, thickened by arthritis, began to probe gently. "You hurt?" she asked solicitously.

Lisa winced when Mrs. Moore touched her shoulder. "You must have hit that when you fell over from the chair."

It suddenly came back to Lisa why had she fainted. She began to cry softly, her hair falling about her face.

"Poor dear!" Mrs. Moore moaned in sympathy. She got up stiffly and came back with a partially dampened towel. This she gently applied to Lisa's face.

"The pen! Where did you get the pen?" Lisa croaked.

Startled, the woman glanced about. "What happened to the danged thing?" she murmured. Spotting it on the floor, Mrs. Moore groped for it with some difficulty. She then handed it to Lisa, who turned the pen so that an inscription was visible.

"There," Lisa whispered, barely able to speak. "You see, it says, 'To Peter from Lisa.'"

How many pens would bear that exact inscription? It had to be the gift she had given her father on Christmas the year before he disappeared. She had picked it out herself, a white pen with red lettering.

The fact that she had found this pen in a house along the Nantucket shore had implications too awful for Lisa to contemplate. She already knew the answer, but had to ask it anyway.

"This pen. Where did you find it?" she whispered.

Mrs. Moore gingerly took the pen in her damaged fingers and looked at it, wondering what it had to do with the girl's strange behavior.

"It's a good pen," she muttered. "Had it a long while. Haven't used it much. Not with these fingers going bad on me."

"Did you find it on the beach?"

"No. It was in something."

Mrs. Moore studied the inscription as if seeing it for the first time. "I 'spect it was in the suitcase John brought home that night, the one I was telling you about, when the *Doria* went down," she said.

Eyes closed, Lisa's head rolled back against the sofa. Her heart ached. She wanted to run outside and wail her sorrow and anger at the world. Was there nowhere she could hide now that she knew at last how her father had died? It was all too unbearable. Mrs. Moore was looking at her oddly and Lisa came back to herself. Despite her throbbing head, she felt she owed this woman some explanation for why she was acting so strangely.

"I'm sorry I frightened you," she said. "I've never fainted before."

"Had worse frights than that, girl."

"It's my father. He's been missing since that summer the *Andrea Doria* sank. He never came home from Europe. No one knew he was aboard. Until now, we never knew what happened to him."

"Could be someone stole his pen," Mrs. Moore said.

"Possibly," Lisa said, "but in his last telephone call to me from Europe, he said he was bringing me a small painting, a portrait of a man, a Van Dyck, he called it."

Mrs. Moore drew back, alarmed. She pointed to the painting.

"You thinkin' it's that one? But it's mine, now," she protested. "Finders keepers!"

Lisa sought to mollify this woman. She'd been so kind. "I'm sure it is yours," Lisa agreed. "There's no way of knowing if that was the painting Daddy mentioned. But the coincidence of the pen and the painting is too much for me not to accept the truth, that he drowned in that awful collision you spoke of."

"I'm sorry for your loss, girl, but many's the man I knew when I was a child was lost to the sea," Mrs. Moore. "We didn't find out about it, sometimes for years, always expecting he'd come home. But that's cold comfort to you, young lady, when you've lost a father you seem to have loved dearly."

It occurred to Lisa that there might be something else of Peter's still in the cottage.

"The suitcase," she asked, interrupting Mrs. Moore's last words, "do you still have the suitcase?"

"John and I never threw anything away if it had value," she replied, "although that suitcase was a poor excuse for one."

She thought back, then murmured, "Sorry! Ditched it a long time ago."

Mrs. Moore continued to search her memory. "But there were other things. I been trying to think what they were."

She left Lisa sitting at the table while she went back into her bedroom. In only a few minutes, though it seemed a lifetime, Lisa was turning over a small notebook in her hand. It had a black leather cover. She leafed through it with trembling fingers, seeing a type of shorthand she didn't recognize.

"May I keep this and the pen?" she asked tremulously.

"A'course! All told, I don't remember anything else 'cept old clothes and these we gave away because they didn't fit John. The cloth weren't worth my altering. It surprised me, such a nice painting and such cheap clothes in the same suitcase together."

"Thank you," Lisa said. She membered the reason she held a pen in her hand in the first place. "We haven't written your letter," she said. "Let's do it now."

"You sure you're feeling up for that?"

"Yes."

For the next several moments Lisa forced herself to listen carefully to what Mrs. Moore wanted to say to her sister, writing down every word on paper. When they were done, she asked, "How do you want to sign this?"

"Can't sign anything with these hands," the woman answered somberly. "Just write, 'Love, Mary.'"

Lisa signed as requested, addressed and sealed the envelope, and applied the stamp Mrs. Moore managed to hand her. Then she stood up. She needed to put her own clothes back on.

When she was ready to leave the cottage, the old woman regarded her with affection and then to Lisa's surprise, draped an old slicker about her shoulders.

"You'll need this," she said, adding, "Come see me again, child. I'll be here until September when I close up this place and Catnip and I go back to town. When you come visiting, why, just ask in town for Mary Moore. Easy to find me." She bent and awkwardly lifted Catnip to share in the goodbye.

Lisa attempted a smile. Rain or not, it was time to go and hopefully meet Ben. And begin to deal with the belated truth about her father's death.

Chapter 18

Woods Hole, July 29, 1967

Upon her return from Nantucket Lisa buried herself in work. Ben had waited for her in Nantucket Harbor, but on the ride back to Woods Hole, Lisa had huddled under the canopy, trying to stay dry and avoid conversation with him. After his attempt to force himself on her, she wanted nothing to do with him, so she said nothing about her encounter with Mary Moore or what she had discovered in the old woman's home. The nor'easter that had swept the cape and islands gave way to a heat wave, and New Englanders began flooding coastal resorts seeking relief.

Now that she knew the truth about her father, the awful way he died, she debated with herself about who she should notify. It was a short list. Peter hardly spoke about his family except to once say his mother had died when he was young, a tragedy that paralleled her own. As an only child, Peter's references to his father made it clear that he worshiped the man. Unfortunately, she never knew that grandfather. He died before Lisa was born.

What would Claire say if she called with this news, this woman who had treated her so badly? Her stepmother had stripped her of her inheritance, and she didn't want to hear her voice. Not that Lisa cared much about money, but it hurt to see the Warden name tarnished in the newspapers when Claire drove the gallery into bankruptcy. Still, she had an obligation to let Claire know. A letter would do.

That left Uncle Tony. Russo, wasn't it? Strange that Sarah Dreyfus had revealed his last name just the other day. Where would she find him, she wondered, this man who seemed to lead such a mysterious life? She remembered her father used to joke about how Tony managed to land on his feet with each assignment, but what kind of assignments Peter never said. She had a feeling Tony did something clandestine for the government, but what precisely she didn't know.

When Uncle Tony sought her out that summer evening in 1956 at a gallery exhibit, she recalled he patted her on the head and praised her for remembering her father's last message from Europe. Then, he, too, disappeared from her life. Until Sarah Dreyfus mentioned his name saying she knew him, he had always been Uncle Tony.

Naturally, Sarah Dreyfus needed to know about Peter. Hadn't Sarah repeatedly told her that the Wardens, father and son, had been friends of hers and her late husband?

Lisa phoned Sarah shortly after her return from Nantucket and asked if they could get together, either at Quissett Harbor or in Woods Hole, not wanting to break bad news over the phone. "Wonderful," Sarah had said. "Be sure to bring your paints and easel. Quissett Harbor is paintable now that we have sunshine to give it color. We'll have all the time in the world to talk. My daughters have gone home to New York. I'm all alone."

The following Saturday, she and Sarah sat outside on the deck facing the harbor and sipped lemonade. Sarah had brought out a tray with tall glasses and a beautifully etched glass pitcher, but before Lisa could bring herself to mention her father, she stood for the moment looking over the harbor studying the view, thinking how she could transfer the brightness and color she saw onto a canvas.

She heard Sarah say: "I'm thinking of expanding this house, using an architect, of course. I wouldn't dare make changes myself." A pause. "Did I tell you that Ruth is expecting her first child and my Rachael is about to become engaged?"

Lisa listened, the glass in her hand, as Sarah went on to speak about her plans for the house.

"I'm just like everyone else. My neighbors are adding on. Can you believe the houses around this harbor are getting bigger while most of us are here only for the summer or on holidays? Size never mattered to David and me. We fell in love with this Cape Cod house the moment we set eyes on it and never changed it.

She paused. "Now, with my family growing, I have to make these architectural decisions without him."

Lisa heard the sadness in Sarah's voice. Was this the time to tell her about Peter?

"You said you were my father's friend," she began, "that you shared a purpose. I didn't want to say anything over the phone, but I need to tell you about him." Lisa described the storm that led to her encounter with Mary Moore, the simple cottage she'd come across. She barely mentioned Ben's role in this, but instead spoke of Mrs. Moore's arthritis and her cat named Catnip. She hadn't meant to mention the painting. It just came out, part of her story because of the impression it made on her.

Sarah's eye widened. "What kind of painting?"

"A beautiful painting, Sarah," Lisa said. "I recognized the style. The technique is Flemish, one of crusts and glazes. It is a portrait of a man with a mustache wearing a blue shirt."

"A blue shirt?" Sarah paused a moment and added: "I used to own a painting of a man with a blue shirt. He was looking to his right and he wore a gold chain over the shirt."

"Why, yes," Lisa said. "That describes the painting."

Sarah leaned toward her, blue eyes bright, "About nine inches by seven inches?"

"Yes?"

Sarah took a deep breath. "I'm sure there are many copies of that Van Dyck." Then she saw a strange look on Lisa's face.

"Van Dyck?"

"From your description, Lisa, I would guess you saw a copy of a Van Dyck."

"Daddy said he was bringing me a painting. A Van Dyck, he called it."

"That last phone call, that's what you mean?"

"He's dead!" She blurted it out finally.

"Dead? Your father? How could you know?" Sarah half rose from her seat.

"There's more," Lisa said, her face pale. Haltingly she told the older woman about finding the pen. As Sarah listened, riveted, Lisa went on then to speak of the suitcase, the fisherman, John Moore, hauling it aboard his boat the night the *Andrea Doria* sank.

In a choked whisper, she added: "Daddy drowned that night."

"Oh, my dear!" Sarah could barely accept what she was hearing. She stood up and, gently lifting Lisa to her feet, hugged the girl.

"I'm so sorry," Sarah said, her voice husky. "You may think you have no one, but you have me."

When Lisa gently pulled away from the woman's embrace, struggling to control her voice, she asked, "Why do you know about that painting? You describe it so well."

Sarah stared at Lisa. "My God, it could be *the* Van Dyck!" she said. "What you saw in that woman's cottage is a self-portrait of the painter. The chain around his neck was a gift from the king of England."

Sarah's eyes moistened. "If it is *the* Van Dyck, it was a favorite of mine. It hung in our bedroom in Paris."

Too agitated to sit down, Sarah held the back of her patio chair tightly and faced Lisa. She took a deep breath and said,

"I don't think you believed me when I told you your father was working for the United States government."

"You're mistaken, Sarah. No way my father was a spy! Daddy was an art dealer. When he traveled, it was on business."

"That's what he wanted people to think."

Anger engulfed Lisa. "You're telling me he died because of some paintings?"

Sarah paled. "It's true. Peter didn't know the danger he faced. Everything I told you when you first came to my house is true. Even before you were born, David and I had bequeathed the collection to the United States. But unfortunately, my David delayed its removal from Paris even after the Germans breached the Maginot Line. He was convinced that as an American citizen, they wouldn't dare touch him."

"How could anyone afford a collection like that?"

"David could. He was very successful, a dealer in all the commodities that had to do with the growing auto industry in the United States, rubber, copper, steel, oil. His market was international."

Sarah looked Lisa in the eye. The young woman's understanding meant so much to her.

"David told me that his father had emigrated to the United States and was somehow related to the French officer, Alfred Dreyfus. The officer had been arrested on false charges, his name dragged through the mud. Although he was later vindicated, even so, David's father, a successful merchant, decided after the Dreyfus affair he no longer wanted to live in an anti-Semitic country. He brought the family to America, settled here, and invested in businesses."

Lisa had a hard time believing her story. "You say your husband procrastinated, but you managed to leave in time," she said.

"Only because of the girls. At the last minute, David made arrangements without my knowing it. He then persuaded me to board the ship at Le Havre just before the Germans broke through, saying he would be on the next ship. He told me he needed to stay and pack the collection properly for shipment and would accompany it to the States. Said he had some business to conclude."

"Why would he risk his life for some paintings?"

"I often asked myself the same question," Sarah said. "But, of course, you didn't know my husband."

"No, I didn't, but I don't understand what all this has to do with my father," Lisa said, her frustration bubbling over.

"I know you appreciate fine art. You paint. It gives you pleasure, doesn't it?" Sarah asked.

At Lisa's nod, she said, "Well, David's great joy, besides his family, was in acquiring wonderful paintings, which he did with the Warden Gallery's help. He spent much of his fortune that way. He told me over and over again how art restored his soul when he was troubled by the duplicity and meanness he saw around him, especially when the Germans began to take over Europe and impose their brutal regime.

"And he told me that people, ordinary citizens, had a right to enjoy the beauty in those paintings as he did. It's all about money, too, Lisa. That's what drove the Nazis' thievery. The Dreyfus Collection is worth hundreds of millions and will only increase in value. Peter and your grandfather saw to it we bought only the best."

"But if you give away a fortune in paintings to the government, what's left for you?"

"My David took ample care of his family."

Lisa stared at the harbor without seeing it. She was having difficulty processing what Sarah was telling her, the connection between the Dreyfus Collection and her father, a connection that cost him his life.

At last, breaking the strained silence between them, she said, "There is one other person I want to find, tell him what happened to Daddy. But I don't know how to get in touch with him. I always called him Uncle Tony, but you said his last name is Russo. He's not my real uncle, but he was a friend of my father's."

"I know Tony," Sarah said. "We met several times in New York when Peter and I tried to figure out what happened to the collection. He's a government agent of some kind—please don't let on I blew his cover. I believe he was authorized by Congress, which oversees the National Gallery of Art, to find the collection. And yes, he was also an old friend of your father's. Perhaps that is why he enlisted Peter's help, especially as Peter was multilingual and knew exactly what the collection contained."

Lisa listened, conflicted.

Sarah said, "Your father told me once that he had been tapped to be a Monument Man, part of team sent by the United States to Europe during and after World War II to locate missing art and restore it to the rightful owner. He didn't enlist. He said he felt he could be of help in other ways while conducting the business of his gallery."

Sarah gasped suddenly and leaned toward Lisa, eyes wide.

"My God," she said. "If Peter found the Van Dyck, then it means he found the collection. We have to let Tony know about this."

Lisa turned away. "I guess," she replied in a flat tone. What difference did it make to her what he found now that she knew her father was dead?

Chapter 19

Woods Hole, August 1, 1967

Anthony Russo stopped short on entering Matt's office. He looked as if he'd seen a ghost.

The same long dark hair, the dark sloe eyes.

Sarah Dreyfus stepped forward. She had been watching for him.

"Looks exactly like Ann, doesn't she, Tony?"

Lisa couldn't help herself. She ran to Uncle Tony and embraced him. Startled, Russo hesitated, then put one arm about her. Matt, for his part, simply stared at the scene being played front of him, wondering what it was all about.

Russo held Lisa gently, looking over her head to the others, his dark eyes inscrutable. "It's good to see you, Lisa. I hear from Sarah you had a tough time growing up."

"Only because Daddy wasn't there," Lisa murmured.

She pushed her hair back from her face. "I can't believe you're here in Woods Hole. Matt didn't tell me who was coming this morning. Just asked me to bring what I found on Nantucket."

"Sorry, Lisa," Matt interjected. "I was told not to say anything. Besides, I had no idea you knew him."

"Oh!" she murmured, seemingly surprised at the secrecy.

Russo led Lisa to Matt's leather couch. "I want you to know that your father was on assignment for the U.S. government when he disappeared. I was his contact."

"Yes, I know that," Lisa said in a subdued voice.

"Do you also know that his mission was to find a German SS agent, the leader of an ERR confiscation team that killed David Dreyfus and stole his collection in Paris?"

Lisa heard Sarah gasp.

"Sorry, Sarah," Tony said. "I never told you about that."

"I know that Peter had identified this SS agent when he went to Paris just after it was liberated. Apparently, this man, Hans Kunz, had disappeared. We think he was captured by the Russians, probably sent to Siberia."

Tony looked at Lisa. "Peter didn't follow up on his leads in 1945. He came home instead because your mother, Ann, had just been killed."

Lisa nodded dumbly. This all made sense.

Tony continued, "Peter went back in the summer of 1956 because we asked him to attempt to find the collection one last time. But then he disappeared and we had no idea what happened to him, but now we do. I think he was on board the *Andrea Doria*."

Ben didn't even knock. He burst into Matt's office, startling everyone, and stood there, surprised by all the people he saw.

"Hey, what's going on!"

Immediately, Russo turned to Matt, his eyes hard. "Who is he?"

Matt reassured the agent. "I know him. He works here. Has clearance just as I do. He may possibly have information that bears on the subject we're discussing." Matt's excuse was lame, but Ben would never forgive him if he was kicked out of this meeting now that he knew it was taking place.

Ignoring Ben for the moment, Tony again addressed Lisa and Sarah.

"I spoke again to an official in New York in charge of the Italian Line and he insisted that no one by the name of Peter Warden was aboard the ship. So I think we need to assume that Peter was traveling under an assumed name.

We also need to assume that he wasn't traveling as an American, because the Italian officials say they identified all the Americans who were injured or drowned the night the *Andrea Doria* went down."

Russo turned to Sarah to make his next point. "We both know Peter spoke Italian fluently."

"Of course," said Sarah. "He spoke several languages fluently."

Tony nodded and continued, "There were many Italians, men and women, traveling in C-Deck who were killed when the *Stockholm* sliced into the *Andrea Doria*. We are going to investigate further, but I am operating on the assumption that Peter was disguised as an Italian and that he went down with the *Andrea Doria*. That's the only explanation for how his pen and notebook ended up washing ashore on Nantucket Island."

"But is there any way we can prove he was on board?" Lisa asked anxiously.

Sarah leaned forward. "And it would be great to find evidence about where the Dreyfus Collection is. Peter might have put something in the purser's safe aboard the ship, something that will help us find those paintings!"

Tony held up his hand. "Yes, that is a possibility."

Ben couldn't help himself. "Did you know that the purser's safe has been blown apart? I saw it myself the last time I dived on the *Andrea Doria*."

"Interesting," Tony said. "So that rules out that possibility."

"Maybe not," Ben said. "There may have been a second safe on board the ocean liner. Maybe that's where Peter Warden stowed something."

Tony rubbed his chin. "Hmmm, I'll see if I can find the captain of the *Andrea Doria*, see what he knows. But—"

Ben interrupted. "Does Washington know about the trouble we've been having with those Russian fishing trawlers? In case no one has noticed, they're sitting right over the *Doria* half the time."

"What has that to do with Peter?" Tony asked pointedly.

"Nothing, probably," Ben said. "But why are they so belligerent when anyone gets near the site? They recently tried to ram an American fishing boat!"

Tony lifted an eyebrow. "Interesting."

Ben wasn't done. "And does Washington know they have put a foreign marker at the *Andrea Doria* site?"

Russo looked up sharply. But before he could respond, the phone on Matt's desk rang, surprising everyone. Matt picked up. His eyebrows shot up. "It's for you, Mr. Russo."

"Thank you. I left word I could be reached here," Tony said as he reached for the phone.

When he hung up, he was clearly perturbed. For a moment, he seemed lost in thought and then he said quietly, "I didn't get the chance to mention that we sent two agents to Nantucket to interview Mary Moore."

Lisa stood up, agitated. "How could you, Tony!" The thought of Mrs. Moore being bothered by strangers repelled her.

Tony looked sheepish. "I'm afraid I have worse news. My agents found Mrs. Moore unconscious and the cottage ransacked."

Sarah cried out, "The Van Dyck!"

Tony nodded, "It's gone."

"Oh, no," Sarah breathed.

Lisa couldn't care less about the painting itself. But she did care about Mrs. Moore. "Is she okay?"

"Don't worry, she's been taken to Nantucket Hospital and her condition is good," he reassured her. His eyebrows drew together in thought. "The question is how they knew about Lisa's visit to Mary Moore and her discoveries. Perhaps they were alerted when you filed for a death certificate for your father. Or perhaps they have been watching you all along."

Lisa shivered. Imagine being spied on like that. All of a sudden, she remembered that foggy evening in May when she had stopped briefly in Mattapoisett and her sense that someone was following her. The realization that not only she, but the elderly Mary Moore had been dragged into this sordid mess made her angry. She turned on Tony.

"Where were you when I needed you?" she said, her voice shaking. "If Daddy was your friend, why did you let him get mixed up in your silly espionage games and risk his life when he was the only family I had?"

Tony looked contrite. "I'm sorry, Lisa, but your father volunteered. He wanted to track down the collection and find his friend's murderer. We're going to put things to right. After Sarah called to let me know what you found, I got authorization for the navy to dive down to the *Andrea Doria* to see what they could find. I'm expecting some Navy SEALs to come up in a few weeks. We'll get to the bottom of this."

Lisa shrugged. She just wanted all of this to go away. She wanted to go back to her life as a graphics designer and put all of this behind her. But she could see that others in the room felt differently. While Matt gazed at her with compassion and understanding, Ben's eyes danced with excitement.

"I'd love to go on that dive," he said. "I'm a certified diver and I've already been down to the *Andrea Doria.* Maybe I could help the navy divers find the safe!"

Tony looked exasperated, as if he didn't know what to do with Ben's enthusiasm. "I'll think about it." He glanced around at everyone in the room, his mien stern. "In the meantime, let's keep a lid on what's going on. Okay?"

Chapter 20

A week later, Lisa again mounted the stairs to Matt Chambers's office. She'd gotten word that Tony Russo was flying up from Washington and wanted her to meet him there. Matt's secretary waved her in, saying Matt would be back in a minute or two. Tony hadn't yet arrived.

While waiting for them, Lisa wandered about the director's office. She fingered a seashell, beautifully colored, streaks of pink and yellow through it. It lay on one of the bookcase shelves. She then studied the watercolor sketches of crustaceans that he'd hung on these walls and couldn't help but compare them with her own drawings. She walked over to yet another bookcase on the far wall and found that the titles of most of the books dealt with myriad aspects of oceanography. They were written by scientists, many of whom worked at the institute.

Absorbed as she was, she didn't hear his footsteps before Matt appeared in the doorway. He seemed pleased at seeing her. She thought him handsome but a bit shy and wondered if he had someone special in his life. She had noticed before that he wore no wedding ring on his left finger. Matt had just begun asking her about the work she was doing when Tony appeared, dapper as usual, suited in charcoal gray with a maroon print tie. His dark hair, slightly tinged with gray, was carefully combed.

Ben burst in after him. "Heard you were going to be in the building, Tony, and frankly couldn't stand the suspense," he said. Tony frowned but said nothing. He had hardly closed the office door when Ben asked, "What did you find out about the *Andrea Doria?*"

The agent had his briefcase with him and laid it on Matt's desk, then took his time before he turned toward Ben to answer him.

"A few things," he said. Waving Lisa over to Matt's leather couch, he indicated he wanted her to sit down. Only then did he expand on his remarks. "First of all, I talked to the captain of the ocean liner and he acknowledged that there was a second safe, a small one in his cabin. But he doesn't remember any American by the name of Peter Warden asking to store something. He does, however, recall getting a small package wrapped in plastic from an Italian traveler and putting it in his safe."

Ben's eyes lit up and he turned to Lisa. "We all know your father wasn't traveling under his own name. It sounds like he may have stored something in the captain's safe, something that could help us find the Dreyfus Collection!"

"Perhaps," Tony answered for her. "It makes sense to at least try to find the captain's safe and see if there is anything still in it."

"Why would anyone but us care what it's in a safe hundreds of meters below the ocean?" Lisa asked irritably. She herself couldn't care less about finding a collection of rare art; it wasn't going to bring her father back.

Tony gazed at her somberly.

"Well, the collection has only become more valuable with time. It wouldn't surprise me if other governments are looking for it."

"How much do you think it is worth?" Ben asked excitedly.

"In today's market, we're talking close to a billion dollars," Tony said. "So I could understand it why the Soviets might make every effort to locate the collection. They might want a few of the more priceless paintings for their Hermitage and they could make a lot of money selling the rest of the art on the private market.”

“It’s a bloody race, isn’t it?” Ben said. “Who finds it first.”

Matt interrupted. “What are you planning to do next?”

“Well,” Tony replied, hesitating, obviously uncomfortable at sharing privileged information. “I have the exact plans of the *Andrea Doria*; Genoa, the company that owned the ocean liner, sent them to me.”

Lisa saw Ben’s eyes widen. Tony pointed to his briefcase and said, “We can pinpoint the location of the captain’s cabin and his safe. I’ve been given the authority to have the navy send divers down to investigate. I also have the combination to that safe. The captain kept a record of those numbers. My guess is, with corrosion after so many years, the tumblers won’t fall in place and divers may have to blow the door to the safe off, but of course, that may damage whatever is still there.”

Ben took a step forward and exclaimed, “If the parts are stainless steel, it’s possible they will work. The problem at that depth is that narcosis will make it damn difficult for a diver on compressed air to think clearly enough to use the combination.”

Ben added, envy in his voice, “Your navy divers use helium, not like us poor slobs.”

Matt looked worried. “Have you thought of what you might find there, Tony? Ben tells me water pressure at that depth has caused a buckling of the walls. You might have to cut through steel to find the safe.”

“It’s possible,” Tony acknowledged. “The navy seems to think they can cope with any situation they find. After all, the ship is pretty much intact from all reports, even if the wheelhouse roof is partially caved in.

“When is all this going to happen?” Ben asked.

“Soon, I hope,” Tony said. “We’re waiting for a ship with a decompression chamber aboard. We need a doctor who has worked with divers, and, of course, experienced navy divers.”

Unable to restrain himself, Ben blurted out, “Look, Tony, I’ve been down. I know the layout. Let me dive with those boys.”

Lisa saw the dismay on Matt’s face, that Russo was seriously considering Ben’s request.

“Why not,” the agent said at last. “Your intuition about the second safe seems right, Ben. You made one successful dive on the *Doria*. I guess you deserve some payback. It won’t hurt if you have a look at the plans.”

Tony took them out and spread them across Matt’s desk. Then while Ben bent to study them, he picked up Matt’s phone to make a call. Meanwhile, Matt’s secretary appeared at the door with a question and the acting director turned his attention to her.

A small paper had fallen to the floor when Tony had removed the plans from his briefcase. Tony didn’t notice it, but Lisa saw Ben pick it up. She guessed it was important because the blood drained from Ben’s face.

Suddenly a sharp noise filled the room. Startled, they realized they were hearing the blast of a ferry departing its slip. Ben looked over at Tony. When the agent went back to speaking on the phone, Ben pulled a scrap of paper from his pocket and, using the pen on Matt’s desk, quickly wrote something down. He stuffed the scrap in his pocket and then replaced the original paper that had fallen out of the briefcase.

Lisa was just about to ask Ben what he had found when Tony finished his call. Ben shot her an imploring look, as if to say please don’t say anything; I’ll explain later. Lisa shrugged. She didn’t trust Ben, but she also didn’t completely trust Tony.

For a while, the three men stood over the desk, studying the plans intently. Lisa felt like an invisible fifth heel. While she hoped the Dreyfus Collection would one day be found, if only to make her father's ultimate sacrifice worthwhile, she didn't share Ben and Tony's excitement about the search. Now that she knew her father was dead and how he had died, she didn't really care who found the Dreyfus Collection. She just wanted to get on with her life.

"If you're finished with me, Tony," Lisa said, "I'd like to leave now. I have work to do."

"Wait—we're done here." Tony folded the plans up and put them back in his briefcase. "Let me walk out with you." He turned to Matt and Ben. "You'll hear from me soon. I think I can arrange for both of you to board the navy ship when she heads for the site of the *Andrea Doria*."

Chapter 21

Woods Hole, August 15, 1967

Lisa walked quickly along a deserted Water Street just before dawn. She was on her way to an office at the Oceanographic that happened to overlook Woods Hole Harbor, hoping to finish an oil painting. It depicted the harbor at sunrise. Hardly anyone was on the street at that hour. The ferry slips close by were silent and empty, the ships overnighting at berths on Martha's Vineyard. The boats would begin ferrying islanders to the mainland at 6 a.m.

It was now mid-August and the summer had begun to wind down. Fewer cars waited in stand-by and some college students were abandoning jobs earlier than promised, leaving exasperated employers short-handed through Labor Day.

Upon entering the lobby of the Bigelow Building, Lisa stopped in surprise, seeing a young intern whose name she knew. Wasn't it a bit early for interns to show up for work?

"What's up, Sam?" Lisa asked.

"Seen Ben around?" Sam was a tall, broad-shouldered young man; Lisa guessed he was around nineteen or twenty years old.

"Not yet," she said.

"Guess what?" There was excitement in his voice. "I took the day off and I'm meeting Ben. Came to get some gear."

"Oh." Was that all? Lisa was well aware of Ben's penchant for diving.

Seeing they were alone, Sam whispered, "Don't say a word. Ben says it's a secret but you're his friend and I don't mind telling you. We're going to dive on the *Andrea Doria* that's lying off Nantucket."

Lisa frowned, recalling the meeting in Matt's office. Ben had asked Tony's consent to dive with the navy, but why would he take a novice like Sam along on such a dangerous dive?

"Yes, I do know about the dive, Sam, but you're misinformed. Ben is supposed to dive with the navy."

Sam looked puzzled. "Ben didn't say anything about any navy . . ." He clammed up.

Lisa was bewildered. What was Ben up to now?

"Where are you meeting Ben?" she asked.

"Eel Harbor," he answered and, looking at his watch, grinned and hurried off carrying a mask and snorkel.

Lisa watched him leave. Their unexpected meeting had used up precious time. For a moment, she stood there wondering if it might be too late now to capture the sunrise. Annoyed, Lisa picked up a newspaper from the pile delivered earlier to the lobby desk and went up to her office. As she quickly set up her easel at the open window, she glanced at the headlines in the paper. The news was much the same. "Talks on Vietnam Still in Impasse," and "Charges Traded" with a brief subtitle account heralding "Triumphant Negotiations by the Soviet Politburo with Recalcitrant Czechoslovakia." She noticed yet another headline that seemed old news, the headline similar to the one she'd seen in newspapers bundled on the step of a store closed for the night in Mattapoisett that foggy May evening when she first made her way to Woods Hole. "Russian Trawlers Again Reported off the Cape and Islands."

She heard footsteps then and looked up. A figure passed in the hall, then turned back. It was Ben, surprised to find her there.

"Have you seen Sam Norris?' he asked.

"He was looking for you," Lisa said. "Said he expected to meet you here or at Eel Pond."

Ben tensed up. "Did Sam say why?"

"Something about a dive on the *Andrea Doria*. I thought you had it worked out with the navy, Ben. What's going on?"

For a long moment, Ben was silent. Then he shrugged. "Hell, who knows when the navy will turn up. I've been waiting for them all week but I've run out of time. Nils and Matt are insisting I be aboard the *Gosnold* tomorrow, late morning, or I'm out of here. I figure to do the dive and be back in time."

"Just you and Sam?" Lisa's voice rose an octave. "Who's going to bring extra tanks to the decompression level if you need them?

"Not your concern!"

"You're committing suicide," she retorted.

"Come off it, Lisa!" Ben refused to be rattled. "I know what I'm doing."

Was she making too much of this? She tried to stifle her fear.

"How are you getting there?"

"I was hoping to take Alex's boat, but he says something's wrong with the engine. Has a mechanic working on it, so I rented one. I've arranged for tanks from the dive shop to be waiting for us on the dock."

Lisa made her decision. "I'm going with you," she said. "Admit it, you need a third person to help you out there. As you know, I know how to dive."

Ben looked at her appraisingly.

"Okay," he agreed finally. "I'll see about a wet suit and equipment for you. Meet me at Eel Pond Landing in ten minutes and don't keep us waiting."

He left. Lisa remained only long enough to phone the Personnel Office and tell its answering machine that something important had come up and she had to take the day off. Ben and Sam were leaving too early that morning for Lisa to run it by Matt, knowing he wouldn't be at his desk for at least two hours. Would he have sanctioned the dive? Would Tony? She didn't know where Tony could be reached. Besides, there was no time. If she delayed, the two men would leave without her and Lisa was convinced she was needed. She put away the easel and half-finished painting and ran to join them.

Lisa sat alone in the rear of the motorboat Ben was piloting as it traveled at top speed through the waters of the Atlantic, heading south from Nantucket Island. She turned once to look back at the island and, noticing a distant flag, realized the wind had changed direction and begun to blow from the southeast. She watched as Ben showed Sam how to operate the boat. He then called for her help and together they unrolled a bolt of canvas and erected a partial sunshade from a side railing to the pilot house. Ben explained he wanted to shelter the gas-filled canisters from the sun.

"They mustn't overheat," he said. "The tanks could explode."

As soon as the canvas was in place and the canisters relocated under it, Ben began his check of the equipment, getting down on his knees to use a gauge. He then laid out the wet suits looking for tears in the rubber. The thoroughness with which Ben examined the regulators and gear he and Sam would take down with them helped calm Lisa's uneasy feelings about their dive. From the pilot seat in the cabin, Sam unexpectedly called out, "Hey, does Lisa know our song?"

Ben sat back on his heels. "What song?"

"The WHOI Song!"

Then, without prompting, Sam sang off-key, "WHOI, WHOI. Baby, let me take you on a sea cruise." Ben laughed for the first time that morning.

A few minutes later, Sam spoke up again. "Hey, how about some grub?"

"Hell, no!" Ben stood up. "No one eats before a dive. I'll have enough to do without you getting sick on me two hundred feet down. You had a big breakfast and I saw you munching on something from your pack while I was at the controls."

No reply.

Ben continued to move about the boat further, checking equipment until he seemed satisfied there was nothing more for him to do. They were ready.

"Time for you to take the wheel," he told Lisa. "You need to free up Sam."

"Are you kidding?"

"Not to worry," Ben said. "All you have to do is stand there, keep an eye on the compass, your hands on the wheel. Just make sure we stay on course."

Lisa sighed. She was stuck; after all, hadn't she signed on for this cockamamie trip of her own volition? She stepped inside the cabin, where Sam gave her some brief instruction.

Once Sam joined him on deck, Ben cleared a portion of it and using some chalk he had brought with him began drawing an outline of the sunken ship.

"Now watch carefully," he told Sam.

Both men alternately squatted and stood as they moved about the deck, slowly following his chalk markings.

"The *Andrea Doria* is two hundred and twenty-five feet deep, position forty degrees north, sixty-nine west," Ben said. "It is right in 'Track Charlie,' the route south of Nantucket all the big ocean liners take to Europe and back. The ship is lying on its starboard side where the big gash is and it is pointed to the north. Luckily, it landed on the Continental Shelf, not down in the Atlantic abyss.

"Our suits are heavy-duty," he continued. "Ought to keep us warm against the forty-six-degree water temperature.

There's a current below, one to two knots. When you first get down there, you'll need to keep from being pushed along."

Seeing the worried expression on Sam's face, Ben added, "Once inside the corridors, we won't be troubled by any current."

Ben sketched in the ship's upper decks and the location of the captain's cabin. He squatted and drew, then got up and explained where in the ship they would be. He reminded Sam, "We'll have little more than fifteen minutes on the ship so we need to know exactly what to do. Once the narcosis hits, we won't be able to think out a new plan. You're to stay with me and do what I do."

Ben pointed at the rough map.

"These doors are open," he said. "We swim through this corridor until we reach here." He indicated the second X mark, saying, "I've memorized the combination to the safe . . . can almost say it in my sleep."

"A safe?" Comprehension dawned in Sam's eyes.

"Yes, Sam, a safe. The tumblers may not work, so I'm taking dynamite."

Sam sat back in shock, his mouth open.

"Oh, yes," Ben said. "You can use dynamite underwater if you know how, and I happen to know how." He watched Sam struggle to take it all in, these new and frightening revelations, his face paling as he said, "Hey, Ben, you never told me you were going to blow a safe."

"So what? I know what I'm doing." He added: "If it doesn't work, we'll make our ascent and let the navy finish the job. But it'll be nice to score one on them, wouldn't it?"

"What navy?"

"I guess I didn't tell you."

Ben put down the chalk and faced Sam. "Look, kid," he said calmly. "You don't have to do this if you don't want to. I can dive alone. I've done it before. You can hang on the line at fifty feet with extra tanks."

Sam swallowed. "No. I'm game, Ben," he said. "It's just that I've never been down so deep before and I guess I'm a little shaky at the thought of using explosives."

"I told you I know how to handle the stuff."

Ben stood up and studied the sketch again. When Sam stood also, he asked, "Think you can equalize your ears fast enough?"

"Been practicing all summer."

"Then try not to lose sight of me. We both have watches. Mine has a signal. When it goes off, we come up regardless of what's going on."

Lisa heard him add: "On the way up, we decompress at each knot. I know the exact minutes we need to wait there, so I won't burden you with the numbers. Just stay with me. Our tanks will be close to empty at thirty feet."

He raised his voice. "And that's where you come in, Lisa."

She didn't turn around, but nodded.

"You were right, Lisa," he said. "We need you." He paused, then asked, "You sure you want to do this. You've never dived under these conditions before."

She considered his question. Certainly, she was afraid. Still, she heard herself say, "I promised I would help."

Ben smiled in relief. "Okay, listen up, you two! Like I said, by the time Sam and I reach your station underwater, our tanks will be almost empty. We'll be depending on you, Lisa, so, twenty minutes after we descend, mark that, twenty minutes, take two tanks to the thirty-foot level and wait there for us. There'll be a knot on the line. Is that clear?"

"Yes."

"And Sam, when you reach the ship, you may have trouble with slimy surfaces. Try not to kick up any sediment with your flippers, and don't forget your knife. There's a heavy tangle of cables and fishing nets at the wheelhouse. You may have to cut your way free at any time. Make sure the handle of your knife is tied to the sheath so it doesn't slip away from your fingers."

Ben paused, no doubt thinking what else he needed to tell them. He looked about at an ocean seemingly devoid of any other boat and said, "We're damn lucky the weather is holding."

Chapter 22

Woods Hole, August 15, 1967

Matt walked into his office, carrying a container of coffee. He'd had a bad night, troubled with dreams. The dreams in crazy sequence had involved Lisa and Ben; even Tony figured in them. He realized the specter of the sunken *Andrea Doria* had disturbed his equanimity and made him anxious to put an end to this misguided adventure. Hopefully, once the navy uncovered the truth, he'd be able to get a decent night's sleep.

He sat down heavily at his desk and willed himself to get on with the day, As he was about to pick up a note that lay on his desk blotter and read it, the phone rang. It was Tony Russo. The agent had landed at Otis Air Force Base the night before and was staying at a local motel. Tony advised him that a navy ship was expected to dock that day in Woods Hole. He should be at the Coast Guard pier at seven the following morning.

Hanging up, Matt remembered the note. It was from Ben, saying he was taking the day off. He wanted Matt to know he had decided to ship out on the *Gosnold* when it left on Thursday. Relieved by this welcome message, Matt now turned his attention to an in-box loaded with papers. The morning seemed to drag until he realized how little he was accomplishing and decided to see what the Oceanographic's library had to offer him. He needed a book sufficiently dull to lull him into sleep at night. As he approached the Lillie Building, it occurred to him that perhaps this library, one of the most comprehensive in the nation on oceanographic subjects, might have a copy of Alvin Moscow's *Collision Course*, the classic story of the sinking of the *Andrea Doria*. The author had written his tale almost immediately following the tragedy. Ben had read it.

Entering the large room, he looked around and saw Alexander Kirov standing at one of the tall bookshelves, fingering some books. Since he wasn't in the mood to engage in scientific conversation, Matt tried to escape his attention. However, Kirov spotted him and walked over, smiling broadly.

"Good morning, Dr. Chambers."

"Good morning, Professor."

They spoke briefly of the weather and then Kirov said, "Sorry I couldn't be of more help to your cousin. I would have liked to accommodate him when he asked to borrow my boat for today, but it's having engine trouble. A mechanic is working on it."

Matt tried to hide his surprise that Ben had wanted to use the professor's boat again and wasn't entirely successful. Seeing this, Kirov said, "You didn't know he took the day off. But, of course, that's Ben's way. Independent. He did say he would make other arrangements."

Matt felt a sudden rush of fear. "Did he say where he was going?"

"No, all he said was that he intended to do a dive."

If Kirov didn't know what Ben intended, Matt did. His heart began to pound.

"Thanks for the information, Alex," he managed to say. Then, ignoring the reason that originally brought him to the library, he smiled weakly, excused himself, and exited the room.

Fifteen minutes later, back at his desk, he phoned the local dive shop to verify that Ben had picked up several compressed air tanks and taken them aboard a motorboat.

With him, the owner said, was a tall young man and a young woman with dark hair. He had watched them pack the equipment aboard and leave before seven that morning.

Matt first called Ben's office and then the laboratory. He was told by a lab technician that not only Ben, but an intern, Sam Norris, had taken the day off. He then tried to reach Lisa, only to discover she had called in a personal day, evidently forgetting she had promised to sketch some specimens that afternoon for one of their important visitors. Everything he learned pointed to one conclusion: Ben, Sam, and Lisa were on their way to dive the *Andrea Doria*. Matt groaned. They were in danger. He picked up the phone again and dialed Tony Russo.

"Something unexpected has happened, Tony. Ben is on his way to the *Andrea Doria*."

After listening a moment, Matt responded angrily, "It's not 'so what!' He took one of our biology interns with him. He also took Lisa Warden. I'm almost certain he is planning to make the dive with or without the navy's help."

Her name must have caught Tony's attention because the agent suddenly started talking about taking one of the destroyers out after them. Matt listened for a moment and finally broke in, "What I want to know is can we catch up with them?"

Seconds later, Matt replied, "The Coast Guard pier today. Noon. I'll be there."

Chapter 23

Nantucket Sound, August 15, 1967

As they neared the site of the sunken ship, Ben took the wheel.

"I'm going to miss you," he said. When she looked confused, he said, "Not the dive. Just that I'll be away for a month or so aboard the *Gosnold*. Will you still be here when I return?"

Lisa drew a breath now that she understood him. "I'm not going back to New York, if that's what you mean."

He reached out and took her hand. "Lisa, listen. I'm sorry I got off to a bad start with you. If I had any sense, I would have realized that day on the beach you were special. I was wrong to hit on you."

Though his words sounded rehearsed, Lisa realized he was sincere. She tried to withdraw her hand, but Ben held on to it.

"I plan to see more of you when I get back," he said. And there was no mistaking his meaning. "Ben . . ." Lisa hesitated. She didn't want to have this conversation with him, not while he was about to go on a dangerous dive. She merely said, "Let's talk about this when you return from the expedition. I'll still be here."

Just then, Sam yelled from the deck, "What's that up ahead?"

He pounded into the cabin and pointed directly ahead. There were boats in the water.

"The navy, maybe," Ben guessed. "Got here before we did."

"How many boats were they planning to send?" Sam's voice climbed an octave.

Ben made no reply but kept the boat on course, eyes fixed on the horizon. As they approached, he said, "Looks like a fishing fleet."

He swore then, turning to Sam. "Damn! That means nets. Just be sure you have your knife."

Lisa squinted at the boats. "They're not flying the American flag."

"Shit, I bet we've run into those Russian fishing trawlers."

As their boat narrowed the gap, Ben checked and rechecked his position.

"Looks like they're sitting on top of the *Andrea Doria*," he said finally. For a moment, there was stunned silence.

"Jesus, Ben," Sam said, his voice strained. "Maybe we should cancel this dive. Where's the navy?"

"Don't know," Ben said. "But I know this: we dive as soon as we anchor and we're not waiting for any navy. Who the hell knows when they'll turn up?"

As he approached the site of the sunken ship, Ben reduced the boat's speed. Most of the fishing boats sat off from where Ben had determined the *Andrea Doria* to be. Only one boat, apart from the others, loomed close by. The boat's fathometer suddenly indicated a marked difference in depth and Lisa wondered if they could be over the sunken hull.

"This is it," Ben said with certainty. He pointed to a marker barely seen under the waves. "Just like the one I cut loose when I made my first dive in June." he said. "The one I brought back to Woods Hole to be examined."

He idled the engines, then ordered, "Drop the anchor, Sam."

Lisa watched as the line, uncoiling, slithered over the side at a tremendous pace. It gave her goose bumps to think of the depths through which the anchor traveled, seeing the line cleave the murky dark blue-green waters until, at last, it came to a halt. Glancing up, she saw a single fishing boat, barely a hundred feet off, the crew looking them over.

When the anchor seemed to be holding, Ben shut down the engines and joined them on deck to survey the trawler.

"Strange; they don't seem to be fishing," he said. He glanced over at Sam. "Time to get suited up."

"Ben!"

He turned to see Lisa's frightened face.

"Wait for the navy," she implored. "It's dangerous, just the two of you."

Ben's eyes narrowed; it was obviously not what he wanted to hear. He ignored her and entered the cabin followed by Sam. Lisa stood at the rail, staring at the trawler, seeing Russians stare back at her.

It seemed forever until she heard the two men emerge from the cabin and move toward the rail, silent figures in black, like surreal creatures from another world.

Ben, and then Sam, helped one another fasten tanks to their backs and buckle on weight belts. Lisa saw Ben attach a small bag to his waist she took to be the dynamite, then check to see he had on his watch, depth gauge, and knife. The two men made their way clumsily to the side of the boat where a small ladder hung, lifting their feet high to avoid being tripped by huge fins.

Ben's last words before he inserted his mouthpiece were to Lisa. "Don't forget. You've only got twenty minutes. Get your suit on now." He gave one last lingering look at her face, and then, holding his mask in place, Ben dove for the anchor line. Sam followed right behind.

Her eyes fixed on the green watery void, Lisa watched them descend rapidly and become increasingly smaller until they disappeared from her sight. Reluctantly, she turned, picked up the tank meant for her, and went into the cabin to put on the wet suit that Ben had rented for her. Though the tank was not as heavy as theirs, it still proved a load for her slight figure.

Her apprehension growing, Lisa stayed within the confines of the cabin, adjusting her mask, loath to expose herself to the interested eyes of the Russian crew. As she watched the trawler through the cabin window, she suddenly thought what if a shark should find her, lured by fish parts likely discarded by them? She shivered.

It was time. She reached back and turned on the valve, adjusted the regulator, and walked clumsily out of the cabin to the edge of the rail, to the gate that swung open. On her way, she lifted two small tanks tied together, and holding them, one hand on her mask, forced herself to jump into chilly water.

The weight of the two tanks plus the one she wore quickly pulled her down. In sudden alarm, she kicked hard toward the line that stretched into the depths. Her free hand touched the line and she grabbed it, halting her rapid descent. For a brief instant, Lisa felt the line slacken and thought she would faint, but then realized that her weight, tanks and all, suddenly coming to rest on the line, had momentarily dipped the bow of the boat.

She hung there now in the nothingness. Clutching line and tanks, she began to worry that her frightened breathing might deplete the air in her tank faster than need be. She closed her eyes until, slowly, she forced herself to control the fear. Now was no time to hang in a state of panic. Ben and Sam depended on her.

She opened her eyes to discover she had descended so rapidly that she was just below the thirty-feet knot. It bulged above her in the soft green, illuminated by sunlight filtering from the surface. She knew the pain she felt in her ears was from pressure, so she cleared them and then kicked her way back to the knot. As instructed by Ben, she tied the two tanks to the line.

Hanging there in the vast Atlantic, Lisa told herself that all she had to do now was wait.

Chapter 24

Nantucket Sound, August 15, 1967

The August afternoon was sultry, the weather producing little wind and calm seas. Matt, standing alone on the foredeck of the navy vessel, was grateful for this bit of luck. If the next twenty-four hours continued fair, it meant Ben's projected dive would prove less hazardous, though Matt was certain Ben would attempt the dive even under adverse conditions.

A little while later, he looked up once more and frowned. Clouds had begun to gather on the horizon. The ship plowed steadily through Atlantic waters, doing twenty-five knots, a speed he figured would bring them to their destination, fifty miles south of Nantucket, within two hours at most.

In checking Eel Pond, he had learned the boat Ben chartered was unlikely to exceed ten knots. Matt had calculated Ben would reach the site of the *Andrea Doria* around one thirty or two o'clock in the afternoon, while their ship should arrive at about three. If Ben dove immediately, he and Tony would arrive too late to stop him.

As the ship left the shoal waters of Nantucket Sound behind, Tony joined him at the rail.

"I know you're anxious, Matt, but as soon as you called me this morning, I reached the captain of this ship and insisted preparations for departure be expedited," Tony said. "He was annoyed, naturally, but acquiesced. He advised me the crew couldn't possibly get ready much before noon when the divers were expected from New London, where they train. Fortunately, the equipment was already on board."

Matt continued to look out to sea.

"The divers are down below, getting ready now," Tony added.

Matt nodded. It galled him that there was nothing personally he could do. He felt useless and guilty. Once Ben had become fixed on finding some elusive evidence on a sunken ship, he should never have given him an ultimatum about going on the *Gosnold.* Knowing his cousin as he did, he should have known better.

Tony interrupted Matt's thoughts. "If what you say about Ben is true, I made a big mistake showing him the plans of the *Doria.* It's not that I'm worried about Ben's loyalty. But he's certainly an impulsive son of a bitch, isn't he!"

Matt winced. Too true.

"Any further clues from Peter Warden's notebook?"

"Not a one. Lisa was probably right when she said it could be a game he played. Maybe Peter thought he'd have some fun in case the notebook was lost or stolen. I mean, maybe it isn't meant to be important. Perhaps he wanted to use the book to divert any search away from what he stored in that safe. Who knows."

The two men stood quietly for a time, looking at the horizon.

Tony spoke after a while. "You remember I told you we could be grasping at straws. We do know we've got foreign agents after the Dreyfus Collection. I don't think they ever stopped searching for it."

"You've got to be kidding!"

Tony smiled obliquely. "Believe it!"

His expression hardened. "I'm convinced there are people now on the cape looking for clues that would lead them to the paintings. How else can you explain the theft of the Van Dyck? Foreign agents searching for the collection would know its value and what its existence on Nantucket meant."

Matt stiffened suddenly and turned away from Tony. A large ship, sunlight shining on its metal superstructure, headed toward them at full speed. He looked back at his companion, whose eyes showed no surprise.

"Must be the destroyer escort the navy is providing us," Tony said.

"Escort?"

"There's been a submarine sighting in the area. Not ours, or I wouldn't bother to mention it to you. Furthermore, a fleet of Russian fishing trawlers has been spotted as well. We had a plane fly over early this morning. All highly suspicious, of course, even if foreign trawlers fish these waters frequently."

Tony paused. "What do you think? Coincidence?"

"What are you implying?"

"If it's not coincidence, they know."

"Know what?"

"That possibly the answer to where the collection is may lie in the sunken ship. With all those Russian boats out there, our project could become hazardous. We don't know what might happen. Hence, the escort."

Matt swallowed hard. That would make any diving Ben did in the area all the more hazardous. He stared at Tony in anger.

"Why are you just getting around to telling me all this? I should have been informed earlier!"

Tony ignored his outburst. Matt couldn't help but feel incredulous about this entire undertaking. How did a nonpolitical scientist, a mind-your-own-business guy like him get involved in so much government intrigue? And even if they did learn the location of the so-called Dreyfus Collection, he wondered, how could they ever retrieve the paintings? From a totalitarian country like the Soviet Union? Tony had to be kidding him.

"Short of invading a foreign nation, the United States will never be allowed to bring the collection back to America," Matt said. "Don't you read the papers? Doesn't everyone know there's a Soviet army in East Germany at this moment, all kinds of troop movements, all intending to intimidate. Is the United States willing to drive a hole through the Berlin Wall to get those paintings out of East Germany?"

Tony grinned. "Hah! You're up on the news. You don't just read scientific journals. And you've hit the nail right on its head. We don't know how the hell we can make it happen with the communists controlling East Germany, but so what. Right now, we don't even know where the paintings are, except that Peter sent Lisa a card from Quedlinburg, a town in the Harz Mountains, and Hans Kunz's sister was murdered not far from Hasselfelde, again in the Harz. We do know her murder has never been solved."

It pained Matt, this talk of murder. It made him even more anxious about Lisa, Ben, and Sam's safety.

"All I care about is getting my cousin and his friends out of harm's way," Matt said tersely. Tony Russo, he thought but didn't say, was one cold fish.

Chapter 25

Nantucket Sound, August 15, 1967

As she hung on to the line thirty feet below the surface of the ocean, Lisa peered anxiously into the depths. She could see nothing and had to keep telling herself to be patient. A little water in her mask made her purge gently, holding the mask against her face with her free hand. This small task kept her from acknowledging for the moment that she hung two hundred feet above the rusting hulk of a famous ocean liner, the one that had taken her father with it in its final plunge. Her fear grew, fed by the knowledge that her father had drowned in this very place. What was keeping Ben and Sam?

Then she saw a figure in the murky depths. But he was not moving up according to plan along the anchor line that stretched away into the void. Horror-stricken, she realized he would pass perhaps twenty feet from where she hung, going directly to the surface. She knew that if he didn't stop to decompress, he could die from an embolism, nitrogen bubbles blocking the flow of his blood.

Lisa let go of the rope and swam to intercept the diver ascending rapidly now to the surface. She positioned herself spread-eagle in the water directly above the rising figure, weights balancing her own buoyancy. He shouldered her aside in his ascent, but Lisa grabbed one leg and held on to it. It felt slippery. She reached for the neck of his cylinder and, fastening her fingers around it, pulled the inert figure, with a strength she didn't know she possessed, to the anchor line.

For the moment she hung breathless, then turned him and looked directly into the concealing mask. It was Sam. He was unconscious.

Glancing at his mouthpiece, Lisa was dismayed to find it half out of place. Still, she could see he was breathing through it, though probably swallowing water. She pushed the mouthpiece firmly back into his slack mouth, wondering what more she could do, anything but bring him to the surface before he decompressed.

As they hung together, she decided to try to make an exchange of tanks, worried that in the process Sam's mouthpiece might slip and he would drown. Still, she floated up with him a foot or two, reached for one of the cylinders hanging there, and untied it.

It was then that she saw him struggle for air in a semi-conscious state. Certain now his tank must be empty, Lisa quickly fitted his regulator to the new tank, letting the old one disappear into the depths.

Sam had swallowed some water. Still, Lisa watched him begin to breathe regularly from the second tank, relieved she'd made the exchange in time. She managed to stay close by his side, arms encircling him as best she could, ready to reinsert the mouthpiece if it should slip from his lips.

Ben had said seventeen minutes at the thirty-foot mark. She was to move up to the next knot for twenty-three more minutes. Ben! Where was he? Lisa's throat constricted, and for a moment she hung with Sam on the anchor line, dazed, until she remembered that the man beside her depended on her for his life. It was then she brushed against Sam's leg. Slippery still, it dawned on her that the grayish film beginning to coagulate was Sam's blood.

Lisa floated out and looked at him and that's when she saw the gash that stretched from his knee through his calf. She felt faint with a new fear. Blood drew sharks. She'd been told the fearsome creatures could smell blood miles away and Sam had left a trail, she guessed, from the *Andrea Doria* to where she hung perched beside his bloody leg, exposed.

Still, she dare not leave him, convinced he would die without her help. Nor could she bring him to the surface, not yet.

As both hung there, Sam stirred.

Lisa looked at his eyes. They fluttered. He was regaining consciousness.

Good! It was past a quarter hour. Time to move up to the next knot. She would need his help. Looking steadily through her own mask at him, Lisa watched him focus and then, her eyes meeting his, she tried to infuse courage into him from a source she hardly knew existed in her. Slowly she began to push him up.

His breathing had become rapid and she wondered, with his consciousness returning, had he suddenly remembered what had happened below? His eyes were awful to behold. When he finally looked at her, Lisa directed his glance to the knot so he would understand he was in the process of decompressing.

Yes, Sam did understand. Alternately moving upward with her, clinging to the line now himself, his eyes told her Ben was still below.

Just then, Sam turned his head. He seemed to be listening intently. Suddenly, Lisa heard it too, a tremendous sound. It filled the waters surrounding them, growing increasingly louder as if the world were coming to an end.

She and Sam saw it at the same time, a huge hull, plowing directly toward them, and it was Sam this time who realized their peril. He clasped her tightly around her hips and, facing the two of them down, dove deeply, taking her with him. In their wild plunge, both managed to reach a safe depth, avoiding the keel of the boat that passed directly over their heads, propellers wildly thrashing the waters in which they had hung only a moment earlier.

Lisa heard a horrendous crash and knew the other vessel had plowed into their boat. She saw the surface waters roil as both boats lurched from the impact. The attacking boat then backed away only to gather renewed speed and return to knife completely through the small craft.

Once again Sam pulled on her sharply and Lisa needed no further urging as both swam feverishly out of the path of plummeting wreckage. They watched in horror as the anchor line they had clung to moments earlier slowly snaked its way down to a resting place beside the *Andrea Doria*, carrying with it the front portion of their boat.

The fragmented hull had no sooner disappeared into the depths when Lisa saw that Sam was in great pain from his injured leg and breathing rapidly, having used it in his desperate effort to carry them safely beneath what was probably an onrushing trawler.

They began ascending. It was Sam who pulled Lisa back as she tried to regain the surface and made her understand he didn't want the Russians, for it had to be them, to know they had survived, at least not until they ran out of air.

The two waited barely ten feet under the bright surface of the ocean for what seemed an eternity to Lisa. Finally, Sam took her hand and they moved up. Surfacing, they found themselves in the midst of floating debris, all that was left of their boat. Though the ocean was relatively calm, swells rose and restricted their view of the trawlers. Fortunately, the same swells prevented their being sighted as well.

Sam removed his mouthpiece. Lisa did the same. The fresh air tasted delicious in their dry mouths.

"Thank God that trawler didn't hang around," Sam said.

Lisa nodded, shivering. She watched Sam try to float on his back, but the tank made that difficult.

"Why don't you drop the tank and float?" she suggested.

"Good idea!"

He dropped the tank and began to tread water, using his snorkel to breathe.

"It's easier for me to float face down. I need to conserve my strength." His eyes sought hers. "Stay close to me. I may pass out from the pain in my leg."

"I will," she promised.

Lisa reached for a cushion floating near them. She recognized it, having sat on it earlier, in another lifetime, it seemed.

"You hold one end and I'll hold on to the other," Lisa said. "That way we won't get separated."

Lisa also unstrapped her tank and allowed it to drop away. Then, she took Sam's hand in hers and squeezed it. Reinserting her snorkel, she too lowered her head in the water, closed her eyes, and prayed someone would see the wreckage and rescue them.

Chapter 26

Nantucket Sound, August 15, 1967

Commander James Wilkins had been staring out the window of the wheelhouse at dots on the horizon for some time now. He finally turned away and instructed the operations officer to find Tony Russo and Matt Chambers. The captain had a suspicion what the dots could be, but he wanted the two men there with him. His ship was at Russo's disposal, and any decisions about how to proceed would come in consultation with him.

Despite his long years of service, it was reassuring to have a naval escort. The reports of submarine sightings in these waters were unsettling, though he'd had plenty of experience with them in the Pacific during the war. He'd learned a few tricks. Still, he'd be a sitting duck this time once the navy divers went down and he strove to maintain the ship's position.

Tony walked into the wheelhouse, followed by Matt. The captain pointed to the specks on the horizon.

"Yes, I've been watching them myself the past quarter hour," Tony said. "I think we can count on their being Russian trawlers. Their numbers jibe with the information I received when we left Woods Hole."

Matt interrupted. "Have you seen any small craft headed this way?"

"So far, nothing." Wilkins waved a leathery hand in the direction of the fishing fleet. "I understand our primary aim is to open and recover whatever is in the captain's safe. Then, if there is time, divers will take a second look at the purser's cabin. Dr. Thomas tells me his men are ready to descend as soon as we are in position and let down the lines."

"Sounds good," Tony said. "We'll be depending on that escort vessel to keep those trawlers out of our hair." He frowned, then asked, "How soon will we reach our destination?"

"Another ten minutes should bring us to the spot."

Wilkins turned away to check his ship's depth-finder, and as Matt's eyes followed his, he saw a change in the sea bottom. A contour emerged. Matt caught his breath as an outline appeared of what was deemed to be the sunken ship. Wilkins immediately ordered a dye marker dropped and the sleek ship turned, 180 degrees. It moved ahead then dead slow until the fathometer showed once again they were over the spot. At his signal, the crew dropped the lines.

Wilkins peered out the window. "Those trawlers are now a little too close to my ship, that one in particular." He pointed to it.

Matt stared at the trawler. Then, glancing down at the vessel's deck, he noticed that navy divers, fully clad in wet suits and gear, had assembled and were standing by at a station. Within minutes, he watched them enter the water and begin lowering themselves to the sunken ship.

Tony turned his eyes from the scene to Wilkins. "Please ask the escort to keep those boats away while this operation is in progress. I don't care how it is accomplished but I want it done and quickly."

Wilkins phoned orders to signal the escort by blinker and then invited his passengers to step out on the bridge. Standing at the rail, the three men noticed that the trawlers had slowly begun to move off.

"Look!" Matt pointed to the fishing boat separate from the others. "They're hauling something aboard on the far side."

Tony and the captain moved quickly to the starboard rail to see what Matt was referring to.

"Bloody hell!" Tony swore. "That Russian trawler is pulling divers aboard!"

"It's moving off!" Matt cried out.

At that moment, a bridge lookout waved to Commander Wilkins. The sailor was pointing into the ocean in the direction where the lone trawler had been. In its wake the three men saw debris scattered about. Wilkins squinted in that direction and said, "Looks like a wreck of some sort. Could be that's what left of the boat you've been looking for."

Matt grimaced. "I hope not! We'd better investigate."

Wilkins barked into his bullhorn without waiting for a reply, "Stand by to lower the starboard lifeboat. On the double!"

Seeing Matt's horror-stricken face, the captain asked: "Would you like to accompany the lifeboat crew? You might help identify things. Might not be the wreckage you think it is."

Matt nodded. He badly wanted to believe the captain's words.

The crew was already in the lifeboat when Matt stepped into it, followed by Operations Officer Salvatore. He watched the side of the ship gradually rise above him as the lifeboat was lowered into the waves. Lines were cast off and the sailors began rowing in the direction of the departing trawler. As they approached the floating mass, one man leaned from the bow and drew from the water a long seat cushion. He passed it to Matt, who examined it for markings. It came from a pleasure craft.

They were now deep into the debris, and Matt could see floatable pieces disappear from sight and reappear on the crest of the next swell. Several buoyant cushions lay in the water as well as a strange humped object that turned out to be a picnic hamper. It was upturned, its contents washed away. Trapped air had kept it afloat.

Salvatore pointed to yet another cushion some ten yards from their boat. At his command, the men rowed closer. Two large black objects floated, partly submerged.

"Bodies!" Matt heard one sailor whisper to another. Matt gasped, his heart in his throat.

The sailors maneuvered the lifeboat alongside the forms, and a sailor reached for what was clearly a body clad in black rubber, floating face downward, a snorkel showing. Hanging half over, a second sailor holding on to his legs, the man grasped the figure under the armpits and struggled to pull the body up and over the gunwale. A cushion that was held in one rubber-clad hand started to come too. A third sailor lent a hand and the crew discovered yet a second figure linked to the first.

Seeing the second body rise, Matt reached over and wrapped his arms around the much smaller figure. He lifted it out of the water and across the gunwale. His hands felt the soft swell of breasts in the tightly fitted wetsuit. The woman's chest was miraculously heaving. He turned her over onto his lap and pulled the mask from her face. It was Lisa.

Matt cradled her in his arms and wept in relief.

For a long time, he held her like that, until, feeling her stir, he lifted his head and saw the look in her eyes when she opened them in wonderment for a moment. Then she slipped back into unconsciousness. Matt bit his lip to keep from crying out. At least she was alive.

Sam lay stretched out on the boat's floor, a cushion under his head. He also was unconscious. Matt noticed that Salvatore was bent over his body, examining his leg. When he looked up, he said, "We better get back to the ship. This man's wound needs looking after. He's lost blood."

"But there was one more person on the dive," Matt said desperately. Salvatore shook his head. "My men have looked through the debris. There's no one else to be picked up," he said.

Matt caught his breath. It couldn't be. Ben gone! He lowered his head to hide the anguish reflected in his eyes.

The sailors rowed back to the ship and shortly afterward, their lifeboat was hoisted aboard in a reverse operation. Once on deck, Matt remained loath to relinquish Lisa. She was breathing but still unconscious. Dr. Thomas finally took the girl from him and had her carried on a stretcher to the sick bay. He had already given orders for Sam to be taken below.

The doctor started to walk away, but then he turned back to Matt.

"Frankly, you don't look so good yourself," he said. "Why don't you come with me? You know these young people. When they regain consciousness, we sure as hell could use some information."

Tony, who had just come back up from below, peered at the two stretchers and stopped the doctor momentarily.

"Sam sustained a knife wound, didn't he, Doc?" he asked, and then muttered, "I wouldn't be surprised if this doesn't have something to do with those frogmen we saw climbing aboard the trawler just before it moved off.

Dr. Thomas nodded. "I'll let you know after I examine him more carefully."

Tony climbed once more to the bridge to ask the captain to alert the lookouts to search for one more body. "We're missing Ben Williams," he said. "Only Sam Norris and Lisa Warden were recovered. I hope the divers that went down will find him."

As Wilkins and Tony watched from the bridge, they saw a second naval destroyer steam toward their escort ship some distance away.

"What's going on?" Tony asked.

"Commander Early has evidently requested a second ship to help him pull off his plan. I think I know what he has in mind."

The two men watched Tony as both destroyers moved rapidly toward the trawlers. At a hundred yards, the first ship turned sharply, the second following his right-angle lead. Smoke poured from the stacks as these two ships increased their speed and began circling the fishing fleet.

Watching through binoculars, Commander Wilkins grunted in satisfaction. "I've heard of this kind of operation being done by two British Royal Navy destroyers to trawlers snooping on our NATO maneuvers a few years ago."

They watched as the two destroyers steamed around and around the Soviet fishing flotilla, creating a tremendous wash that then came sweeping against the trawlers' hulls. As the wakes of the destroyers began generating tons of water, the smaller vessels pitched and tossed like corks.

"Gad!" Tony said. "I wouldn't want to be aboard those trawlers now."

"They'll keep it up until either we finish here and leave or the Russians give up and move off," Wilkins said.

Tony rubbed his chin. "I would think that if they had gotten what they came after, they wouldn't stick around, not with that kind of punishment."

Wilkins shrugged. "They still may want to see what we're doing here. I must admit when you told me the reasons for this undertaking as we were leaving Woods Hole, I thought you might be pulling my leg. You know, that that was a cover for some other intelligence operation you didn't want the navy to know anything about.

He smiled at Tony. "But I believe you now. Congress must want these paintings pretty badly."

Just then, a sailor appeared on the bridge. He had a folded paper with him.

"From Dr. Thomas, sir."

Wilkins read it, then thrust it into a jacket pocket. "The doctor expects his divers to break water soon," he said. "Thinks perhaps we might want to be there to greet them."

He leveled his binoculars again. "Why don't you go along. I plan to stay and watch the fun from here."

Tony was only too happy to comply. He was anxious to see what the navy divers might have found. He arrived on the lower deck just as the first navy diver climbed aboard. An inflatable life raft had been lowered into the water and from it the divers were now beginning to climb a ladder to the ship's deck. Several sailors stood ready to lift off their tanks and help strip away the black suits that would soon become uncomfortable in the summer heat.

Two more divers followed the first one. Then a sailor climbed down into the inflatable to steady it against the ship's hull while the last diver climbed out of the water. As Tony squinted at the life raft, he saw two other bodies already sprawled in it. Six? He was certain only five men had made the dive. He turned to Dr. Thomas, who had come up to examine each man as they removed their gear.

"How many divers did you send down to the wreck?" Tony asked urgently.

"Five," Dr. Thomas responded without looking up.

"But there are six!"

The doctor moved quickly to the rail to see for himself.

"You're right," he almost shouted, "there are six."

"Sir!" One of the divers finally got the doctor's attention. "We found a man below and brought him up with us."

Tony exhaled sharply and watched as the men in the raft handed the limp figure in black to the sailors on deck. The sixth diver still wore his mask, but the lips, unencumbered by any mouthpiece, twisted grotesquely as if his final moments had been torturous. Dr. Thomas bent over the body and removed the mask.

It was Ben.

"This the man you were missing?" the doctor said. Squatting, he placed his fingers on Ben's lids and covered the eyes. The navy divers stood in silent tribute until Dr. Thomas said sternly, "If none of you needs further decompression, and you all look fine to me, scat! Lay down to the galley for chow, then stand by for questions."

Dr. Thomas then ordered Ben's body be carried to the sick bay.

For several moments, both men remained on the deck together. This exercise, this ephemeral hunt for evidence of lost paintings, was turning out to be a nastier business than either one of them had expected. It was Dr. Thomas who broke the silence.

"Glad none of my boys need the decompression chamber, especially since I put Sam Norris into it, just in case. He was a little hazy when he came to, about whether he had decompressed long enough. I figured I wouldn't take any chances with him."

Tony took a deep breath and asked, "How's the girl?"

"She's fine," Dr. Thomas said. "Exhausted from her experience, but otherwise, okay. She's sleeping now. I gave her a sedative."

He added, "We got the whole story from her and the divers. Whatever it was you were looking for on the *Andrea Doria*, my men didn't find anything in the captain's safe or anyplace else."

Chapter 27

Nantucket Sound, August 15, 1967

It was well after eight o'clock that same evening when Dr. Thomas, Tony, and Matt entered the wardroom and sat down for a meal. The destroyer's officers and crew had already eaten and gone about their duties. The three men sat silently in a place that normally buzzed with conversation. The doctor and Tony dug into their food. Only Matt, pale and distraught, had no appetite; Ben's death lay heavy on his conscience.

Finally, Matt turned to Tony and said, "I'd like to bring my cousin home. What more do you expect the divers to find here?"

Tony ignored the frustration in Matt's voice. "We need to think this through again. The divers found Ben's body in the captain's cabin. The safe had been open, by combination, it appears, and I don't know how the hell Ben knew those numbers. No dynamite was used, though they found a small bag of it in the cabin. Sam verified these facts when he regained consciousness. He says Ben opened the safe and took something out after rummaging around inside. Sam couldn't see too well because the visibility was poor even with their battery-powered lights. He remembers being relieved they wouldn't need to use dynamite."

Matt leaned forward. "Sam told you Ben took something out?"

"Yes, but whatever he found, we don't have it." Tony paused and in a subdued voice, admitted, "Ben didn't die accidentally. He was murdered."

Matt pushed back his chair, stunned. He couldn't have heard right!

"How do you know that?" he managed to say.

"You remember those divers—not ours, theirs—the ones we saw climbing aboard the trawler before it joined the fishing fleet? Well, Sam's not certain, because he found himself fighting for his own life. He thinks they either grabbed Ben, pulled out his mouthpiece, or else shut off the air valve on the tank he wore and held his arms until he drowned."

"My God!" Matt gave a wrenching cry.

Tony looked down at his empty plate, then continued, "Sam thought at first the men in black were our divers until he saw Soviet insignias on their wet suits when they attacked. He was certain Ben would never have let them come so close if he had known who they were.

"When they attempted to pinion Sam, he said he kicked at them with all one hundred and ninety-five pounds, knocking off a mask or two, which slowed his attackers. He was making his escape to the surface when one of the men followed him up partway and managed to gash his leg. The Russian turned back, probably figuring sharks would finish him off."

"So Ben lost his life for nothing." Matt's voice was racked with pain.

Tony nodded. "If Ben had found anything, the Soviets must have taken it away from him." He shook his head wearily. "I've wired the head of my agency for permission to search the trawlers. I can hear the indignant outburst from Moscow now. In any event, permission will have to come directly from the president. I'm waiting for instructions now."

Matt dreaded the thought of having to tell his aunt what happened to Ben. He needed more information, more time to process this tragedy.

"Did they find anything at all that would make sense of what happened?" he asked.

"I'm told that Ben's knife and a glove were found," Dr. Thomas said. "They were on the cabin floor beside his body. Our divers brought them back. He must have pulled the knife out to use against his attackers."

A thought suddenly occurred to Matt. "The Russian trawlers didn't leave the scene immediately. Perhaps their divers didn't find what they were looking for. Perhaps Ben concealed something on his person."

Tony narrowed his eyes. "The Russians are known for their thoroughness."

Dr. Thomas stood up in excitement. "Rather difficult to be thorough two hundred feet down in the cold Atlantic. I think we should take another look at Ben. We haven't removed his wet suit yet."

"Okay, Doc." Tony stood and pushed back his chair. "If you think so, let's do it!"

Reluctantly, Matt stood up too. He and Tony followed the doctor deep into the ship, to the reefer where they kept the ship's frozen stores. Ben's body lay in isolation on a long packing case, the black suit covering all of him except his face. Tony looked first in Ben's glove, but it was empty. Dr. Thomas then began to feel around the torso. There seemed to be no unexplained bumps, no creases.

"He must have had the suit made for him. Fits perfectly," the doctor said.

The three men glumly left the storeroom, but as they stepped out the galley door, Dr. Thomas asked Tony, "What else did you notice on his person? You think anything could have been attached to his belt?"

"No, you yourself told me it was a quick-release model, no place a cylinder could be concealed."

The doctor stood there, thinking out loud. "He wore a depth gauge and a watch, a whistle and a knife strapped around his thigh. Wait a minute," he exclaimed. "The knife was lying beside him on the floor in Captain Calamai's cabin, right!"

There was a momentary stillness and then he and Tony turned simultaneously toward each other, inspiration on their faces.

"The sheath!" Dr. Thomas shouted. "He wore a sheath, but the knife wasn't in it."

The men hurried back to the supply room. Dr. Thomas pushed the door open and went to the table in the corner where Ben's effects had been placed. He pushed aside the regulator and snorkel to find the sheath, the knife lying beside it. He reached into the sheath as far as his fingers would allow, then, frustrated, turned it upside down on the table and banged it hard.

A small object, wrapped in plastic, fell out and rolled off the table onto the floor. Inside was a tape.

The weather changed in the next hours. The wind came up under cloudy skies and waves began to build. The Russian trawlers were seen moving out to sea. Wilkins's ship headed back to the Massachusetts coast and Woods Hole, followed by one of the destroyers.

While everyone else tried to catch a few hours' sleep, Matt stood on the deck alone, oblivious to the rain pelting down, overwhelmed with grief and guilt. As the ship made a cautious turn into Woods Hole Harbor, Matt couldn't help but think how the somber sky and the darkened buildings of the town lent themselves to the sad proceedings about to take place. In the distance he could see an ambulance waiting on the pier to claim Ben's body.

He drew a deep breath. There were things he needed to do. His aunt and mother had to be notified, funeral arrangements made. He wondered how Lisa Warden was, hopefully sleeping comfortably.

Matt looked at his watch. It was barely 5 a.m. Then he saw the *Gosnold* nestled against the pier and remembered it was due to sail at noon. So, he thought sadly, Ben's wish not to sail with her had been granted.

He was startled when Tony appeared at his side. The agent had shaved and looked rested. His voice was solicitous. "Anything I can do to make things easier?" He hesitated, then added, "Want me to arrange Ben's burial?"

"No, thanks, Tony. I'll handle it."

Tony rested a hand on Matt's shoulder. "Ben is a hero," he said. "He got to the tape before the Russians did and hid it well. I listened to it in Wilkins's quarters. Felt eerie hearing Peter's voice after all these years. He describes exactly where we can find those lost paintings in the Dreyfus Collection. Amazing how the tape withstood seawater immersion and pressure at that depth, but it did."

"So, are you going after the paintings?" Matt asked in a voice devoid of interest.

"I'd sure like to, but I'm not sure what can be done to retrieve them at this time. As you're well aware, we're in a cold war with the communists."

The two men suddenly noticed the upcoming pier and each grasped the railing as the naval vessel, drifting into position, jarred against the pilings. They watched the subsequent burst of activity as sailors doubled up the lines, adjusting huge fenders to a proper height to protect the ship and pier against the rough waters even as the rain began to subside. A gangplank was rigged to bridge the narrow gap from deck to pier and Matt saw the ambulance back up to it. He stiffened as white-jacketed figures came aboard, one carrying a folded stretcher, and watched them disappear into the ship.

A moment later, Matt saw Lisa emerge from a passageway followed by Sam Norris, who was on crutches. Lisa wore a faded pair of blue jeans tightly belted to keep them from falling down from her slight figure, and a shirt several sizes too big. The white sneakers on her feet looked ludicrous, but she had them tightly laced and was trying not to trip over them. She carried an umbrella and was attempting to shield Sam from rain with one hand. But the intern was finding it difficult to keep his balance on the deck of the heaving ship.

Both men quickly moved to help him. Matt placed one of Sam's arms around his own neck while Tony took hold of the other. Lifting together, both men raised the big fellow so his leg barely touched the deck. Then, carrying him off the ship, the pair gently deposited him on the front seat of the ambulance bound for Falmouth Hospital.

Lisa handed the crutches to the driver and walked over to Sam's side, ignoring the drizzle. "You're sure you don't want me to go with you to the hospital?" she asked.

Sam smiled wanly. "You saved my life, Lisa. Isn't that enough?"

Lisa backed off and then turned and fled, stumbling over her sloppy sneakers toward Water Street. She'd had enough of the ocean and this abominable search for lost paintings.

Chapter 28

Woods Hole, August 18, 1967

In the quiet of her office at the Oceanographic Institution, Lisa Warden's eyes took in the view of Woods Hole Harbor. She had begun to spend extra hours at work, anything to avoid dwelling on Ben's death. She had been working on a sketch of a plankton recorder, commissioned by the engineering department, which wanted a drawing of the newly developed instrument. But they hadn't provided a model, only a blurry photograph. She needed a better picture and remembered that similar photos had appeared in one of the latest oceanographic periodicals the library routinely kept. She decided to check those periodicals out.

In the Lillie Building library, she was leafing through a magazine for pictures of plankton recorders when she felt a presence. Looking up, she saw Alexander Kirov standing nearby.

"I was hoping to find you," he said.

"Find me?" Had he followed her there?

"Yes, I was hoping you would know the arrangements for Ben's funeral. I'd like to come."

"I'm not certain there will be a funeral," Lisa said. "I think Matt is planning to scatter his ashes somewhere." It pained her just thinking about it."

"Of course, but I did hear there would be a memorial service at some point," Kirov said gently. "Do you know when?"

Kirov added, "Ben and I knew one another at Columbia. We were friends."

"Oh, I'm sorry." She was apologetic. "There is a service four p.m. at the church tomorrow. I expect Ben's family and friends will be there."

"Thank you," the professor replied. "In all the years I've known Ben and considering what a splendid swimmer he was, I never quite expected the end would come by drowning."

Lisa froze. She continued facing away from him, trying to conceal the shock she felt at his words. Matt had said no one had been told about the manner of Ben's death. Then her body began shaking and she found herself crying.

Kirov reached out to her and touched her shoulder, offering consolation. Instead, Lisa, not trusting herself to speak, brushed him off and skirting the library tables, exited the room. Surprised, Kirov did not follow.

She fled to the administration building, hoping that Matt would be there. His secretary was away from her desk, but to her relief when she knocked on his door, he opened it and invited her in. Noting her distress, he closed his door.

"What happened?"

"Tony was right, I didn't want to believe him," she said.

"About what?"

"I was just in the library and Kirov came in and said something that made me realize he could be the spy you're looking for."

"What did he say?"

"He said he didn't expect Ben would die by drowning. How would he know that? Are you sure no reason was given for Ben's death, just that he met with an accident?"

"Yes, Tony was adamant on that point," Matt said.

"But anyone knowing Ben, and Kirov does know him, wouldn't it be natural to assume he drowned? After all, he was out in the Atlantic in a boat when it happened. He's a diver. Word could have gotten out."

"Anything's possible," Matt agreed, "but Tony tells me he took every precaution. Only his men handled Ben's body and no autopsy was made. The navy isn't talking and Sam has been instructed to say nothing. It may not mean a thing. Ben was a friend of Kirov's despite the difference in their ages. Tony feels Ben could have easily used Kirov as a sounding board, perhaps for certain scientific ideas he had, particularly since Kirov made himself available here in Woods Hole this summer. Tony's only guessing that Ben may have told him about the Van Dyck. Anyway, we'll never know about Kirov unless we catch him red-handed trying to steal the tape."

Lisa swept back the long dark hair that stubbornly clung to her skin. "I'm sorry to be difficult," she said. "You can't know how hard I'm trying to carry off this frightful business for you and Tony, only I hate it. I like Alex. Ben was his friend. Suppose we're mistaken. We could ruin his reputation, his career as an oceanographer and professor."

"Tony assures me nothing will be done to implicate Kirov," Matt said firmly. "He will have to implicate himself."

At that moment, Matt decided that she should know all of Tony's plan. He said, "By this time, a rumor's been floated that something important was found on the *Andrea Doria* and has been placed for safekeeping in my office."

"It is?"

"Not the actual tape. A substitute his agency made up with a false location. Tony tells me the one Ben found is safe in Washington."

Lisa's mouth dropped open. "Wow, are you trying to entrap Kirov?"

"Kind of. Kirov knows I will be taking the day off for Ben's memorial service. So, if Kirov is our spy, he will try to find the tape when I am out of the office. I haven't hidden it well."

"My God!"

"Don't worry, it will be fine. Either he finds the tape, and I hope he does, and escapes with it to the Soviet Union and then spends fruitless years trying to find the collection, or Tony's men close in on him in the act. Finding the tape on him will be proof enough."

Lisa suddenly thought of Ben, how smart he was to have known where the tape was.

"He made all the right guesses, Ben did, didn't he, except the one that might have saved his life."

Uninvited tears welled up in her eyes. Matt reached out and sat her down gently on his couch, then sat down beside her and, turning, took her in his arms, her small figure nestled in the bigness of him. It felt so right to be in this man's arms. Neither moved for a long time.

Finally, she made an effort to extricate herself and Matt released her. She stood up and smiled at him.

"The memorial service! Will I see you?" he asked.

"Yes," she answered, and walked out the door, thinking to herself that seeing Matt could become habit-forming.

Chapter 29

Nantucket Sound, August 19, 1967

Matt was only alive because he had persuaded Alexander Kirov that it was too dark for him to navigate the Cape Cod waters by himself. He and Lisa had returned from Ben's memorial service to find Kirov just about to leave his office, the fake tape in hand. He had bargained for Lisa's life by telling the professor that he would accompany him to his rendezvous offshore, and that there was no way Kirov, who was not as familiar with the waters off Cape Cod as he was, would find his way there by himself in the dark.

Now, Matt was attempting to get his bearing as he peered through the cabin windshield at the barely visible seas. Kirov had refused to permit any lights to be shown, including the boat's running lights. Matt finally found a star or two and then spotted a barely visible moon. Fortunately, Kirov's boat was large enough to handle the swells in the North Atlantic. Kirov was seated behind Matt and he didn't have to turn around to know the professor held a gun on him.

Thank God, Kirov had left Lisa alive, her mouth taped shut and her hands bound so she couldn't escape his office too quickly. Matt had insisted upon it, in return for promising to get Kirov to his destination. He had recalled Ben once telling him how inept Kirov was around boats and what a poor navigator he was.

Standing at the wheel in the darkness, Matt knew Tony Russo would find Lisa eventually. He'd know for certain then the spy he was seeking was Alexander Kirov. Even so, Matt couldn't understand what had happened to Tony's men. He had been led to believe a trap had been set for whoever might be after the tape. Instead, it had been Matt and Lisa who surprised Kirov as he was attempting to leave with the tape.

Now that Kirov's cover was blown, Matt wondered whether he had been deliberately planted in New York to make every effort to find Peter Warden. When that failed, his next assignment may have been to remain in New York and keep watch on the Warden Gallery, Peter's daughter, Lisa, and perhaps, Sarah Dreyfus as well, all in an ongoing search for the valuable Dreyfus Collection.

For his part in exposing the Russian, Matt expected to pay with his life. He clenched his fists as he held the wheel. He wasn't going to be led like a lamb to the slaughter. Kirov would have to work to kill him. Except for the steady throb of the powerful engines and the slamming of the bow into waves, and occasional directions from Kirov, it had been quiet in the cabin for the past hour.

Kirov broke the silence. "I made a good bargain in accepting your offer. You do know these waters at night."

Matt was aware the Russian had been studying a nautical chart using a small flashlight.

"Only if I have a direction," Matt said. "You haven't given me the coordinates."

"Soon."

Matt knew he needed to force the issue. "I have to make adjustments for direction, and I need to get radio bearings. If I make even a small mistake, we'll go off course."

There was silence behind him. Matt decided to change the subject.

"Why is the tape so important to your government?"

Kirov snorted in derision. "Have you any idea as to the value of the Dreyfus Collection? Those particular paintings are worth hundreds of millions, and each year they grow in value because they are irreplaceable."

"But they were stolen," Matt said. "They don't belong to the Soviet Union."

"Hah!" Alex snorted. "You forget who took them first. We didn't. The Nazis did! We only wanted to save them, naturally, or sell them when the Soviet Union needs cash. Like gold, art can be a priceless asset."

"Doesn't it matter that this collection belongs to the United States?"

"Who cares? The Nazis stole Mother Russia's treasures when they invaded us. Enough of this."

Kirov stood up, steadied himself, and once more checked the chart using his flashlight. "We rendezvous at 41,40.6'N latitude; 69,46W longitude. We should be there in about a half hour, that is, if we're on course, and according to that last buoy, we are."

"What should I look for?" Matt asked.

"A submarine, naturally. Whether it will surface before or after we get there, I can't say." Kirov added, his voice flat, "After that, if you're not interested in accompanying me, you'll take the boat back."

Matt recognized the lie and didn't respond. Instead, he continued to peer through the windshield hoping for a break in the clouds, moonlight that would give him some indication of what lay ahead. He wished for the moon. It would enable aircraft to spot the submarine at night when it surfaced. Matt needed to keep their conversation going. He asked, "Which type of submarine is meeting us?"

"I don't know. All I know is that it will be here."

Matt tried another subject. "What made you believe the tape could be aboard the *Andrea Doria*?"

"When we couldn't find Peter Warden back in 1956, we concentrated on those who were close to him in the event he would try to contact them. We never suspected he was on the *Andrea Doria*. After all, we had men watching people board that ship in Naples. It wasn't until his daughter filed a death notice in 1967 that we connected the dots."

"But how did you know Lisa had found evidence that her father drowned when the *Andrea Doria* went down?"

Kirov barked. "Ben had one too many when we were on the town one night. That young man always trusted me."

"It was your people who ransacked Mary Moore's cottage," Matt said.

"Yes."

"Then you have the Van Dyck."

"Yes, I have the Van Dyck. It will be extra payment for my services to my country."

Matt knew he should keep his mouth shut but he couldn't help himself.

"So, the spy steals from the Soviet Union who stole from the Nazis who stole from helpless people!"

Behind him, he heard Kirov's indrawn breath and realized his life was double forfeit. He wouldn't want anyone alive to know he had the painting.

Matt's eyes ached. He had been straining them, needing to see as best he could what obstacles lay ahead of this swiftly moving craft. He kept his tongue now, not wanting to provoke Kirov any more. As they approached the point of rendezvous, Matt considered the possibility of escape. If he dived overboard and managed to dodge a bullet, the chances of his remaining alive in these waters were problematic. However, he had always been a strong swimmer, and he guessed he might be able to stay afloat for a while. Fortunately, the ocean in late August was reasonably warm.

Suddenly the clouds parted and Matt saw the submarine, the moon identifying its huge bulk. It lay directly across their bow not three hundred yards ahead. The greater mass, he knew, was submerged, but it rode high enough in the water to expose the superstructure and he could make out figures on the deck.

"The sub's directly ahead," he said.

"Yes, I see it," Kirov said. "Idle the engines so I can give my signal."

An idea that had been simmering in Matt's mind burst full bloom. He would have to act quickly. He waited until he saw Alex's shadowy figure in the bow, his arm holding aloft the flashlight to transmit identification. As soon as Matt saw him lower the light, he threw the throttles full ahead. The boat lurched forward and Matt quickly set the automatic pilot on a course straight for the sub, then grabbed the nearby fire extinguisher and struck and jammed the controls.

The motorboat gathered speed and he could hear the urgent heavy running once Kirov had regained his footing after being thrown against the rail. Matt frantically stripped off his jacket and the pilot's cap he had worn facetiously and draped them in the dark about the wheel. Then he backed away toward the cabin door and flattened himself beside it, listening for his adversary.

Except for the thrust of the boat's powerful engines, he heard nothing after the abrupt halt of footsteps outside the cabin door. The door was flung open and bullets slammed into the wheel, knocking his jacket and cap to the floor. Kirov rushed the fallen cloth only to pitch forward when Matt tripped him. Matt then flung himself out of the pilot house, taking only a second to jump over the boat's rail and dive out away from the racing vessel and its churning propellers.

Underwater, Matt kicked off his shoes and struggled to the surface. Treading water, he turned to face the submarine. The moon, completely free of clouds now, revealed the scene. He saw no one on the deck of the motorboat as it hurtled toward the submarine. Matt guessed Kirov was attempting to wrestle the controls. The submarine began to move at last, trying to outrun the oncoming boat. There were flashes as the submarine's guns made its abortive attempt to blow the deadly oncoming vessel out of the water. Seconds before impact, Matt thought he saw the professor race for the stern of the boat and fling himself overboard. Then the air vibrated with thunderous sound as the collision sent geysers of water into the air. A few seconds later, the gas tanks aboard Kirov's boat exploded and the sky lit up.

Matt felt the shock waves and swam as hard as he could away from the wreckage. As he crested the waves, he saw the submarine's nose beginning to lift as the weight of incoming tons of water midship slowly pulled the sub to a grave on the floor of the Atlantic. It was really happening. Matt knew that the crew would have had time to temporarily seal off the stern and had probably already done so, trapping whatever crew hadn't moved forward quickly enough.

The submarine was not more than a hundred feet long, certainly not one of the Soviet Union's large new models. If the crew had trained, they could eject themselves from the bow. It would then be about fifty feet to the surface, allowing the men to reach its safety. No oxygen would be needed.

As if to confirm his guess, he soon began to hear the calls of sailors in the water. These must be the men who had been topside and jumped. The others would probably wait until the submarine touched the ocean floor before they began to desert their ship.

Matt realized that if he stayed here and waited for rescue, he might be found and killed by the Russian sailors. His best bet was to put distance between the crew and himself. Hopefully he would be picked up by the Coast Guard or navy, ships he expected would shortly be steaming toward the survivors, given the impact of the collision and the light from its fiery explosion.

Matt began swimming toward Cape Cod.

It was Adam Stillwell, Ben's fisherman friend, who saved Matt. Adam had been heading out in his boat at his usual early hour and would have missed Matt's frantic calls if he hadn't just turned the helm over to his son and gone back to inspect the nets. He heard the shouts and called to his son to idle the engines.

Adam threw Matt a line and hauled him safely aboard. He threw him a towel, and after Matt told him what had happened, Adam radioed the Coast Guard.

"Coast Guard says to bring you right in," Adam said. "So much for the day's fishing."

Twenty minutes later, as an exhausted Matt rested in the stern, he heard the sound of a helicopter. It dropped down and hovered over the boat. The voice on the bullhorn instructed the fisherman to heave to. He then invited Matt to grab the ladder that had been dropped to the deck.

As soon as Matt was buckled into a seat, the helicopter veered off toward the cape. Looking out the copter's window, Matt realized he hadn't swum all that far from the collision. He saw specks in the water and two ships steaming toward them. He sank back into his seat and closed his eyes.

The next thing Matt knew, someone was shaking him awake. It was Tony. The first words out of Matt's mouth were, "You found Lisa?"

Tony laughed. "Couldn't miss her, she made such a racket. Almost kicked your door down with her hands and feet tied."

He sat down next to Matt. "I'm glad you're alive."

Matt filled him in on what happened. And then added, "When you pick up the Russian sailors, look for Kirov. He may have survived."

Evening was well under way when Matt awoke. As soon as he got back to Woods Hole, he had stripped off his dry and salty clothes, taken a shower, and fallen into bed. He had slept for hours and would have gone back to sleep, except that he heard his stomach rumble, reminding him that he hadn't eaten in more than twenty-four hours. He dressed and went downstairs to raid the refrigerator. When he was eating, he heard a knock on his door.

It was Lisa. She wore a simple summer dress with thin straps over her shoulders, pale green, a color that emphasized her dark hair and eyes. She carried a small box, and he could see it held a container of coffee and a sandwich.

"I'm so glad you're okay," she said. "You saved my life—thank you."

Matt turned beet red and found himself tongue-tied.

Lisa smiled. "I'll let you get back to your dinner. I just came by to tell you that Tony has been trying to reach you. He intends to stop by your office this evening, around ten o'clock. He said he wasn't able to reach you by phone."

Lisa headed for the door and then turned back. "You're safe. That's all that matters," she said.

It was closer to ten-thirty by the time Tony walked into Matt's office. He wore a suit as usual, an impeccably cut summer linen, and he had the look of a man completely satisfied with himself. He said he had flown to D.C. for an important meeting and returned that evening.

"You look a hundred percent better than the man I greeted in the helicopter earlier today," Tony said. Without waiting for an invitation, he sat down on Matt's couch.

His arrogance irked Matt. He seemed to feel that everyone was obliged to serve him and yet he had failed Matt and Lisa.

"What happened to the men you said were staking out my office? Lisa and I are lucky to be alive," Matt said.

Tony didn't respond to his question. Instead, he said, "I'm here to give you some follow-up and discuss—"

Matt interrupted him. "Did Kirov survive?"

Tony grinned. "Funny you should ask. The answer is yes. However, he's pretending to be one of the crew and none of them dare give him away. Of course, I know who he is."

Matt couldn't believe the man's temerity. "Did you find the tape he stole from my office?"

"We had him strip on pretense of a hot shower and dry clothes," Tony said. "As soon as we got our hands on his clothes, we found the cylinder in one of the pockets of his jacket. We had some fun with him and delayed returning the tape, said we needed to dry everything first."

"Was that wise?" Matt asked. "You told us that tape gives false directions to the Dreyfus Collection. Why play around with him?"

It was clear Tony didn't like being challenged. "Don't worry," he said. "We didn't burn any bridges. We handed his clothes back to him with the tape still in the pocket, although the saltwater may have ruined it for him. The thing is, we don't want him and his men searching in those mountains anytime soon. I don't want him interfering when we begin our own search."

Matt nodded; that made sense. "When will you begin your search?"

"My agency wants me to find the Dreyfus Collection as soon as possible even if they haven't quite figured out how to get the paintings out of East Germany."

Matt had a disturbing thought. "American operatives poking around in Soviet-controlled territories could precipitate a hot war, couldn't they?" he asked.

"Hell, we could wait for the cold war to end and negotiate, but I may be in my grave by then," Tony said. He paused and added, "Sarah Dreyfus and I have come up with a plan."

"Sarah?"

"Yes. Believe it or not, she's coming with me to East Germany."

"I see. Does Lisa know?"

"Lisa knows almost as much as you know about my plans. I should tell you, Lisa offered to go with us. She said she wanted to finish the job her father started."

"What!" Matt was surprised and dismayed; Lisa had hated all the skullduggery that led to her father's death; why this sudden change of mind? He didn't trust Tony and didn't want Lisa going along.

Tony must have seen Matt's pained expression, for he quickly added, "Hey, don't worry. Taking one lady along is enough for me. I need Sarah to identify the paintings. She's willing to take the risk. But I won't subject Lisa to danger."

Matt was happy to hear that. "So what are you going to do with Kirov?"

"I think we'll keep our friend in the States awhile longer. And now I've got to go." Tony picked up his briefcase. Matt walked him to the door, glad the agent was leaving. He was grateful Tony was not involving Lisa in the search any longer and that he himself could put all of this craziness behind him. Enough was enough.

Chapter 30

Hasselfelde, August 30, 1967

Tony Russo pulled up in a rented Volkswagon van in Hasselfelde, East Germany. The town lay nestled in the upper part of the Harz Mountains close to the West German border. Sarah sat alongside him, and four young intelligence agents occupied the rear of the van. They all looked Aryan and were fluent in the German language. Their story would be that they were Tony and Sarah's sons, members of a middle-class German family. Tony had arranged to meet with a land agent about leasing some farmland.

"With luck, some isolated property close to the Kunz farm will be available," he told his fake family. "That's what Herr Ulrich led me to believe when I phoned. Once we settle in, our job is to determine if Peter Warden's instructions as to where to find the cave are accurate, if in fact a cave exists."

They had driven from Berlin, a distance of about 160 miles, and Sarah was still dealing with jet lag. But she was glad she was here; they were getting so close.

"Okay, let's keep our appointment with this Mr. Ulrich," Tony said, and opened the door to the van. He and Sarah entered the building while their sons remained in the van.

An older man, somewhat overweight with a pot belly, dark hair streaked with silver, and smooth-skinned with a round face, greeted the pair. He'd been expecting them following Tony's phone call, though he had no way of knowing it came from the airport in Berlin. The realtor introduced himself as

Herr Ulrich.

"Guten Tag," he said, and looked them over. "And you are the Krouts?"

"Yah!" Tony replied, then proceeded in flawless German to tell Herr Ulrich exactly what they were looking to lease. He explained in an earnest voice that the family was turning its back on the crowded cities and wanted to reestablish themselves in the country, where they could farm for a living.

The German smiled broadly, his small eyes almost disappearing. "Ah, I have just the place for you," he said. "The farmhouse has been vacant since spring. The owners are anxious."

He glanced at Sarah, who hadn't yet spoken. Seeing the look, Tony explained, "My wife's German is poor. She grew up in France, but returned to Germany when Herr Hitler came to power, wanting to be with our people."

"Ja!" The man understood. He then showed them a photograph of the farmhouse. It had a steep roof and was built of brick, obviously old. He hesitated as if deciding what to say next.

"I don't want to mislead you. The tenants who moved complained about its condition. A superstitious lot they were!"

"Superstitious?"

"Some fool neighbor told them it was the scene of an unsolved murder, a woman whose family lived there a long time."

Sarah saw Tony's eyes widen, almost in disbelief, but only for a moment. He quickly gained control of himself and asked, "What was their name?"

"The family name was Kunz." Ulrich added, all business now, "Under these circumstances, we've lowered the rental price."

"Naturally," Tony responded. "My sons and I were looking to farm, contribute to the state. We don't frighten easily."

Ulrich reached into his desk for the proper papers and pulled them out, having obviously gotten them ready in the hope the farmhouse would suit. He said, "The repairs to the house are your responsibility. The owners who inherited the farm insist on that. They live in Magdeburg."

"Agreed."

Ulrich prepared the papers and Tony signed them, putting down an appreciable amount of East German currency. Sarah knew it was money they would never recover.

Twenty minutes later, following Ulrich's directions, they arrived at the Kunz property. The land, overgrown with tall grass, stretched from the farmhouse to a looming forest. The group carried their suitcases into the neglected and mostly empty farmhouse and then Tony got back in the Volkswagon and drove alone to Hasselfelde. There he found a shop where he was able to trade the Volkswagon for a closed truck, though it cost him a hefty sum of East German money. He located a used furniture store where he quickly bought what he needed and had them put the items in the truck. He bought several lanterns and then purchased groceries at the food store. He was surprised by how cheap food was and how poor the selection.

When he returned to the farm, the summer sky was beginning to darken. The "boys," hearing the truck drive up, emptied it and began moving the furniture Tony had purchased, chairs, a table, and narrow mattresses for all of them, into the farmhouse. The six of them ate the meal Sarah prepared on a small gas stove, and then everyone, still feeling the effects of jet lag, prepared for sleep. Sarah took the only first-floor bedroom in the farmhouse for herself, surmising it had been Hildegarde's.

After breakfast the next morning, Tony took off alone for the mountains, intent on following the trail at the edge of the property that Peter Warden had spoken of on his tape. Sarah cleaned the house while awaiting Tony's return. She wore a simple cotton dress that fit the role she was playing. She had cut her blond hair short and eschewed makeup. No point in calling attention to herself.

On the flight over, Tony had confided his concern that Peter's instructions might be wrong or insufficient. They could well be on a fool's errand, their search fruitless, he warned. He also confessed to being anxious about reputed Soviet troop movements in the region. It was all the more important, he said, that they conclude their search as soon as possible.

As Sarah waited for him to return, standing by the weathered front door and enjoying the mild weather, her eyes scanned the mountains. With barely a hint of the fall to come, she couldn't help but sense a wild and melancholy beauty that seemed to emanate from its peaks. Tony had told her tales about the Harz Mountains, that they were notorious for spawning legend and superstition. Its tallest mountain, Brocken, had been rumored for centuries to be the haunt of witches.

She shivered. She had given Lisa and her daughters a lame excuse for why she couldn't be at home with them over Labor Day weekend. She said that she had received a last-minute invitation to visit an old friend in Paris. Tony had insisted she not tell anyone where she was going.

It wasn't until afternoon when Sarah finally saw Tony emerge from the trail and walk toward the farmhouse. Their four "sons" joined her at the door to watch his approach. Once inside, Russo put aside his walking stick and sat down wearily. Then, looking at their expectant eyes, glumly admitted, "No luck! Couldn't find the cave, though I think I may have passed close to it.

He then added, "But there's always tomorrow."

He withdrew to the far corner of the room to communicate with his agency on a transistor radio. His voice at first was low-keyed, but then he must have heard something that concerned him, because his voice grew louder.

Sarah walked over to him. "Something happened, Tony. What is it?"

"Damn fool Lisa."

"Lisa?"

"She's joining us."

"How did she manage that?" Sarah asked.

"The foolish girl convinced my superiors she had important information, insisting her father had given her specifics to finding the collection."

Sarah concealed a smile and wondered why he was so reluctant that Lisa join them.

"Couldn't Lisa have told the agency what she knows? They could radio it to us, in code, of course?"

"She wouldn't tell them. Insisted they fly her to East Germany."

He turned away and said, almost to himself, "Lisa's coming here is the last thing I need right now."

Lisa drove up to the Kunz farm that night just before dark. She stood in the doorway, dressed modestly in a cotton dress, dark hair framing her pale face. While Sarah and the four young agents smiled at her in welcome, Tony glared at her.

"Sorry, Tony, I told you I needed to be here to help you find the paintings," Lisa said. "I feel like I owe it to my father."

Sarah interrupted. "Have you had dinner?"

"No, I wanted to get here before it got dark," Lisa said.

"Well, then, let's see what I can do." Sarah bustled over to the stove.

Lisa, who hadn't eaten anything since her transatlantic flight, ate quickly and faced Tony, who had seated himself at the table across from her.

"I owe you an apology," Lisa said.

"An apology?" Tony was clearly taken back.

"When Daddy first disappeared and you came to see me at the gallery, I didn't give you his full message."

"What!"

"I'm sorry, but I was upset and not thinking clearly," Lisa said.

Tony's face was inscrutable. "What was the rest of the message?"

"Daddy said to tell you to look for an old pine tree with a small hole at its base big enough for me to crawl into. Then he described a cluster of three rocks beside it. He said they looked like sentinels."

Tony sank back in his chair and closed his eyes. "Thank you for that, but you could have told Washington that," he chided, but his anger was gone.

"Yes, but I wanted to be here in person."

Sarah intervened. "I'm sure with what Lisa has told us that we'll find the collection now."

One of the agents, a man named Jim, offered to move his mattress into Sarah's room for Lisa; he said he could make do otherwise. Lisa felt very grateful for his kindness and accepted his offer.

As the two women prepared for bed, Sarah felt comforted by Lisa's presence. She was glad she had come after all.

Chapter 31

Harz Mountains, September 1, 1967

The next morning, Tony and two of his "sons" hiked back up the trail to find the sentinel boulders Peter Warden had described to his daughter. When they returned in the afternoon, Sarah could tell by the elated look in Tony's eyes that his quest had been successful. He told her and Lisa that after a climb of less than an hour, he had indeed discovered the hidden entrance. It led to a small interior space and perhaps to a larger cave that could conceivably contain David Dreyfus's collection. Tony advised the other agents to pack all necessary digging equipment into the truck and they would leave for the site at first light the next morning. It was only after they had eaten dinner that he shared his other finding.

"There needs to be a burial before we can dig through the rubble inside the opening. I found a hand and arm belonging to a body," he said, eliciting gasps from Sarah and Lisa. "An animal must have been attracted by the smell and uncovered them."

Despite being shaken by his bizarre announcement, Lisa declared, "I'm going with you tomorrow."

"No, you're not!" Tony said. "It'll be a long day of digging. You'll just be in the way."

"I can be a lookout. Please! I want to go with you."

"No!"

Sarah intervened. "Why not, Tony? She'll be useful. She can watch outside while all of you dig. I'll stay here just to make sure we don't get any visitors."

Tony was silent for a long time. Finally, he muttered, "Okay." He added, "I received information today that Alexander Kirov has been released from United States custody along with the surviving members of the submarine crew. The Soviet Union applied pressure and the State Department folded. I've no doubt the KGB agent is heading straight for East Germany and these mountains."

The window for finding and rescuing the paintings had suddenly narrowed.

As the sky began to lighten the next morning, Lisa and the young men climbed into the truck, now loaded with digging tools and baskets. Tony jumped into the driver's seat and started the engine.

"We're going up a dirt track I found yesterday," Tony said as he began driving. "It's quite close to the cave, and I can see why Kunz picked that location. It allowed him and his helpers to move the paintings without undue strain. The entrance is impossible to see from the track."

Their trip was rough, the road eroded, forcing Tony to drive slowly up the steep incline. The road finally branched off onto an earthen track that was even worse. Jostled about in the cab, Lisa could smell the damp scented air and hear the song of birds in the forest. Finally, Tony pulled over and parked the truck beside a heavy stand of trees. They piled out and Tony directed each man to pick up a shovel and basket for the rubble Tony warned them they would find.

He led them to a barely discernible slit behind a huge boulder. Lisa stared at it, realizing she would never have seen the opening if he hadn't pointed it out, concealed as it was by several large boulders and an ancient pine tree.

Tony and the four men squeezed into the opening and began digging. After a time, Tony came out and reported they had found three bodies in the dirt. Two of the young agents, Jim and Tom, dug a rough shallow grave nearby on the ledge, deep enough to bury the remains. The burials accomplished, they joined Mike and Ted working to excavate the remaining debris from where the three dead Germans had lain. Standing beside the sentinel boulders, Lisa watched the side of the ravine slowly fill with the excavated soil and rubble the men brought out in baskets, seeing it dribble its slow way down the slope.

It was late morning when she heard the thunder. Startled, she glanced up at the sky where trees parted to allow her a view and realized how dark it had suddenly become. It was about to rain, and as if on cue, Lisa felt the first drops. She barely had time to reenter the cave when the skies opened up and the rain came down in torrents. In the short time she stood within the rocky enclosure, she began hearing a noisy runoff. Water had begun to cascade from the higher reaches of the mountain.

Lisa peered out and saw that the heavy rain was producing waterfalls that increasingly flowed into the ravine to the stream below. She realized she should tell Tony that the stream was rising. She walked through the partially excavated cave, calling for him. Tony heard her and followed her to the entrance. He peered out of the cave and then called back to the men, "Hold up for now. We can't empty debris with this runoff. I guess this is as good a time as any to stop for lunch."

The heavy rain didn't taper off for another hour. The trees were dripping water when Lisa took up watch again. She wondered about the mud on the mountain road they had taken earlier. Would the track be passable?

Just then, she heard the hum of a motor and stiffened. Someone was approaching on a motorcycle. The next minute Lisa saw the vehicle make slow progress toward them as it skidded about in the mud. Alarmed, she slipped inside and touched Mike, who was carrying a load to the cave's entrance. Her finger to her lips, she pointed out.

Mike understood. He dropped the basket he carried and looked out toward the track. A man was examining the truck they had parked nearby. He had a walkie-talkie in his hand but wasn't speaking into it, not yet.

"Tell Tony," Mike whispered. "I'll do what I can."

Lisa disappeared into the newly created tunnel and came back out with Tony, the three other agents following. Peering through the opening, they saw Mike walk toward the man and heard him call out in German. Lisa didn't understand what he was saying, but Tony and the others thought they did.

"Mike's probably telling him he's a hiker, Tony said. "That's what I told the boys to say if anyone came by, that he's lost his way, that he needs directions off the mountain."

Tony paused, listened, then explained, keeping his voice low, "That stranger seems to be having trouble understanding Mike. Evidently doesn't know German well."

He listened some more. "From the little I hear, he's speaking Russian. He's asking why Mike's clothes aren't wet if he was hiking. And of course, Mike is stalling, pretending he doesn't understand the language."

Tony again whispered, his voice strained, "The fact he has a walkie-talkie means there are others on the mountain searching for us. Kirov got here sooner than I expected." He then moved back away from the entrance to let his men assess the situation. Mike might need help.

Ted understood and edged out, unseen at first. He ambled down to the pair standing by the truck, another hiker. The Russian surprised both him and Mike when he drew a gun. Before he could aim it, Mike rushed him, knocked him down, and kicked the weapon away. He was after the walkie-talkie next, but it was Ted who wrestled it away as the man tried to regain his feet. Then Ted stood back while

Mike hammered the man and was about to intervene as the two fought on the edge of the ravine.

Suddenly the Russian slipped, tried to grab hold, and, failing, disappeared from sight. Mike was sliding off as well until Ted, dropping the instrument, quickly reached for his hand and pulled him back. The earth they had been dumping into the ravine had turned to liquid mud.

As soon as the Russian slipped over the edge, Lisa followed Tony as he and the other two agents rushed out from their concealed place to peer into the ravine. Lisa saw the man roll and slide down the steep slippery slope toward the stream below, unable to stop himself. At the same time, she heard a deafening roar and saw a sudden wall of water erupt below.

Horrified now, she witnessed a flash flood envelop the man and quickly carry him away out of sight, having first hurled him violently against the huge rocks in the stream at the ravine's bottom. Lisa stood frozen, shocked by what had just happened.

Tony recovered his wits first. He walked over to the truck and picked up the walkie-talkie Ted had dropped. "If he survives, at least he won't be able to communicate his position to Kirov right away," he said. "Time's running out. Let's get a move on!"

Lisa remained stunned by the violence she had just witnessed. As she stood looking down into the ravine, a strange thought assailed her. Sarah had mentioned the legends about witches as they prepared for bed the night before. If indeed witches inhabited these mountains, hadn't they just intervened on the side of the Americans?

An exhausted but elated group of Americans drove slowly back to the Kunz farm as evening approached. They had discovered six wooden crates deep within the inner cave. Tony had decided not to open the crates there since time was of the essence, but he was convinced they contained the Dreyfus Collection. When they arrived at the farmhouse, Tony directed Jim and Tom to jump out and open the barn doors. He then drove slowly into the sagging structure. There was a full moon and he didn't want any prying eyes to see what the crates contained.

"Mike, grab that crowbar," Tony said as the group gathered around the truck bed. Sarah had come out of the farmhouse and her eyes now shone with excitement. Mike hopped onto the rear of the truck and began to pry open the nearest crate. The top lid parted just enough to reveal paintings packed inside.

Mike lowered the crate to the ground with Tony's help. They could see how the frames, the corners carefully affixed against movement, held the art in place. The paintings were mounted, one on top of the other, separators between them. With both hands, Tony reached in and gently pulled one of the top paintings halfway up.

Scarcely daring to breathe, Sarah leaned forward and saw a painting set off by the flashlight, its colors unbelievably brilliant. It was a Cézanne, a favorite of David's.

They had found the Dreyfus Collection!

As Tony carefully lifted the one next to it, she recognized that painting also, a Vermeer. It was all too much. Sarah turned away, sobbing.

Tony gently replaced the paintings. He and Mike lifted the crate back onto the truck. They opened the barn doors, and after Sarah and Lisa had emerged, closed and locked the doors behind them. In bright moonlight, the four Americans walked in silence to the farmhouse.

Chapter 32

Harz Mountains, September 3, 1967

A summer mist enveloped the forests and fields of the Harz Mountain region when early the next morning the Americans packed their few belongings. The four young agents took care to fasten the six crates even more securely using additional rope and bungee cords.

Tony, who had been supervising the operation, turned to Jim and Tom. "I'm changing our game plan. You two will remain. It's only a matter of time before Kirov and his cohort appear, especially after the disastrous episode yesterday. Your presence here will put them off, give us time to get the collection safely away. Delay is the name of the game," he said. "Pretend to operate the farm. In a few days, make your way back to the States."

The men nodded. "You can use Lisa's car," Tony added. Lisa, Sarah, and the two other agents piled into the cab, with Tony driving. Not until he left Hasselfelde behind and took the turn in the road that pointed in a northeast direction did Tony finally explain what he had in mind.

"It's too dangerous to attempt to escape East Germany at any border crossing," he said. "We'll be stopped and the truck searched."

"What's the alternative plan?" Sarah asked.

"We drive two hundred miles to the Baltic coast," he said. "We'll bypass the city of Rostock for the small East German seaport town of Warnemünde."

Lisa looked at him. "What then?"

"A ferry will take us to Denmark. I've been advised the Warnemünde–Gedser ferry carries vehicles. Once in Gedser on Danish soil, the collection will be safe."

"Won't there be guards at the ferry?"

"Probably, but I'm told we have a better chance to elude the authorities there. A cargo plane is waiting, even now, at the Copenhagen airport to airlift the paintings to the United States."

Hours later, Sarah spotted the smokestacks of Rostock impressively outlined against a blue sky. But that was all they saw of Rostock, for Tony took the bypass. It led to Warnemünde, a coastal town beside the Baltic Sea. They stopped only to buy gas and use the restrooms, eating whatever food they had packed as they drove.

As they neared Warnemünde, Tony said, "If we're lucky, we could arrive in time to catch the one o'clock ferry. If not, there's another ferry an hour later. Washington radioed me a schedule."

He paused. "We may yet outfox Kirov. But he could have raised an alarm, and that would alert border guards to look out for us."

Sarah tensed; they might still lose David's collection.

Warnemünde was a pretty town of shops, cafés and beaches with the Baltic Sea glinting in the distance. Tony drove along the busy waterfront looking for the ferry terminal. They found it, in time to see visitors disembarking and a long queue of vehicles waiting in line to board the next ferry to Denmark. He got in line.

Lisa smiled at the familiar sight. "Don't the cars lined up here remind you of the ones taking the Nantucket ferry?"

"Yes, they do," Sarah answered. "Makes me feel right at home."

Only then did Lisa spot uniformed guards. She paled.

Tony had just returned from buying ferry tickets when Sarah noticed a lone inspector. This man approached each vehicle in line awaiting its turn to embark and was questioning the occupants. She pointed him out to Tony.

He nodded and called softly to Ted and Mike, who were sitting in the back of the truck.

"There appears to be only one inspector on duty," he said. "The others may be at lunch. If the inspector insists on checking our cargo, it will be up to you, Ted, to take care of him. But I don't want him killed."

He turned to Mike. "Get out of the truck and wait for me in the rear."

Unfortunately, the East German inspector believed in thoroughness. Peering through the open cab window at the three of them sitting stiffly, he told them he needed to inspect the truck's contents.

"Of course!" Tony spoke affably. He looked around and, seeing that other guards patrolling the pier were engaged elsewhere, he stepped out of the cab, a large map in his hand, and walked to the rear. Lisa and Sarah each watched from the truck's side-view mirrors.

From her vantage point, Lisa was surprised to see Tony ignore the inspector, turn him over to Mike instead, and approach the car that had pulled up behind them. A lone occupant sat behind the wheel. Mike opened the truck's rear doors, and when the inspector looked into the dim interior and became curious about the crates he saw there, Mike suggested he climb into the back to get a better look and in fact, helped the man up. They heard the slight sound of a scuffle in the rear of the truck and that was the last they saw of the inspector.

In the meantime, Tony had engaged the driver of the next car in line and pushed a map of Denmark through the driver's open side window. The map obscured the windshield as Tony distracted the man by asking him directions. As soon as Mike shut the truck rear doors from within, Tony thanked the driver of the car behind them and returned to the truck cab.

When it was their turn to embark, Tony started the engine and pulled slowly onto the ferry. The driver in the next car, finding the inspector nowhere in sight, followed them onto the ferry.

Lisa stood by the rail as the ferry made steady passage toward the Danish seaport of Gedser. Breathing in the fresh sea air reminded her of the ferry ride she had taken to Martha's Vineyard with her father. He would be so pleased to know they had finally recovered the paintings he had assembled for his friend, David Dreyfus. But at what a cost.

Inexplicably, Matt Chambers's face supplanted her father in her mind. She realized she was in love with him and couldn't wait to see him again. Matt was smart, sensitive, and caring, or at least he seemed to really care about her. He had been upset when she called and told him she was going to East Germany to help find the Dreyfus Collection, but by the end of their conversation, he understood she wouldn't be deterred and had wished her well.

The crossing took about two hours, just as Tony predicted. As soon as the ferry docked and the truck disembarked, Tony pulled next to a building that had an outside telephone. He left the cab saying he needed to call ahead to the Copenhagen airport to alert the American pilot that they were on their way. While Tony phoned, the women left the truck to buy sandwiches at a roadside stand, Sarah using what little German she knew to make the purchase.

The sun was still shining in that northern Scandinavian region when the tired refugees at last reached Copenhagen. Tony drove directly to the airport and right up to the American cargo plane that was waiting for them, a "Hercules," Tony called it. It stood out on the tarmac, away from the terminal, huge and impossible to miss.

Mike and Tony jumped out of the rear of the truck and removed the crates. They had hidden the bound and muzzled inspector under a rug, and no one noticed him. The crew of the Hercules then carried the crates on board. Tony told Mike to drive the truck to a Danish suburb far from the airport and park it inconspicuously.

"Not a scrap of evidence must be left behind," he said. "Make sure you wipe the truck clear of prints. After that, make your way to the United States embassy in Copenhagen. Once you're there, you can anonymously notify the Danish authorities about an abandoned German truck. The embassy staff will arrange your return to the States."

Tony shook his agents' hands and watched them leave. He then motioned Sarah and Lisa aboard the giant aircraft. As they mounted the steps, he informed them, "Pilots refer to this plane as the Herk and sometimes, Fat Albert."

Entering the huge cabin, Lisa looked about, amazed at the military and communication equipment the plane carried in its belly. It was only after she tightened her seatbelt in the forward cabin that she realized there were hardly any crew members aboard. No one to operate the plane's equipment. The Americans she remembered seeing unload the crates had disappeared.

She turned to Tony and asked, "What happened to the rest of the crew? There's only Sarah, you, and me, that navigator who just introduced himself, and whoever is occupying the pilots' cockpit aboard. Where are the men who originally flew to Copenhagen aboard the Hercules, the ones I saw help you move the crates?"

Seated across the aisle, Tony shrugged. "They have other work to do," he said.

Chapter 33

North Sea, September 4, 1967

Sarah relaxed against her seat in the cabin of the huge plane as it flew over the European mainland toward the North Sea. The Hercules was bringing her home and, despite the odds, it carried David's collection aboard. She closed her eyes and remembered the day she and David had met by chance at the Metropolitan Museum in New York; how she stood studying a Camille Pissarro painting until suddenly she became aware of a man who in turn was studying her. His concentrated gaze made her blush. He drew near and apologized, saying he was delighted to find someone else who could become so totally absorbed in art. He told her that the artist, Pissarro, had been a free thinker and would be pleased, were he still alive, to know how much he was appreciated.

Now, Sarah looked over at Tony, who was seated across the aisle. "I hope you'll accept an invitation to the opening."

"What opening?"

"Why, when the new Dreyfus wing opens at the National Gallery of Art. You'll be there?"

Tony didn't answer right away, so Sarah pressed him. "Won't you come?"

He looked at her strangely and finally replied, "Of course."

Sarah turned to Lisa, her eyes alight. "Did you know there will be a Peter Warden Gallery? I intend to see to that."

Lisa was dumbstruck, that Sarah would honor her father like that. "Thank you, Sarah, that's so kind of you."

After a time, they all fell asleep and Lisa didn't wake up until the huge cargo plane landed in Newfoundland for refueling. Tony unbuckled the seat belt and vacated his seat as soon as the plane taxied to a halt, away from the main terminal. Lisa and Sarah took turns going to bathroom and washing their faces. Bagels and other breakfast food had been left out for them in the galley, so they helped themselves.

It wasn't until the plane was about to take off again that Tony returned to his seat and buckled in. As the plane sped down the runway, Sarah asked the question uppermost in her mind: "When do we land in D.C.?"

For a moment, Tony seemed to be considering his answer. "The crew's orders have changed."

"Changed?"

"The military wants the Herk to fly to Homestead Air Force Base south of Miami. This plane has been assigned a new and secret mission. Nothing to do with us."

Sarah was speechless with frustration.

"Not to worry," Tony said. "A light transport, a Beech 18 Expeditor, is being flown to Homestead. It will be there waiting for us. The collection will be transferred to this smaller aircraft. We'll be on our way to D.C. almost immediately."

Lisa sat up and stared at Tony. "That doesn't make sense," she said. "Why fly to Miami when Washington is on the way?"

Tony grimaced; he was not used to explaining himself. "The Hercules is being rerouted on a special mission, an immediate one out of Florida," he said. "It's a military priority. The collection's arrival in D.C. has become secondary."

He paused. "Once we transfer the crates onto the smaller plane at Homestead, I promise you we'll take off right away and be in D.C. in a matter of hours. Naturally I'm not happy either, but military needs take precedence."

Sarah found her voice. "Ridiculous! We could easily land in Washington and remove the collection. This plane could then continue on to Florida."

Tony shrugged. "Ours is not to wonder why, ours is just to do or die!"

Lisa felt as though something were off; Tony had been in such a hurry to get the collection stateside. Why this unwelcome diversion now?

"When did you learn of this change?" Sarah asked sharply.

"By radio, while we were refueling."

"Why did you wait until takeoff to tell us?"

Lisa tried a different tack. "Daddy always told me you could make things happen. Why not now?"

"Whoa!" Tony said. "Both of you, take it easy! The crew is under orders and I can't explain this change any more than you can."

Sarah unbuckled her belt and stood up. "Put me on the radio, Tony. I know a few congressmen who might be able to get the military to back off enough to land us at National Airport or at Andrews Air Force Base."

She added, "After what we've been through to rescue the collection, the government owes us." She blinked back tears.

Tony stared up in surprise at her sudden defiance. "Sarah, I'm just a cog in the wheel," he said. "I take orders. I don't dish them out. We're only talking about a short delay. Nothing to get worked up about. As for radioing anyone, we're under military restrictions, especially as this plane's secret mission has commenced."

Sarah remained skeptical. She had always believed Tony to be omnipotent, remembering how Peter had marveled at the way his friend operated. Why couldn't he pull rank now, when it was crucial to bring the Dreyfus Collection safely home?

"Tony," she pleaded, "with all your contacts, can't you reverse those orders?'

"No."

Sarah sat down heavily. Lisa's hand reached out and squeezed hers, but she was too distraught to return the gesture.

The Hercules landed smoothly at Homestead Air Force Base south of Miami, Florida, later that afternoon. Traveling the full length of the runway, it then taxied away from the fighter planes lined up on the tarmac and slowly rolled toward an aircraft parked off to one side and isolated. When the Hercules finally came to a stop, a ground crew maneuvered a tall ladder to the lofty cabin door and the plane's navigator swung the door wide to allow the three passengers to emerge into the daylight. It was the first time since boarding the military plane in Copenhagen that Sarah and Lisa were exiting it.

They were immediately assailed by Florida's hot, humid air. Lisa squinted from the glare, and as her eyes adjusted, saw the small plane sitting nearby. Once the women reached the tarmac, they stood watching the three Hercules crew members and an officer they took to be the pilot of the Beech carefully remove the six crates from the Hercules's huge cargo bay. The men then transferred them into the small transport, the taller ones barely clearing its cabin door, finding it necessary to stoop in order to make it through the opening. Tony supervised each step of the operation.

As soon as the crates were transferred, the Hercules's crew shook Tony's hand and, nodding to the women, reentered their plane. The bay doors closed and the big ship rolled toward the fueling station, leaving the pilot of the Beech,

Tony, Sarah, and Lisa standing beside the smaller aircraft. There was no one around, although they could see activity at a distant building.

As the Hercules taxied down the runway, Tony turned toward the group and made introductions.

"Our pilot, Captain Jim Comly, U.S. Air Force."

He pointed to Sarah. "This is Mrs. Dreyfus. The young lady is Lisa Warden."

"So. You're the ladies Mr. Russo and I get to take with us," Comly said, revealing a brisk manner that seemed to fit his close-cropped military haircut.

"Call me Tony," the intelligence agent corrected him.

Sarah ignored their exchange. "How soon will we be on our way?" she asked.

Tony didn't answer her. Instead, he turned to Lisa. "We don't have room on the Beech for all four of us. Lisa, you will be flown back to Woods Hole on another plane."

Sarah drew back. "No!" she said sharply, "I want Lisa to come with us."

Lisa stared at Tony, confused. "The Beech can only handle a certain weight," Tony explained. "It can't safely take both the collection and four people."

He addressed the captain. "Isn't that so?"

The women turned to look at Captain Comly and saw that he seemed reluctant to speak up. Lisa guessed the captain might risk insubordination if he openly refuted Tony. The captain gave an almost imperceptible nod, his eyes disguised by the sunglasses. Yet she could tell by the captain's stance that he didn't agree there was a weight problem. Why was Tony acting this way?

Sarah glared at him. "Tony, I hold you responsible for that ridiculous decision not to have the Hercules land in Washington. You've stuck us here in Florida, wasted our time, and made us dependent on this small plane."

She added, "Lisa is going with us."

For several long seconds, Tony glared back before saying firmly, "No."

She stiffened. "I'll call Washington and raise Cain if need be."

This time, Tony shrugged, hesitated briefly, then capitulated, "You win, Sarah."

Lisa glanced at Sarah, surprised by both Tony's strange demand and her friend's intervention.

"You're sure about this, that you want me tagging along?" she asked Sarah. "I don't mean to create a problem for anyone."

"As sure as I will ever be," the older woman said.

Tony interrupted. "I've got to radio Washington. We're not scheduled to take off for at least an hour or two. Why don't you and Lisa go grab a bite to eat in the mess hall? The captain will stay with the airplane."

An hour later, Tony joined them back at the plane. He had a bottle of Champagne in his hand. "It's time to celebrate what we've accomplished," he said. As Captain Comly initiated flight checks and talked to the air controller, he poured the bubbly into glasses for Lisa and Sarah. "To the Dreyfus Collection!" he said, and raised his glass.

Chapter 34

Lisa's mouth was dry. She thought her head would burst, it ached so. Her eyelids were heavy as she struggled to open them. Where was she?

As consciousness returned, Lisa realized she was seated in the co-pilot's seat of an airplane, her arms fastened behind her, her body lashed to the wheel. Her head rested on it, and when she lifted it to try to see behind her, the cockpit curtain was drawn.

What in God's name was going on?

The last thing she remembered was toasting the success of their mission, hers, Sarah's, and Tony's, with Champagne. Against all odds, the three of them had returned to the States bringing the Dreyfus Collection safely with them.

Champagne. Suddenly, she understood. She had been drugged!

What about Sarah? And Tony? Were they lying somewhere close by, drugged as well?

As Lisa's mind began to clear, she thought of the pilot. Comly, his name was. She pictured him at the controls waiting to take off. Where was he?

Struggling to free her arms to no avail, in her despair, she heard someone mount the steps to the cabin and enter.

"Tony?"

The cockpit curtains were drawn back and she saw a man's hands work at the ropes that held her to the wheel.

The same person lifted her from the seat then and turned her around. She needed support her legs felt so weak.

"Tony!"

Elated, she asked, her voice unsteady, "Are you okay? Is Sarah okay?"

She saw his eyes, inscrutable and focused on her.

"I was drugged," she said plaintively. "I think it was the Champagne."

And then she shivered. Tony's eyes were cold and dismissive. It was as if he had become a different person. She might have fallen had Tony not continued to hold her. She stared at him. Had he had some role in rendering her incapacitated? It frightened her that she had such thoughts about her father's old friend.

"Tony," she asked, her voice weaker than she wanted it to be. "Sarah. Where is she?"

He smiled crookedly, "Sarah's a lucky woman. I let her live."

She knew then.

He carried her over to a passenger seat in the cabin, hands still tied, and pushed her into it, all the while towering above her. Turning her head away, not wanting him to see how frightened she was, she gazed sightlessly at the darkness outside the plane's windows before realizing in shock that the crates that had leaned against them were gone.

"The collection!" Lisa could hardly breathe. "What did you do with it?"

He leaned against the far side of the Beech while he kept watchful eyes on her. There was a smugness about him when he replied, "The collection is safe. I had it moved."

He paused. "It belongs to me now."

What was he talking about? Lisa struggled to erase the fog in her mind. She knew she needed to be alert. "Where are we? Weren't we supposed to fly to Washington?"

"We're on Tortola, Beef Island Airport."

"The Caribbean?" Lisa stared at him in disbelief.

"Proper destination, wouldn't you think?" Tony said. "Pirates and all that!

He shifted his stance. "You spoiled my scenario, Lisa. I had intended Sarah to be where you are now, and though I like the woman, I had no compunction in fitting her into my final plan."

"Final plan?" Lisa's voice quavered.

"My agency expects me to deliver the collection to Washington. However, at this moment they have no idea where we are. Hopefully they never will. The collection and I will be long gone and so will the plane."

"And me?" Her throat tightened in fear.

Tony's eyes bore into her.

"If you hadn't stupidly insisted on joining us in East Germany, and then, damn it, you refused to go back to Massachusetts, you'd be safe now."

"Safe?"

"I can't have witnesses, Lisa." He paused. "But I never wanted it to be you."

"But what about Sarah? She's a witness," Lisa said. She shivered, afraid for her friend. "And Captain Comly. What happened to him? You didn't share Champagne with him, did you? Not if he was to fly this plane. I heard him speak to the air controller at Homestead."

"Oh, yes, Captain Comly," he said. "Well, just before takeoff, I knocked him out, taxied over, and left him unconscious in the shadow of a hanger. I didn't want my old buddies in the air force on my neck for murder. He'll have no idea when he regains consciousness where we've gone or what went down. And neither will Sarah. I left her beside him, drugged and unconscious, just before I took off with you. Like I once told Matt Chambers, taking one lady along is enough."

Tony appeared to want to say more. He said finally, "Peter gave his life for these paintings. You deserve to profit from his death."

He placed a hand on her shoulder. "Come with me, Lisa. Share this new life I'm about to begin. We have much in common despite the difference in our ages. When I sell off a few paintings, we'll be rich. You'll enjoy a life beyond your imagination."

He stopped, and looked for some response, eyes bright in expectation. After all, his offer was hard to refuse.

Lisa's head was ringing, the pressure at her temples intense. How could she answer him when her very life was at stake? Yes, she could pretend to agree, let him think she could be as greedy as he, hoping to be enriched by valuable paintings.

But then it hit her. Once implicated in his scheme, she could never go back to the life she loved in Woods Hole, never return to Matt. Once a thief, always a thief, that's what she'd be, just like Tony.

She changed the subject. "You flew us here?"

"Naturally!"

"Tony, are you telling me the truth?" she asked. "Is Sarah alive?"

He nodded. "She'll be fine. You should be proud of yourself that I brought you instead of her. You're the one I care about. I would never have made the proposal to her that I'm making to you."

"Proposal?"

"Lisa, in my business, you have no friends. Peter was the exception. I grew fond of you. For Peter's sake and your own, go with me. You won't regret it. But make no mistake, I intend to enjoy the rest of my life. Those paintings will ensure the style of living I've always looked forward to. And I want you to share that new life."

Lisa needed to think, but there was no time.

"Why?" she asked. "What will you really gain, isolating yourself from the world you've always known, looking over your shoulder each day?"

He frowned. "You don't believe I can carry it off? Hey, you know me better than that. Don't act foolish," he said. "I know you can be stubborn, but this isn't the time."

"You can't sell them," she said.

She needed to convince him. Her survival depended on it. "Sarah told me that every auction house knows where they belong. She and my father made such a fuss over their loss. It's common knowledge in the art world the United States owns them."

"You forget, there are private individuals who want the rarity, the beauty, for themselves and will pay a hefty price for those particular paintings."

Of course. Lisa knew such people existed.

She tried a different tack. "Look, Tony, you work for our government, always have. Why jeopardize your career?"

"This fell into my lap," he said. "I've been waiting for an opportunity like this ever since Peter disappeared. It had to present itself before Washington got its hands on the collection."

Lisa's heart shrank that she'd misjudged him so badly.

"All these years," he continued, "I planned to appropriate the paintings, just as the Germans and the Russians once did. I just didn't know how I could make it happen.

"Thanks to you and Peter, I finally found the collection. When I got in touch with my agency by radio from East Germany, I learned by chance they and the air force were planning a special mission that needed a long-distance Hercules. I also learned that for a very brief time, the plane could be available. That's when I proposed they detour the Hercules to Copenhagen to pick up the collection. And since the Herk's original mission was to start from Homestead, I then suggested a smaller cargo plane be sent to meet it in Florida, telling my superiors the collection could then be safely transferred and flown to D.C."

"But why?" Lisa repeated, knowing Tony's defection would be huge.

"I am about to retire from the agency," he admitted. "Fatigue sets in early in this game—that is, if you survive. I was never one to save money. I've always lived well and I intend to continue living well, something my government pension will not allow me to do."

"They'll hunt you down," she said, remembering now that Peter had joked about Tony's extravagant ways when she was a child.

"They will have to find me first."

Lisa looked out the window at the darkness. The only thing she knew about the Virgin Islands was what Rob Flanders had told her when he taught her to fly. All she could see were the lights of houses shining from the mountains that surrounded the airport.

Tony noticed her looking. "You can't see much, can you?" he said. "We're on Beef Island on Tortola. It's a narrow stretch of flat land sandwiched between Drake's Passage and the waters of the Atlantic Ocean. It got its name because pirates kept their livestock here for meat."

He searched Lisa's face for a response, but she turned away from him.

"There's a bar nearby. Mr. Carty's Bar," Tony said. "His wooden shack stands at the side the runway. A popular hangout. Has a little shed on top of the bar roof where the local air controller sits protected from rain. Fortunately, plane landings and takeoffs end at six p.m. when the airport shuts down."

He smiled. "All I had to do was wait till darkness to remove the paintings."

Lisa looked out at the starry night and guessed it might be midnight or even later. She'd begun to lose hope. There was no doubt in her mind that unless she agreed to join him, Tony would kill her. He was a false friend. And a turncoat to his government!

Lisa made up her mind. "If I don't come with you, what will you do with me?"

His lips tightened. "So far, no one knows what happened to the Beech," he said. "They're expecting it to land in Washington at some point. Once Sarah and Comly regain consciousness and alert the authorities, my agency will search for it in the States."

He continued to stare at her, his face expressionless, and added, "Now that the collection is safely stowed, the evidence needs to disappear. So, what better way to end any search than to make certain the plane and you and I are never found?"

"How?" She could hardly get it out.

"Just like the days of old, Lisa, you're going to walk the plank!"

"The ocean!" Lisa shivered with fear.

"Smart girl!"

"But how do you intend to do away with me?"

"We take off and fly away into the wide-open spaces until the Beech runs out of gas."

"And you?"

"The flight will take us over Anegada. It's the furthest island in the British Virgins. Flat land, easy to parachute onto. And, as I drift toward my new life, I'll be sure to wave goodbye while you continue on over the ocean."

"And the collection?"

"Will be waiting for me."

"I'm not going with you, Tony," she blurted out, wondering if there was anything she could say to save herself. She couldn't accede to his demand that she join him in the theft. Becoming a fugitive would put her at Tony's mercy for the rest of her life. And even if she escaped him, she would be his accomplice in her eyes as well as in the eyes of the law.

Was she a fool not to accept the chance of survival he was giving her? They were only paintings, the Dreyfus Collection. Still, she couldn't shake the thought that being Tony's accomplice negated all her father had stood for as well as who she thought she was.

Her stomach tightened with fear, knowing Tony intended she drown as her father had.

But she could not say the words that would save her. The sense of shock at Tony's betrayal was too enormous.

"It's your choice," was all he said. If he had any scruples about killing her, he displayed none now.

Tony moved quickly to the rear of the plane. Her hands still bound behind her, she struggled to turn in the seat. She saw him lift a parachute hanging there and put it on, adjusting the straps, watching her all the while.

"Sorry, Lisa, there's only one parachute aboard," he said with a crooked smile, "but this one would have held two."

She suddenly realized why Tony couldn't allow himself to be the only survivor at the same time the paintings went missing. It would have made him a prime suspect. Once the collection disappeared, Tony would want his agency to think it was all the fault of Russian operatives. Washington would naturally assume he and Lisa had become Kirov's victims despite anything Sarah might say.

She watched as Tony entered the cockpit and sat down in the pilot's seat. She saw him adjust the seat to accommodate the bulky parachute for a better pedal position and then proceed to rev up the twin engines. Noise filled the cabin as he continued to check the controls, and after several minutes, she felt the plane shudder like an anxious animal and slowly move toward the runway.

Lisa decided to try one more time to dissuade Tony. She raised her voice so she could be heard over the engines.

"Once you jump from this plane over Anegada, without a pilot, it will plunge into the ocean. It's probably not deep off that island and the plane may float for a time. On the chance it is recovered and my body found, they'll know you never flew to Washington, that you're the one missing, the one person still alive."

Her throat constricted. She could barely mouth her last words as she fought to contain a sudden hysteria.

Tony didn't bother to turn around. "Good try, but I've accounted for that."

He positioned the plane at the edge of the runway to follow the few guiding lights that were on though the airport had shut down for the night.

"Not likely you'll hit the water anywhere near land," he finally said. "This plane was refueled while you were still unconscious. Has a range of over seven hundred miles, more if it's lightly loaded."

A few seconds later, he said, "There's still time for you to change your mind."

"Don't do this, Tony. It's not worth it. You can't be sure you won't drown."

"You trying to frighten me?"

"No," she said, "but I won't go with you."

"So be it."

Lisa briefly closed her eyes. She heard Tony throttle to maximum power for the short runway. The plane took off, lifting sharply. Feeling the pressure, Lisa opened her eyes and watched from the window as the aircraft circled and began to bank away from the mountainous terrain. As Tony made his turn and gained altitude, the Beech rose easily into a dark sky brilliant with stars. The few lights she saw below were from boats anchored along the shore.

It surprised her that Tony would be flying away from Anegada. But as time passed, she realized he intended to hold off abandoning her until dawn when he could see to make his jump. She knew she needed to keep him talking, anything to stall his plan.

"You said the paintings were stowed. That sounds like they're on a boat of some sort."

For what seemed a long period, he didn't answer.

"Naturally," he said at last.

"So, when you get back to Tortola, you will board a boat and take the collection somewhere else."

"Right you are!"

There was a pause. "Too bad you turned me down," he said. "You and I could do well together."

For a time, Tony continued to fly in a direction that apparently took them away from land. Then as the stars began to fade, he banked the Beech and turned back toward the Virgin Islands. It occurred to Lisa that if Anegada was a small island, Tony could easily miscalculate his jump and wind up in the water with no hope of rescue. She was certain he had no idea she could fly. But what did it matter when she was tied up so securely?

Lisa peered through the cabin window. The sky had slowly begun to lighten. Islands were again coming into sight, outlined in the distance, the ocean reflecting faint light from the emerging dawn. She saw how placid the water was that morning, free of whitecaps induced by wind.

Lisa turned away from the window and concentrated now on Tony's hands, long and thin as he held the wheel and manipulated the controls. She saw him begin to engage the automatic pilot, slowly moving the on-off lever to the on position. She had never trained with an automatic pilot and only had hands-on experience, wishing now she knew more about it.

She drew a long breath and waited for the inevitable.

"We're at ten thousand feet and coming up on Anegada," Tony said.

He pushed the pilot's seat back and stood up, hoisting his parachute out of the way. Then turning, he made his way to the cabin door. He unlatched and opened the door and poised at the edge, but then, his lips twisted and he said, "Goodbye, Lisa."

Tony stepped out and disappeared from her sight as the plane flew on beyond Anegada into the vast spaces of the Atlantic.

Chapter 35

Virgin Islands, September 5, 1967

Lisa was all alone now in an aircraft flying east over the Atlantic Ocean at ten thousand feet. She felt the pull inside the cabin that air created as it blasted in through the open door; it might bring the plane down at any moment.

She blanched and wondered what it would be like, drowning.

"Daddy, help me!" Her plea, a whisper.

She struggled against the rope that bound her, realizing she was still feeling some effect of the drug Tony had put in the Champagne.

Champagne. In a bottle.

My God, she thought, where is the bottle, the one the three of them had toasted their success in Miami?

Had Tony tossed it?

She shifted in her seat and looked around. Struggling further, Lisa managed to pull free and stand up, legs shaky, hands still bound behind her as the Beech continued on its way to oblivion.

Desperate, her eyes searched for the bottle or anything she could use to cut her bonds. She felt herself buffeted by currents that swirled dangerously within the cabin, frightened they could pull her out the open door.

Slowly, despite her fear, she began edging her way toward the rear of the cabin and now stood beside the cabin door as it swung wildly about.

She took a deep breath and caught the door on a rebound. Using her body, Lisa slammed it shut and, keeping her back to the handle, her fingers succeeded in levering it tight.

For a moment, she leaned there shaken. At last, she took hold of herself and began to search the narrow shelves in the rear of the plane. To no avail.

As she stumbled back to the front of the plane, she saw a glimpse of reflected light from sunbeams now stealing into the cabin. The Champagne bottle lay on the floor wedged between a cabin seat and the fuselage on one side of the plane.

Her heart leaped.

Slowly, Lisa forced herself to kneel down behind the seat, her back to it and with bound hands reached behind her for the bottle, pulling it from where it was stuck. She struggled to stand up then, holding a bottle she couldn't see.

Lifting her arms as far as she could, she smashed it against the seat's metal supports. It shattered and fell out of her bound hands, glass landing all over the cabin floor and on her legs.

She gasped in pain at slivers that penetrated her skin.

Once again, she knelt down. Using her hands to grope behind her, she picked up a large shard and arduously began to cut through the ropes that held her captive.

It took forever, but finally, she stood up, her hands free at last. Her knees were bleeding, but she ignored them and headed for the cockpit. She thought then of the parallel between her father and herself, both of them almost making it safely home only to go down miles off the Atlantic coast.

Tony had levered the pilot's seat far back to accommodate his parachute. Lisa moved it forward and then pushed her long brown hair away from her face.

She looked for the radio but discovered to her dismay it was inoperable. Tony had seen to that. She then studied the auto-pilot and although she had never used one, decided it made sense to move the engaging lever to the off position.

It worked. She could now control the plane manually. Lisa drew a deep breath and rose up slightly to look out the window, expecting and seeing the ocean stretch endlessly ahead. The sun had begun to rise above the horizon completely free of clouds. It also confirmed a direction.

For agonizing minutes, Lisa studied the instrument panel and flight controls, and then decided she had to turn back. She began to bank the plane, slowly bringing it about in the opposite direction. Disconcerted, she saw nothing in any direction but the ocean. A shiver ran down her spine. Would she be able to get back to dry land before the fuel ran out? Then she remembered Tony admitted to refueling the Beech. The gauge confirmed she had a quarter of a tank left. That gave her some time.

At least the sun was no longer in her eyes. She was headed west, hopefully back to the islands. Still, she had no idea where she was at present. She wondered, could she navigate her way back to an airport on the Virgin Islands? The small plane she flew didn't need much runway, but she certainly wouldn't want to try landing on some curved mountain road or on a beach somewhere.

She told herself she needed to stop worrying and concentrate on saving her life. Now that she could fly manually, she decided to increase the plane's height beyond the ten thousand feet Tony had set on auto-pilot. Once the Beech gained greater altitude, she could better see what lay ahead.

She leveled off at a cruising speed of twenty thousand feet, doubting that the plane she was flying could go much higher than that. With the sun behind her increasing in brilliance, Lisa could better see into the distance. But there was no sign of land. And what if the fuel ran out before she made land? How cruel to die so close to deliverance just as her father had.

Her eyes straining, Lisa at last caught sight of islands. Were they the Virgins? As she flew toward them, she decided to drop to a lower altitude.

She was approaching the outermost islands when she recalled Rob Flanders saying there was an airport on St. Thomas named after a president, Harry Truman. She'd heard it was larger than the one on Beef Island. Flying this unfamiliar plane as an amateur, she needed all the runway she could find. Lisa decided to head for St. Thomas.

She continued flying west, trying to remember all she had heard about the Virgin Islands. It wasn't much, only what Rob had told her. She guessed those islands coming up were the British Virgins, separated by what must be Drake's Passage.

Glancing to her right, she observed a flat isolated island in the distance she guessed had to be Anegada. She wondered about Tony; had he parachuted down safely or been blown out to sea? If he made it to land, he must already have returned to Beef Island to take possession of the paintings.

She scanned the horizon for a boat. The paintings he now considered his had been removed to one. She guessed Tony arranged for someone else to pilot the boat, probably the same person who helped him move the crates while she was unconscious. If the collection was on a boat, wouldn't the boat make its way to Anegada to pick Tony up, assuming he survived the jump?

She shuddered. What would happen to anyone unlucky enough to help Tony?

Lisa found herself flying above a wide passage, islands on either side. British or American? She began dropping to a lower altitude. She flew past several islands and saw a large harbor ahead to her right encircled by a densely populated town rising above it. Charlotte Amalie? Spotting cruise ships lined up along one side of the harbor, she was certain she had reached St. Thomas.

And then, she remembered the Caribbean trade winds. They blew from the east so that aircraft needed to take off and land into them. To enlist the trades, she had to bypass the St. Thomas airport, continue flying west, then circle back and land in the direction from which she'd come.

It was a gamble. Would the fuel hold out?

As she flew over Charlotte Amalie Harbor, she noted a sparsely settled island just below to her right, and past that, she saw a second smaller harbor. It surprised her to see a submarine lying at one pier. She then remembered there was a naval base at St. Thomas.

Suddenly, Lisa felt the Beech shudder. Turning her head in amazement, she saw a navy plane flying beside her, close enough she could see the expression on the pilot's face, a puzzled one. Of course; she hadn't been able to radio the tower, so the navy pilot would have no idea what her intentions were. It occurred to her that the appearance of the Beech she flew, reported missing, may have attracted an alert military.

The presence of the plane fed her anxieties. It wasn't just the plane at her side, but she realized suddenly that in landing at the St. Thomas airport, she needed to avoid the "puddle-hoppers" that carried passengers the short distance from San Juan, Puerto Rico, to the Caribbean islands. The same planes flew back and forth to Martha's Vineyard and Nantucket in the summer from the New England mainland.

She groaned. A collision was likely if just one plane made a false move as she tried to land. In the midst of her fears as she flew past the airport, she remembered another conversation she'd had with Rob as they dallied over coffee before beginning a lesson. Hadn't he mentioned that the St. Thomas airport was among the most dangerous in the world for large airplanes because of its short runways? For reasons of safety, he said, airlines preferred to transfer their passengers in San Juan to smaller planes, which then island hopped the Caribbean.

Ignoring the fighter plane on her wing, she slowly banked the Beech and turned back to the Harry Truman airport. She had seen it off to her right as she flew past, its cavernous corrugated steel structure resembling a vast aircraft hangar. As she approached the island, she kept her eyes on the strip of runway rapidly coming up, realizing without turning her head that the military plane had disappeared.

That was when Lisa, nearing land, saw the mountain at the runway's end. It was the mountain that pilots feared when they attempted to land. It was that mountain that gave St. Thomas its short runways and fearsome reputation. Planes regularly overshot the runways and ploughed into it; it was why big airliners were reluctant to land there.

Lisa gasped. Was she destined to be a statistic? Lowering the wheels, Lisa recalled the injunction that the optimum height of approach needed to be fifty feet, and just as she saw the water disappear beneath her, she followed that rule. In seconds she felt the Beech touch down at the beginning of the runway. Quickly, Lisa reversed the engines while raising the flaps. She did all this while frantically searching for planes on the runway, but at the moment of touchdown, she didn't see any.

Only when she'd managed to stop just short of the mountain and turned the Beech toward the terminal building did she notice planes standing off to the side. She guessed then that the air controller may have held them back for her when he saw her unscheduled approach.

Lisa taxied off the runway and parked. Then, experience kicking in, she shut down the engines. Breathing deeply, exhausted, amazed she had survived, she laid her head against the wheel, thinking her father's spirit had been with her to the very end.

Chapter 36

Fall was well under way as Sarah Dreyfus stood on her patio overlooking the harbor. She had returned to Quissett Harbor only the day before, flying from New York to Falmouth in her Cessna. The trees had lost some leaves, though the oaks as usual were late. They still retained their brightly colored foliage. Too soon, winds would cause these leaves to disappear into Quissett's garden beds and woods, rendering the landscape stark against the sky. But at that moment, the harbor had begun to reflect the setting sun's glory. By now, most craft had been pulled out and winterized by their owners or neighboring boatyards. But there were still a few boats moored in the harbor, owned by the few diehard sailors who couldn't bear to acknowledge the season was ending.

Dressed in a stylish burgundy suit jacket and matching skirt, Sarah waited. A car entered the driveway and approached the house, breaking the spell of the sunset. Her guests had arrived.

She left the patio and opened her front door to greet them, delighted to find Lisa standing there beside Matt. A stranger, a Dr. Thomas, stood waiting also.

Lisa didn't hesitate. She reached out with pleasure to hug the older woman. That Sarah was alive meant much to Lisa. Their bond had been cemented by the reality that both survived to see this day. Hugging Lisa warmly in turn, Sarah said, "Come in, come in! I couldn't possibly close down my house without first seeing both of you."

Matt had called her to ask if he could bring the doctor along. He explained he had an obligation to entertain this visiting guest lecturer who was coming to Woods Hole at the Oceanographic's behest.

As she greeted her three guests warmly, she noted that Dr. Thomas wore a naval uniform and seemed pleasant enough. Though taller than she was, he was shorter than most men, especially seen standing beside Matt, who towered over him.

Matt had actually worn a suit. It was gray and he had accessorized it with a white shirt and a red tie. Lisa wore a light green wool dress that set off her pale features and dark hair. Entering the living room, she turned her eyes momentarily to a painting that hung on the wall, the Claude Monet painting, again taking in the blues and purples of that canvas. She stood there wondering if someday she might paint as the Frenchman had, if only a fraction as well as he had.

Sarah interrupted Lisa's thoughts, suggesting that they all sit around the coffee table before adjourning to the dining room for dinner. As they began chatting, she offered her guests some wine, an assortment of cheeses and crackers and a dish of hummus.

Matt now formally introduced Dr. Thomas to Sarah and explained as he placed cheese on a cracker how he had come to know the doctor.

"He was aboard the navy ship with me—the one that sent divers to the *Andrea Doria* site," he said. "He's the one who discovered Peter's tape."

Lisa interjected, "And he took very good care of me and Sam after we were rescued."

Lisa glanced at Matt. He was looking at her with concern. Sarah, watching the pair, saw the meaningful glances they gave one another and deduced that something special had developed between the two in her absence. It was when Lisa reached for and accepted the glass of wine Sarah poured for her that the older woman saw the ring on Lisa's finger.

Sarah's heart expanded. "Is that what I think it is?" she asked.

"Yes." Lisa smiled happily. "It is."

Sarah grinned. "My heartfelt congratulations to both of you!"

Smiling, Matt reached for Lisa's hand and held it in his until she turned back to Sarah, aglow once more. "I'm staying in Woods Hole," she said happily. "Nils asked me to be a permanent employee."

Sarah, beaming, said, "And Matt, what part did you have in that?"

Matt grinned. "Just a bit part," he said, and Lisa laughed. She leaned forward.

"So, tell me, Sarah, now that the Dreyfus Collection is safe in Washington, what are the plans for exhibiting it?"

"It's very exciting," Sarah said. "The trustees plan to engage a noted architect to build a new wing to house the paintings. As I told you aboard the Hercules, I've asked that an alcove off the main room be named the Peter Warden Gallery. After all, he found the collection first and made it possible for us to finally locate it. And I made certain that people in Washington know how you rescued it in the end. But tell me—how exactly was the collection found? Matt told me you were able to fly the Beech and land safely at the St. Thomas airport. But what happened then?"

Lisa pursed her lips at the memory. "As soon as I landed, I alerted the authorities. A small naval ship was temporarily assigned to the submarine base at Charlotte Amalie and was at a dock there. It sailed for Tortola once I told the authorities I thought a boat might be involved."

Hearing all this for the first time, both Sarah and Dr. Thomas leaned forward as Lisa continued.

"The captain in charge of the naval vessel along with British police boarded the few yachts at Beef Island and found nothing there. They then sailed to Anegada on information that a pleasure boat from Beef Island had recently tied up in that harbor."

Lisa paused, her eyes shining. "They found the collection. It was intact, all the crates with paintings in them accounted for."

She added softly, "But they didn't find Tony, as you know. It wasn't likely anyone on Anegada would notice a descending parachute, as it was barely light. Though I understand the authorities searched the small island thoroughly after finding the collection, Tony had disappeared."

Matt spoke up, "When you first told me this, Lisa, I suggested that it's entirely possible the chute went down in the ocean and he drowned."

Lisa frowned. "I don't think so. I was told by the captain of the naval vessel when it returned to St. Thomas that a small motorboat at the dock in Anegada went missing about the time the Americans and British arrived."

The group sat around the coffee table, weighing this last bit of information, until Dr. Thomas asked, "What would Tony do for money if he survived? He can't return to the States without being apprehended, I would think. And he probably can't access his pension."

Matt agreed. "He's under scrutiny, I would guess, from the FBI, if not his own agency. They don't forgive a turncoat."

He looked at the others, trying to conceal a smile.

"If he is alive, I wouldn't be surprised if Tony didn't decide to track down Alexander Kirov. Kirov has the Van Dyck painting and it's worth a fortune."

Dr. Thomas laughed. "One thief steals from another.

Sarah stood up, wineglass in hand. Enough speculation. She wanted to forget about Tony Russo and the ordeal he had put them through.

"I hope you are hungry because I made chicken soup with matzah balls and roasted hens."

Lisa stood also.

"Sarah, when you first invited me to spend Labor Day with your daughters, you told me Ruth was pregnant. She should be due about now."

"In less than a week! This is my last visit to the cape until spring. My daughter will need my help over the winter once the baby arrives. I am closing the house up tomorrow."

She looked sternly at Lisa and Matt. "That is, unless I have to come back for a wedding. Have you set a date?"

"Memorial Day weekend!"

Sarah smiled. "Couldn't be a better time for me. That's when I reopen my house for the season. She ushered them into her dining room. They were just taking their seats when the phone rang and Sarah excused herself.

She returned a few minutes later, her face aglow. "The call was from my son-in-law, Samuel," she told them beaming. "Ruth just delivered a fine boy, eight pounds. He'll be my first grandson."

They heard the catch in her throat when she added, "They tell me his name will be David."

About the Author

Estelle Rubin Brager was a writer, township supervisor and committed conservationist who lived in Bucks County, Pennsylvania, where she was the longest serving Democratic committeewoman in that county's history. The mother of four and grandmother of eleven, Estelle became a certified scuba diver while researching this novel. She is also the author of *Gittle, a Girl of the Steppes*, which is about her own grandmother, an adventuresome Jewish woman who escaped persecution in 19th century Russia by emigrating to America with her family. Estelle passed away in 2014 at the age of 86.

About the Publisher

The Sager Group was founded in 1984. In 2012, it was chartered as a multimedia content brand, with the intention of empowering those who create art—an umbrella beneath which makers can pursue, and profit from, their craft directly, without gatekeepers. TSG publishes books; ministers to artists and provides modest grants; designs logos, products and packaging, and produces documentary, feature, and commercial films. By harnessing the means of production, The Sager Group helps artists help themselves. For more information, visit TheSagerGroup.net

More Books from The Sager Group

#MeAsWell, A Novel
by Peter Mehlman

The Orphan's Daughter, A Novel
by Jan Cherubin

Meeting Mozart:
A Novel Drawn From the Secret Diaries of Lorenzo Da Ponte
by Howard Jay Smith

The Allergic Boy Versus The Left-Handed Girl: A Novel
by Michael Kun

Eat Wheaties! A Novel
By Michael Kun

Miss Havilland, A Novel
by Gay Daly

High Tolerance:
A Novel of Sex, Race, Celebrity, Murder. . . and Marijuana
by Mike Sager

Lifeboat No. 8: Surviving the Titanic
by Elizabeth Kaye

See our entire library at TheSagerGroup.net

THE SAGER GROUP
Artifex Te Adiuva